THE
SERGEANT'S SON

Ashim Choudhury was a corporal in the air force before he crash-landed into journalism and cartooning in 1992. Soon jobless, he got a break with the UN in Delhi, where he hopped several agencies. He also worked at the UN missions in the African states of Liberia and Sudan. An avid storyteller, his dream of becoming a newspaper columnist was never fulfilled. An inveterate traveller and a self-professed environmentalist, painting landscapes still remains his first love.

THE
SERGEANT'S SON

Ashim Choudhury

RUPA

First published by
Rupa Publications India Pvt. Ltd. 2012
7/16, Ansari Road, Daryaganj
New Delhi 110002

Sales Centres:

Allahabad Bengaluru Chennai
Hyderabad Jaipur Kathmandu
Kolkata Mumbai

ISBN: 978-81-291-2110-3

10 9 8 7 6 5 4 3 2 1

The moral right of the author has been asserted.

Typeset in Arno Pro 11/14.5

Printed at Repro Knowledgecast Limited, India

To
Ma and Baba

To Arabinda, my little brother, who left abruptly... leaving a void that never will fill

To Taposh-da, whose departure I do not mourn because in death he escaped a wretched life

Out of the cradle endlessly rocking,
Out of the mocking-bird's throat, the musical shuttle,
Out of the Ninth-month midnight
Over the sterile sands and the fields beyond, where the child
    leaving his bed wander'd alone
                                —WALT WHITMAN

My heart leaps up when I behold
    A rainbow in the sky:
So was it when my life began;
So is it now I am a man;
So be it when I shall grow old,
    Or let me die!
The Child is father of the Man
                        —WILLIAM WORDSWORTH

Contents

PART II: ALLAHABAD

Part I

BOMBAY

Life in Miltry Camp

Every evening, Kalu and his mother would go out for long walks towards the old Santa Cruz Airport in Bombay. The city was 'Mumbai' only for the Marathi-speaking people then, just like it was 'Bambai' for the Hindi speakers. It was not always that Kalu volunteered to go with his mother. Very often he would be playing with friends when his mother would call out, 'Kalu, come—won't you come with me?'

Sometimes, too absorbed in play, he would refuse. But when Basanti had walked a few yards all by herself, he would feel guilty and abruptly abandon his friends. 'Ma! Ma!' He would run up to her, panting for breath.

From early childhood Kalu could never refuse his mother anything. Somehow, he knew that she counted on him when her other sons failed her. These evening walks would take them along a desolate road within the military camp where they lived. Once they were outside the camp, they reached the main road, which was used by very few pedestrians and wore a deserted look, except for a stream of cars going up and down. By the roadside, a lone hawker sat selling fried gram and peanuts. Basanti always bought Kalu something from the hawker. She would untie the end of her sari pallu and give him three paise, and in exchange, the hawker would roll a piece of paper in the shape of a cone and fill it to the brim.

Sometimes, Basanti didn't have money, but even then he would coax them into taking the gram, saying '*Koi baat nahin.*'

A clever fellow he was, because the next day he would take the money without demur. Sometimes an aunty or two from their neighbourhood would accompany them for the walk. Unwittingly, thanks to their gossip, Kalu would be apprised of all the goings-on in the neighbourhood. It would be dark by the time the mother and son returned home.

This road they took ran right along the Santa Cruz Airport terminal. Sometimes, they walked right up to the fencing of the airport. For Kalu, it was enchanting to see the planes land or take off in a blaze of grey smoke. There were various kinds of aircrafts from different countries and he was fascinated by their colours. Among the colours he recognized—besides those of Air India— were the colours of the BOAC, as the British Airways was known then. He could also identify most of the types of aircrafts—Boeing 707, Caravel, Viscount, Fokker Friendship, Dakota, etc. After a few years, enormous hangars started being built, and there was excited talk that the jumbo jets would soon be arriving.

'It will be as tall as a five-storeyed building!' Kalu had heard some of the older boys say. But they left Bombay before the jumbos arrived.

'Ma, can we ever fly in an aeroplane?' Kalu sometimes asked his mother.

'Huh, stop having silly dreams!' she chided him.

Basanti was a fecund woman and had given birth to four sons, Kalu being the third. For a man of his generation, Corporal Samar Biswas had planned his family well—between each son and the next there was a gap of three years. Kalu was the 'darkie' in the house, which explained the choice of his name. Whenever Kalu had a fight with one of his brothers, his name would be the first casualty. They would call him 'Kalia!' with all the disdain the word could conjure. Having taken after their father, the other brothers were fair-complexioned and never missed an opportunity to tease Kalu about his colour. Why, even his mother once said, 'I sometimes think that perhaps you had been exchanged in the hospital.'

Kalu was born in Bengal, at the Barrackpore Base Hospital near Calcutta on an 'amavasya' or new moon night. Amid the bursting of crackers and the beating of dhak—the traditional Bengali drums—Basanti had begun to feel a familiar wet sensation. Her water had broken! The ward ayah, who had been called in to assist with her pregnancy, predicted with all her premonition and experience, 'The baby can come any time.'

But it was only two hours into the noisy night that Basanti felt her bowels churning. It didn't feel like labour pain. She called out to her husband, who was standing by in the veranda just outside the ward. Men were not encouraged to stay inside the 'family ward'. Samar came running and helped her climb down the bed. 'Sister… Sister!' he called out, and the ward nurse who was outside watching the colours light up the sky turned up reluctantly.

'You leave the ward,' she ordered Samar as she helped a pale Basanti walk into the toilet.

Minutes later there was a scream from the toilet, whose door had been left half ajar.

'Sister!'

Basanti had nearly collapsed in the toilet.

'Ayah! Ayah!' the nurse called out, and together they put Basanti on the stretcher with the help of two ward boys, who had materialized hearing the commotion. From there she was wheeled into the operation theatre.

Nearly half an hour later, a ward boy emerged from the OT and announced to a distraught Samar, 'It's a boy!'

Samar's tense face broke into a smile.

The ward sister, on receiving the information, looked up towards the dark sky and crossed herself. 'Thank God!'

She was glad all had gone off well. Had there been a mishap in the toilet, it would have cost her the job.

An auspicious night it was—Diwali for most Indians and Kali Puja for the Bengalis. It was believed that those born on an amavasya night were exceptionally creative in whatever they did, good or bad.

'They mostly turn out to be philosophers and thinkers,' an elder had said. He added to that, 'Sometimes they also turn out to be legendary thieves.'

Others in the family corroborated the theory.

'Why was I born dark?' Kalu would sometimes ask his mother, feeling betrayed by nature.

'It was because of amavasya—You were born on Kali Puja, when the sky is pitch dark,' Basanti once explained to the curious boy.

On other occasions, when she was feeling light-hearted, she gave him an alternative explanation, 'I had to take a lot of black medicines when you were inside me.' That hardly consoled Kalu.

Any new visitor to the house would often remark, 'How come this boy is so different from his brothers?' Which was a polite way of asking, why is he so dark compared to the other siblings? Somehow, Kalu felt he was a source of embarrassment to the family. He grew up acutely conscious of his skin colour.

Kalu was not even a year old when Corporal Biswas got posted out of Barrackpore and the family shifted to Bombay. Childhood for him was Bombay—the life inside Miltry Camp at Kalina. The military camp was like an island of greenery amid the concrete jungle of Bombay. Hilly and forested in parts, it was surrounded by barbed wire fencing on all sides. The camp had all kinds of trees—mango, tamarind, English tamarind, rose berries, guava, plum, dates and many more. But it was predominantly the mango season that the Biswas boys and their friends awaited. They were like children of the forest, playing and growing up among the trees. They not only ate and fought over the fruits that grew wild in the camp, they even played 'jhar bandar' on the trees. Despite living in a city, they grew up in the lap of nature. The camp was roughly ten square kilometres in size and there was hardly any corner of it that the boys had not explored. Among the jungles there also lurked snakes, many of which they had seen being killed. The fear of reptiles became all the more pronounced during the monsoons, when wild weeds grew all over the camp covering the dirt tracks. Roads used at other times of the year were now avoided and feared.

As kids, Kalu and his little friends played many different games, including Market-Market in which they 'sold' all kinds of things such as grains and clothes. The grains were usually procured from wild weeds, and leftover cutouts of stitched clothes served as the clothes.

The children were always on the lookout for items to add to their market. One day, Kalu saw a colourful piece of cloth lying on the ground. Immediately, he thought how useful it would be for their market and bent down to pick it up. But just when he was about to touch it, the cloth appeared to move. Kalu pulled back, realizing that the 'cloth' was actually a small, colourful, coiled snake. The snake moved slowly, giving him a scare, but also gave him enough time to pick up a stone with which he killed it. Having killed a snake for the first time in his life, he was proud and wanted to show the trophy to his friends. He could not hold it in his hands—his mother would fly at him if she found out. So he searched for a stick. Then, hooking it on to the stick, he took the dead snake to his friends Ashok and Nimmi who, thanks to their longer experience with reptiles, immediately told him, 'It is a baby python!'

'How do you know?' an impressed Kalu asked them.

'We know. Our father has killed so many snakes,' Nimmi stated with finality.

The children later burnt the snake because Ashok and Nimmi ordered it.

'The eyes of a dead snake take a picture of the person who has killed it,' Nimmi said.

'So we have to completely destroy the eyes by burning it,' Ashok seconded his sister's opinion.

'And if it is not completely destroyed, the surviving mate of the snake will see the picture and take revenge on its killer,' he added for dramatic effect.

Years later, Kalu realized that none of it was true—for one, a baby python had to be much larger in size. But at that time, when it came to snakes, no one disputed the views of the brother-sister duo. Ashok had told Kalu several tales, including one where an uncle of his had been bitten several days later by the partner of a snake he had killed. The mate had apparently hidden in his shoe and bitten him at the first opportunity. The uncle died. Kalu was terrified of snakes. But burning the snake he had killed made him feel proud, like a grown-up man.

The camp in which they lived was bordered by the Santa Cruz Airport and Kalina, a lower-middle class locality dominated by Goan Christians, on one side. On the other side was Vakola, also lower-middle class but with a mixed population, where people spoke less frequently in English. Towards the Kalina end, the camp was hemmed in by the Air India colony, while towards the Vakola end was the PNT colony—quarters belonging to the employees of the post and telegraph division. The Miltry Camp had two gates—the Vakola gate and the Kalina gate—which were the main entry and exit points. If one walked about a kilometre into the camp from the Vakola gate there was another road coming from the Kalina gate. At this junction there was a third road, and a couple of hundred yards ahead on this road was a steep slope. The residents of the camp referred to this place as the 'double-line quarters'. The double-line quarters were two rows of ash-coloured blocks of houses with sloping roofs, facing each other, separated by a distance of about ten feet.

Further down the road from the double-line quarters came a bend, and then came blocks of houses, which were the MES or Military Engineering Service quarters. Those who knew better also referred to the MES as Money Earning Service. Each of the MES lines housed three to four families. The road here branched out after every few blocks and terminated at large low-roofed bungalows where the army officers' families lived. The officers' bungalows were at a higher plane and stood out in splendid isolation. Behind these, the land sloped gradually. Near the fencing on this slope, the sweepers' quarters faced the airport workshops and the Air India colony—isolated and shielded from the eyes or influence of the higher classes. Life was quite segregated in a sense, with the families of army officers and that of the ORs—short for the Other Ranks—living completely separate, compartmentalized lives. Kalu and his brothers, being sons of airmen, for instance, never ventured anywhere near the officers' quarters.

In front of the MES quarters the tarred road led to a cobbled road, which had rows of houses on either side identical to the double-line quarters. These were meant for airmen who worked in the air force. This was where Kalu lived. The dull grey blocks had six quarters each. Each quarter had a latticed door that opened into the kitchen, which also had a small enclosure with a tap. During the monsoons, when there was rain and storm, water would be sprayed into the kitchen through the latticed doors. And the women, like Basanti, would have a hard time mopping the floor to keep it dry. The kitchen led to a large room with a single, iron-barred window, mostly overlooking green shrubs or woods. Apart from five blocks of such houses, there was another block that had just two quarters each, both of which had two large rooms that opened out to a long veranda. These quarters were meant for the seniormost ranked airmen, and were the envy of others not fortunate enough to occupy them. Samar and his family later came to live in one of these large quarters. Many of the neighbours resented this, as Samar was only a sergeant, despite having put in several years of service. But Samar and his family were the oldest residents of the airmen's quarters. That qualification somewhat mollified the envious neighbours.

The Days of Dry Latrines

None of the quarters had independent bathrooms or latrines. There were common bathrooms in three blocks in front of the two-roomed quarters, beside which, at the far end, was the 'gents' urinal' and at the near end was the 'ladies' toilet'. Since the bathrooms were at a distance of about a furlong from the farthest quarters, and they were dark and dank, very few people used them, the tap-enclosure in the kitchen often doubling as a bathroom. Women, particularly, rarely used the toilet. It must have been an embarrassment, to be watched by idle men while going in or out. The men mostly went to the back of the quarters and took their leaks behind the trees. There were a few common taps out in the open where children and a few men had their baths, the women usually bathing indoors. The latrines were even further away, at the back of the quarters, nearly touching the tall barbed wire fencing. A broken road led to three blocks of buildings on a slight elevation, with tiled roofs, each having six latrines. The one on the left was referred to as the 'ladies' while the two on the right were the 'gents'. One had to climb a few steps to reach the row of latrines, and it would be quite funny if people with flatulent stomachs occupied adjacent latrines. The sound would be something akin to the bombing of Iraq! When two people occupying adjacent latrines stood up after finishing their business they could see one another. Some even exchanged pleasantries!

Going to the latrine was embarrassing for many people. They had to carry water with them—mostly in a discarded tin of baby food or an empty beer bottle. This was particularly galling for those who lived in the quarters farthest away from the latrines, as they had to walk through the entire stretch of houses holding their tin cans. The latrines were 'dry' with no flush system. One sat at a height ensuring that the excreta fell into a tin pot. To get a clean latrine, one had to keep a close watch for when the sweeper, an old mustachioed man from UP called Ram Singh, had finished washing them. And grab the opportunity. A dirty latrine could be quite repelling. But the worst part was when the sweeper would fall ill and the filth would pile up. Using the loo would be a nightmare then, ending only with Ram Singh's return.

Ram Singh was a scrawny sort of man with severe button-like glowing eyes. His semi-bald head and grey bushy moustaches lent his face a stern look. A sharp tongue added to the severity of his countenance. Always dressed in longish khaki-coloured shorts and a white-turned-yellow vest full of gaping holes, he was a man of few words. As the keeper of the lavatories, he held a special place in Basanti's life, and as a result, for the entire Biswas family. Aware of his importance, Ram Singh took full advantage. Done with his chores, which included sweeping the general surroundings and clearing the choked gutters criss-crossing the quarters, Ram Singh often planted himself outside the Biswas quarters.

Squatting on the floor, his spindly legs stretched out, he would demand, '*Bibiji, paani dena!*'

However busy she might be, Basanti could never turn him away. One of the boys would usually fetch the water and pour it into his cupped palms from a safe distance. Having quenched his thirst, he would wipe his face with his red gamchha and pretend to go, but Basanti would hold him back.

'*Baitho, baitho!*'

Asking him to sit meant that tea would soon follow. So, he would once again squat on the floor, and thrust forward his white enamel mug (with black scratches in several places) brought specifically for the purpose. Leaning against a wall he would wait patiently until the tea arrived. Again, care was taken to ensure that the tea was poured into his mug from a safe distance. Often, in addition to the tea, two dry rotis would be flung on to his proffered gamchha. During this exchange of goods, utmost care was taken to make sure that neither Ram Singh nor any of his belongings were touched. If that happened accidentally, and provided Basanti was a witness, a bath had to be taken immediately. It was a given that no one questioned. This is not to suggest as if there was any rancour against the man. As a matter of fact, in strict power terms, it was Ram Singh who held a position of dominance. It was Basanti Bibiji who was meek and servile, always pandering to his demands.

To avoid this delicate balance of power, some just eliminated the latrine from their lives. No wonder an Anglo-Indian lady, Mrs Menezes, was never seen visiting the latrine. It was rumoured that her kitchen not only doubled as a washroom, it trebled as a latrine! Basanti felt revolted by the idea, and it was a crude joke for the children.

'Ohh ma!' she would say, making a face.

Kalu often had the unenviable job of keeping a watch on Ram Singh, and when he finished cleaning the latrines, informing his mother. Basanti would tie the 'pallu' of her sari across her nose whenever she had to pay a visit to the latrine. Before such visits, her mouth would fill with spit out of revulsion. Every few minutes she would spit, as though the act would obliterate the memory of filth from her mind.

She would keep spitting even long after her visit to the latrine until, finally, Samar would shout, 'Will you stop that spitting of yours!'

Basanti would retort, 'I have never seen a man like this—no revulsion!' and make a gagging sound as though she would vomit.

Often, there were times when Basanti felt her bowels churn after dark. On such occasions, Kalu was his mother's natural choice to escort her with a torch. The darkened road leading to the lavatories took on a frightening aspect at night, more so because of the thick vegetation on either side of the road. Kalu was mortally afraid that a snake, emerging from the bushes, would bite him or his mother and they would be dead. With one dim light glowing in each, the latrines looked eerie by night.

'Ma, hold my hand,' he would plead.

Kalu was terribly afraid of the dark, but he couldn't disappoint his mother. So there he was, holding the torch in one hand and with the other his chest, to literally stop his heart from popping out of his mouth. While Basanti went into the loo, he waited outside with bated breath, bathed in the orange-yellow light of the single bulb, hoping against hope that there wouldn't be a snake lurking somewhere. The wait would seem unending, and his eyes would dart around looking for some wild nocturnal creature. One night, terror of terrors, he actually saw a small snake coiled on the rough outer wall of the toilets. It was still, like a statue, and it took him a while to realize it was alive. When he did, he turned back and took to his heels, abandoning his hapless mother. During the rainy season, the incessant croaking of frogs in the rice fields beyond and the singing of crickets in the eerie night made matters even worse for the little boy. Poor child! His fertile mind interpreted these sounds as coming from snakes, making him even more terrified. Whenever he would reach home after these nightly duties, he would feel immensely relieved, as if he had narrowly escaped the clutches of death one more time. On reaching home, they would not enter the house immediately. Even Kalu, who had not entered the latrine but only its precincts, was 'contaminated' and could not enter the house before he was detoxed with water. Somebody from inside, very likely one of his brothers, would fetch a bucket of water while Kalu and his mother waited outside. Washing his own feet with water, he would pour a little water on to the earth, over which Basanti would rub her palms. Then he would pour more water for her to wash her hands and feet with. Only after that, cleansed and purified by running water, did they step into the house. Then the mother would change into a fresh sari, and discard the defiled one.

Changing Neighbours

The Biswases lived in Miltry Camp for eleven years in three different houses. At first, they lived in Quarter No. 37. This was in a corner of one of the two rows with its back towards the latrines. Kalu wasn't even a school-going child then, but he remembered looking out of the window into the dark every night and imagining a thief standing there—a thief wearing a hat, with bloodshot eyes.

One day, while the children were playing outside the house, there was a sudden commotion as Basanti began to scream, writhing in pain. Their father was not at home, and the women of the neighbourhood descended on their house, blocking the entrance. Soon, one of the men arrived with an ambulance, and their mother was taken to the hospital. The neighbours assured the terrified children, 'Don't worry, she'll be fine soon.'

For the next two days, the children had their meals at a neighbour's house, not quite sure what was going on. Then their mother came back, carrying a little baby in her arms.

'It's a new baby boy!' someone explained.

That was their youngest brother, the fourth. He was fair and beautiful, with little pink hands and feet. Kalu, now three, took an immediate liking to the little brother.

'Kalu, keep an eye on him,' Basanti would often say, and he was happy to play big brother while his mother finished her chores.

'Oh, what a beauty!' everyone who saw the new baby exclaimed.

Basanti would dress him in a blue frock and put a black kajal spot on his cheek to ward off buri nazar. After three sons, Basanti had been looking forward to a daughter. A son for the fourth time disappointed her. To compensate for her loss, she grew his hair long and dressed him up in frocks, like a girl. Kalu often had to guard his little brother while he played in the cot, when their mother was cooking. Babu, as they called him, was just three years younger to Kalu, but he was always the little brother, even when he was forty-one years old, when he died suddenly in a train accident.

The Anglo-Indian family of Corporal Menezes lived in the quarter adjacent to the Biswases'. With two sons and two daughters, they mostly kept to themelves. The Menezeses had a certain conceited attitude for being English-speakers. But Kelly, their youngest boy, was an endearing child with an impish face and a naughty smile. Basanti often spoke in whispers about Joan, the eldest daughter, who used to wear short skirts revealing her fleshy legs.

'She's a slut,' Kalu had overheard women telling his mother.

Then there was the family of Sergeant Chakrabarty, who had a deviant son called Kallol and three daughters. The man often got drunk, and his arrival in the evenings would be marked by loud slurred speaking and swearing at nobody in particular. He was a pleasant man when he was sober, though.

There was also the Malayali family of 'Copl' Thomas, who had a daughter called Mercy. Mercy would wear beautiful frocks, and it was said that she had a rich uncle who lived in 'foren'. Kalu vaguely understood 'foren' as some other country that was not their own. In this case, the uncle was in Dubai.

Flight Sergeant Dua was grey-haired and had a demure-looking wife. Since she was barren, it was said that her face should not be seen the first thing in the morning, or it would bring ill luck. They were a quiet and good-natured couple, though a little sad-looking.

There were a number of other families, their names prefixed by the men's ranks. But it was difficult to place them accurately, because from time to time, the neighbours kept changing as people got posted in or out. Postings were occasions which aroused a lot of curiosity among those living in the quarters, more so for those who lived in that particular 'line'. For instance, anything affecting Quarter Nos. 37 to 42 would be of particular interest to the Biswases because they lived in that 'line'. Another point of interest was if the airman's family that was coming or going belonged to one's own state. That marked the beginning or end of a special relationship with one's own people, from one's native place; who spoke one's language, ate similar food and celebrated the same festivals. Regional bondings were strong.

Samar Biswas used to be a corporal when they lived in Quarter No. 37. Once he got promoted to sergeant they were allotted Quarter Nos. 45 and 46 together, which was a rare privilege. But this was to be his last promotion. For the rest of his life in the air force, Samar remained Sergeant Biswas, even as his contemporaries got promoted further and superseded him. Basanti, in particular, used to be very sore because of her husband's 'incompetence'.

'Everyone gets a promotion, but you will remain a sergeant all your life!' she would grumble on occasions.

Samar would sit through these barbs stoically, not paying any heed to them. That would provoke Basanti even more. 'How shameless!' she would often say, murmuring to herself but loud enough for Samar to hear.

Such sulking was often the result of some woman in the neighbourhood who would come announcing her husband's promotion,'We have got a promotion!'

And then, as if to add insult to injury, this would often be followed by the query, 'When is Bhaisaab getting his promotion?'

Basanti felt very let down by her husband on such occasions.

'I can't show my face to the world because of the shame' was one of her common refrains.

For the children, it wasn't an issue that bothered them in the least, but egged on by their mother, they would occasionally ask her, 'Why didn't Baba get his promotion?'

To which she would retort, 'Your father is a permanent Cat-C!'

This meant that Samar belonged to the Medical Category C because of a heart problem. And that, the children were told, debarred him from a promotion. The truth was probably something else—Sergeant Biswas was never in the good books of his officers. He often confronted his bosses when he thought they were not being fair. It was a quality for which Kalu later came to respect his father very much. In the air force, as in the other forces too, one's promotion depended less on competence and more on the ability to keep one's superiors in good humour. That was a quality that Samar Biswas lacked, as did Kalu, inheriting it from his father in generous proportion. He, too, would often be deprived of his promotion, which his contemporaries—much less educated or accomplished—acquired with ease.

When Kalu Was Pampered

Samar was much more refined compared to his peers. While they drank and gambled, Kalu's father was a man of sober tastes. The son of a poor peasant in Pabna—then a district in the erstwhile East Bengal—he had come a long way in life. Even though the family lived in Bombay, Samar regularly subscribed to *Desh,* the leading Bengali literary journal. He would read the magazine from cover to cover. It was because of him that the children got into the habit of listening to the news on radio both in the morning and at night. As the radio chronometer would go *keek-keek-keek,* a booming voice would announce, 'This is All India Radio, the nine o'clock news, read by Surajit Sen…'

It became a regular feature along with dinner. Melwyl D'Mello, Lotika Ratnam and other newsreaders not only added to the children's general knowledge but also improved their English diction. Samar also avidly read Bengali novels and heatedly discussed matters of state whenever he found a man of matching interest. A matriculate of the 1940s, he often lamented the low level of knowledge among the people of the next generation when compared to his own. Kalu, however, was a mamma's boy and didn't much love or admire his father. In fact, all the children were a little afraid of their father. The greater part of their affection was directed at their mother. Even Basanti was afraid of her husband much of the time.

Aloof and reticent, Samar was never demonstrative in showering affection. If his affection for anyone was overtly visible it was for his own mother, who the children only saw as a grey-haired toothless grandmother with wrinkles all over her face. She bore a striking resemblence to her son, and looked beautiful even in her old age.

'Akaloo!' she would call out their father's pet name, and Samar's face would light up with a smile.

'Tell me what you want, Ma,' he would say obligingly.

Every year, the grandmother would come all the way from their native village in Chakdaha, near Calcutta, and live with them for a few months.

On the rare occasions when he was pleasantly disposed towards Kalu, his father would endearingly call him 'Kelo' or 'Kelochand'. Beyond that, Kalu knew no pampering from his father.

In fact, Samar actively discouraged indulging the children, especially with money. Every morning before leaving for school, the children had to plead with Basanti for pocket money. On lucky days, Kalu would get three paise from her. But most of the time she didn't have any money to give the children.

'Your father does not give me a penny, where can I give you money from?' she would say, feeling as sorry for the children as for herself.

On the days he got some money, Kalu would buy a colourful 'logence' (lozenge) with one paisa and gram with the remaining two. The gram-wallah was a grey-haired, middle-aged man with large, yellow teeth, who sold his wares at the gates of St Mary's School in Kalina. He wore khaki shorts and spoke English. 'Buy gram! Buy gram!' he would shout, as one after the other the schoolchildren crowded around him. He used keep a miniature brass tumbler-like container which he filled every time you gave him a paisa, and asked the children to open out their pockets, into which he poured the gram. Even paper packets did not come by easily then. And, of course, the thin polybags, the curse of our times, had still not been invented.

Kalu also bought toffee with his pocket money. This was a sticky but hard cream-coloured paste that had to be pulled out from a large mass wrapped around a block of wood. The boys and girls would endlessly chew the solidified, gum-like mass—sweet to taste—until it disappeared. They also ate pink puffs of candyfloss, which they called buddhi ke baal, and multicoloured meetha saunf available at the shop just outside the school gate. There was also khatai, a dark brown sweet-and-sour paste wrapped in transparent cellophane paper. Among a host of hawkers crowding around the school gate was a man who sold orange-coloured ice creams, and another who sold sweet and colourful ice cakes. With so much and more to choose from, money was always in short supply. It was only once in his entire childhood that Kalu got money from his father, and that too without asking for it.

That was on a Sunday morning in winter. The children were sitting outside the house in the sun, huddled on a charpoy with their school-bags, studying their lessons. Samar sat nearby on a chair, reading the newspaper and keeping a watchful eye on his brood.

All was well until Basanti came on the scene and announced to her husband, 'You know what Kalu did yesterday, when you were not there at home?'

She had not even finished with her complaint, and the next thing Kalu knew was that his father was thrashing him. While the blows rained he screamed, at the same time remonstrating that he had not committed the crime he was being punished for.

'I haven't done anything!' he shouted. That incensed Samar even more.

'How dare you answer back!'

The beating became even more severe. Blinded by rage, Samar finally lifted Kalu by the hair and threw him on the ground. By now, the little boy was like a bundle of rags sobbing inconsolably, at the same time aware that all the people in the quarters were watching the scene.

'I have done nothing wrong,' he wailed between his tears.

He was crying less out of pain and more out of shame. Even in that state he ran indoors and crept under the big bed to cover his shame. Here, he sobbed and sobbed until his body shook. The house was shocked into silence, except for his stifled sobs. His face was wet with tears and a running nose.

His mother then shouted at Samar, 'Is this the way to beat a child!'

Babu, the youngest brother, also began to cry. Everyone started pleading with Kalu to come out of his hiding, but he sobbed even more pathetically because he was convinced that he had been beaten wrongly, that too in front of everyone. The child's pride was deeply hurt. The house fell silent. After a long silence he heard a metallic tinkle as a ten-paisa coin rolled on to the floor and came to rest near him. It was his father who had thrown him the money. Samar was paying for the wrong he had done. That was the only time Kalu remembered being pampered as a child with money.

His Father's Tyranny

Samar's temper was quickly roused by his children's naughty pranks. A strict disciplinarian, he often imposed order on them at the cost of their happiness. But he did so, convinced that it was in the best interest of their future. Among his tyrannical orders was that the children should be back home in the evening soon after sundown, wash themselves, spread out the mat and sit down with their books. No occasion, except Durga Puja, could alter this schedule. He presided over their studies, sitting nearby with a newspaper or a book as the children sat down to study, cross-legged, on the straw mat. They had to read their lessons aloud so that their father could hear them from any corner of the house. In between, he would ask questions pertaining to their lessons, which, if they failed to answer, invited a rebuke and sometimes a slap on their bare backs. (During summers he made sure that the children, like himself, didn't wear shirts when inside the house.) Very often, repeating their hackneyed lines, the children would droop off with sleep, only to be shaken out of their slumber by a harsh slap on the face or the back, whichever was closer to their father's itchy hand.

Towards the end of their study hour Samar would switch on the radio, tuning in to the nine o'clock news—their window to the outside world. The beginning of the news also signalled supper-time, provided that the day's homework was complete. Sometimes the children were hungrier than usual and would want to eat before supper was fully prepared. A little pleading and Basanti would agree to serve up whatever had been cooked till then. But Samar would command, 'You will eat only after the entire meal is ready!'

The 'entire meal' would mean nothing short of rice with courses of dals, fries, vegetable and fish. Such was his tyranny that even Basanti's intervention would not help. Sometimes, the children fell asleep without eating, in which case he would have them woken up. The food would then be thrust down their gullets, even though they were half-conscious and limp with sleep.

Basanti would occasionally lose her patience and say, 'Is there any meaning to this?'

Samar would retort, 'Just keep quiet! It is because of you that the children are getting spoiled.'

He was the master of the house and his word was final.

Supper would usually be concluded with 'doodh-bhat'—rice mixed with milk, sugar and banana. In summer, the banana would be replaced by mangoes. Samar loved to eat, and the family ate like kings, so to speak. It was a common sight to see Samar return in the evenings with two large fish strung to his bicycle handle. As soon as the fish arrived, Basanti would take out the 'bothi'—a typical Bengali contraption that served as a knife and was particularly useful in slicing fish. It consisted of a sharp angular blade fixed on to a flat and long block of wood. One had to grip the wood with one's foot while using the blade to slice fish or vegetables. To this day Bengalis, irrespective of the city they live in, use the bothi to cut vegetables, rather than a conventional knife. Probashi Bengalis visiting Kolkata always make it a point to carry back a good, sharp bothi with them as advised by their wives.

Basanti would place the bothi over a newspaper, next to which she would have a mound of ash. (The ash was bought from an old, wrinkled woman who looked, the children thought, like a witch. The half-mad, half-naked woman, wearing her sari in typical 'ghati' style, like a wrestler in loincloth preparing for a fight, would come to the neighbourhood once a week. Unfolding her plastic sheet, she would sell the ash that had been scrounged from the ovens of bakeries and restaurants in Kalina—as little as a kilo for as much as four annas. The ash was also used for scraping clean the day's dirty utensils.) Swathed over the fish, the ash would make it less slippery and easy to hold. Cutting and cleaning the fish was a tedious affair which Basanti, like any sensible woman, hated. She would often be cross with her husband for bringing home fish at late hours. Often, a battle of words would ensue.

'It is easy for you to buy the fish and dump it! Who is going to sort, cut, clean and cook this thing now?' she would scream.

This was a scene the children feared very much. It signalled the brewing of a storm, often resulting in their father losing his temper and landing a few blows on their mother, after which she would weep bitterly. Kalu couldn't bear to see his mother weep, and he, too, would begin to cry.

One day, tempted by the thought of the koi fish cooked in lau, Samar brought home half a kilo of live kois very late in the evening. The anticipation of the delicacy brought water to his mouth, as he dismounted from his bicycle on reaching home.

But the saliva was quickly replaced by bile.

Basanti took one look at the fish and began, 'I can't cook this fish at this hour! I'm not your slave…'

Before she could even finish her sentence, Samar, his eyes bloodshot, growled angrily, 'You slut!' and threw the entire bag of fish into the gutter at the back of the house.

That night the family ate their meal in absolute silence. The next morning, at some distance behind their house, the children discovered a few of the fish swimming in the gutter. Kois could survive outside water for a long time. Kalu retrieved a few of them, which he put into a glass jar. It became their new obsession.

Sometimes the boys would accompany their father to the market where Samar would haggle endlessly with the shopkeepers. Basanti and the children felt embarrassed accompanying him to the market. The sharp-tongued fisherwomen of Kalina were very rude to him, but being a regular customer, he usually had his way with them.

Once, when he bought fish from one of the heavily bejewelled fishmongers without haggling, the woman looked up in awe and asked, '*Kya baat hai Babuji, aaj jhik-jhik nahi kiya?*' With his children around the remark embarrassed him.

One grocer—a Gujarati man called Suspal—was tired of Samar's haggling in a good-natured sort of way. One day when the family went to his shop, Suspal asked Basanti, 'Your husband is such a miser. Does he give you food at home?'

Samar, who was standing by, responded with a smile. He was hardly a miser, but he made sure that he didn't pay a paisa more to those crafty bania shopkeepers. Haggling was more a matter of principle—or perhaps sheer habit—for him. Just like it was de rigueur for him to check the gills of a fish and make sure they were red before he paid for it.

'If a fish has red gills, it means it is fresh,' he would teach his sons. Like life itself, buying fish was a serious business. There was little to laugh or smile about.

On the rare occasions when Samar did smile, the double canine of his left jaw became visible, and Basanti would tell him with mock seriousness, 'Don't smile, for God's sake! It doesn't go with your grim self.'

Samar was fair-complexioned, but rather short and flabby. He had sharp features and was clean-shaven. There was something handsome and serene about his face when he was not frowning at the children, but most of the time he was. Although generally good-natured, his sons feared him for his angry outbursts, which could also mean a beating for one of them.

If anyone were to ask the children, 'Whom do you like more—your mummy or your daddy?' their unequivocal answer would be 'mummy'. Their father was not a friend to them. He belonged to that old school of thought which believed that children should be scolded and never spared the rod, or else they would get spoiled. This dictum he carried out both in letter and in spirit. It was not very surprising, therefore, that the children looked forward to his absences from home. His absence meant freedom!

Their father's presence at home on a Sunday morning, on the other hand, meant that the boys would be confined indoors with studies inflicted upon them, while their friends from the neighbourhood played outside. While the children slogged away at their schoolbooks, one or two of their daring friends would even lift the curtain—very often an old sari that their mother had at some point discarded—and peep into the house. But the moment Samar turned his head to look, they would scamper away like frightened rats.

Mercifully for the children, their father's agenda for Sunday mornings usually included his weekly outing to the market, before Basanti would begin with her nagging, 'There is no rice in the house… There is not enough sugar… There is no…'

The list was long.

So as the children carried on with their lessons, in their minds there was only one thought, 'When will Baba leave for the market?'

As though he could read their minds, Samar would normally leave with a warning, 'If I find that any one of you has moved out of the house when I come back, you have had it!'

The boys never looked up from their books when he uttered this warning, fearing their faces would betray their thoughts. But within moments of his departure, after he would take the bicycle out of the house and mount it, one of the brothers would tiptoe to the window and signal to the rest that he had travelled off a safe distance. That also signalled the end of their Sunday morning studies. Their father's warnings gone with the wind, the boys would burst out of the house to where their friends were playing.

Basanti would shout after them, 'Let him come back! Let him come back, and I will tell your father everything!'

But who cared? It was a carefree world as long as they had the freedom to play.

The freedom ended the moment the boys spotted their father returning on his bicycle, the bags on either side of the handle bulging with groceries. Almost on reflex, they would run back home and pretend to be immersed in their studies. And Sunday mornings would pass off peacefully.

But it was not always that their mother forgot to inform Samar of the children's misdoings, and sometimes even before he was able to extricate the bags from the handles of his bicycle she would reel off: 'You know what, the moment you left…'

Basanti didn't even need to finish her litany of complaints and Samar, obligingly, would be beating the life out of them. The beatings were in direct proportion to the age of each of the boys. Babu, being the youngest, was mostly spared. Borda, the eldest, received the severest and the maximum amount of beatings.

Borda, the Outlaw

Taposh—the oldest boy, called Borda by his younger brothers—was a renegade. As a rule, the three younger brothers returned home from play after the sun had set, but Borda usually took his own sweet time. The others would be busy with their studies when he would quietly sneak into the house.

'You have arrived, my dear son?' Samar would say to him, his voice dripping with sarcasm. He would get up and follow his eldest son into the next room. And then, with a shoe that was handy or a leather belt that had been specially ordered for the purpose, the blows would rain down on Borda until he writhed and screamed in pain, '*Ma go! Baba go!*'

While all this was going on, the three younger brothers were strictly instructed to not let their concentration wander. They had to continue reading their lessons aloud, without any interruption.

Any fall in the pitch of the reading would invite a loud rebuke, 'What happened...!'

The volume of their reading would then automatically rise. After the beatings Borda would retire to a corner of the room, groaning in pain as his mouth frothed. Huddled against the wall, he would often fall off to sleep. The next morning he would have forgotten all about the previous night's beatings and would go about his affairs as usual. He was a happy-go-lucky boy. His build was rather large, leading his brothers to call him 'jadia' or fatty.

'Fatty fatty bumba latty, ate up all my ghee chapatti!'

Borda was a law unto himself. He bunked his school, had girlfriends at an early age, wore tight pants, grew his hair long, had rich school-friends and rarely passed his exams. He belonged to a different class. While the three younger brothers studied at St Mary's High School in Kalina, Borda went to St Anthony's in Vakola. He had been dismissed from St Mary's for poor results and improper behaviour, after which he had been admitted to St Anthony's. But even here, complaints were regularly noted in his school diary. On these he used to forge his father's signature without ever having actually shown them to any parent—Basanti, anyway, could not read beyond the rudiments. This went on for several months, perhaps, until Samar got a letter from Father Pinto, the principal, that he or the boy's mother should see him immediately in connection with his son.

Samar had to go to work, so the responsibility fell on Basanti to go to the school and answer the complaint. And who but Kalu was chosen to accompany her. Since she did not speak English, he also had to act as her interpreter.

When they reached Borda's classroom, a short-haired lady teacher, wearing a tight skirt, came to the door. 'Yes, how can I help you?' she asked rather sternly.

'We received a letter from the principal…' Basanti petulantly explained the purpose of their visit.

The teacher was hysterical. 'Your son has not been coming to school for the last fifteen days!' she complained.

Shocked, the mother remonstrated, 'But he has been going to school everyday!'

The teacher was angry. 'Really? Where is he today?'

And Basanti, embarrassed that she could not speak English, said, 'Why, he should be in his classroom.'

So the agitated teacher led them to his classroom and summoned 'Taposh Biswas! Where is Taposh Biswas?'

There was no sign of Borda. All the students in the class stared curiously at the two of them and Kalu felt very ashamed.

While they were leaving, the teacher issued a warning, 'If he continues in this fashion, he will soon be dismissed from school.'

It was not an empty threat. And indeed, a few weeks later, Borda was dismissed from St Anthony's. He was in the seventh standard then. It was a dead end, for no other good school would admit him. Dismissal also brought with it a long round of severe physical and verbal reprisals from Samar.

'You can sit at home and become a rickshaw-wallah when you grow up,' Samar said, adding cynically, 'but who will even give you the money to buy a rickshaw? I'm not going to spend a single paisa on you.'

The reprimands fell on deaf ears. If he felt any remorse or guilt, Taposh showed no sign of it. There was also no sign of worry at the prospect of having no school to go to. It was only his parents who were driving themselves ill with worry.

In a resigned sort of way, Basanti chided her eldest son, 'What will happen of you? Will you end up begging for a living?'

The search for a new school was long and time-consuming. Samar took a break from his office and went to a few English-medium schools, asking if they would admit his errant son. Looking at the boy's past records, every school answered him with a firm 'No'. Even some of Samar's friends and colleagues were pressed into service to find a new school for Taposh.

Finally, one of Borda's older friends from Vakola brought news that a new school was opening up very close to St Anthony's, and he could give it a try. Fortunately, New Model, an obscure school that had just sprung up and was desperately looking for students, opened its doors to Borda. Once again, peace was restored in the house and Borda resumed his usual ways. Later that year, when the results were announced, his siblings were pleasantly surprised—Borda had stood fifth in his class!

'How did you manage it, man?' Bappa, the second brother, asked.

'Just like that, man,' Borda evaded the question.

The news was too good to be true. How did Borda achieve this turnaround? Both the children and the parents wondered. Meanwhile, a quiet respect developed for him in the family. But it soon collapsed when Bappa found out that there were only five boys in Borda's class!

'So you came last in your class!' Bappa exclaimed.

Borda laughed with abandon as though he had cracked a smart joke.

While he was in New Model, Borda would often boast to Bappa that he had a girlfriend called Asha.

One day Kalu was playing with his friends when someone said, 'Dekh! Dekh!'

Looking up in the indicated direction, Kalu saw Borda arriving with a girl. It was Asha, wearing a sari. Though a child, Kalu vaguely understood that there was something scandalous about walking around with a girl. He ran home out of curiosity.

Basanti, too, was embarrassed to receive the strange guest, and to escape from the situation said, 'Let me get you some tea.'

The smart girl replied in a typical filmy style, 'No, no, Aunty, I will make the tea.'

All the while she was in the house, there was a half-smile on everybody's face as if they were wondering, 'What is happening?'

Curious neighbours were also looking out of their doors in

the direction of the Biswases' house.

'Who was that *Aunty*?' Ashok's mother finally asked Kalu with a naughty smile after the young lady had left.

It is not known whether Basanti ever spoke of the female visitor to Samar. Perhaps Borda had warned her not to.

Borda had a lot of rich and—it was presumed—'bad' friends. He would tell his brothers stories of hotels and restaurants where he ate lavish meals with them, their splendid cars that he rode, and their grand houses that he visited. The brothers secretly envied him. Sometimes he would come to the camp with his friends in a car, inviting the attention of all and sundry. In those days, only the very rich had cars. And as if that was not enough, he once came home riding in a Chevrolet, following which his stock went up with his brothers. One of his rich friends called Manzoor once brought eight white poodles in his car. Everyone looked agog as the sweet little dogs wagged their flag-like white tails. Manzoor's father, Borda later told his brothers, was in the dog-breeding business. His dogs were often featured in Hindi films.

'They have hundreds of dogs, some as big as tigers and others as small as rabbits,' he told his eager mother and brothers.

Borda's friends would often have tea at their house. Sometimes they even had lunch. Basanti obviously felt flattered serving food to these rich children.

'See, sons of such rich men, but they are so simple. They have no airs,' she would say.

When Borda was in St Anthony's there was once a 'Nine-Nite Fête'. This was an annual event to which students of the school and their families looked forward. Normally, the Biswases never went to these fairs.

'Where's the money to spend at such events?' Basanti would say when any of the children demanded to go. 'Don't forget, your father sends you to convent schools with great difficulty.'

'Ma, just this once...' the children would plead, but to no avail.

Of course, Borda knew how to extort money from their mother and he always had a gala time at these events. Moreover, his rich friends often covered his expenses. The year that he was expelled from St Anthony's—a few weeks before the mishap—Borda invited his mother and younger brothers to come to his school for the fête.

'I'll take care of you,' he promised, when Basanti protested that she had no money to spend on a fête. It was a big day. The children polished their shoes and ironed their clothes. Basanti pulled out a starched, ironed sari from her tin box. Dressed and wearing perfume, the mother and her three sons trooped out of the camp, past the PNT colony to St Anthony's. Borda was to meet them at an appointed place.

But when they reached his school, there was no sign of him. The wait seemed unending and the surging crowds of families made the matter even worse. Finally, the mother and the sons set out among the festive, milling crowds to look for him. They had nearly given up when Bappa suddenly shouted, 'There he is!'

He was pointing towards the sky. It turned out that Borda was taking a ride on the giant wheel, flanked on each side by a girl! The small group was scandalized, but no one said anything. Borda waved to them, unfazed. Afterwards, when Bappa mustered the courage to question him about the girls, he laughed and said, 'Oh, they were my classmates.'

After that, he took them around the stalls, introducing them to a number of his classmates. He bought them bhel-puri to eat. The younger brothers were happy to watch people going round on the giant wheel, even though Basanti didn't have money to buy them tickets. From the loose end of her pallu she dislodged some coins, with which the boys had ice creams and fried groundnuts.

Later that evening, Borda gave Bappa some money.

'Enjoy yourselves,' he said, before disappearing into the crowd of revellers again.

It was a source of awe and mystery to the younger brothers how their Borda always seemed to own so much money, while they had none. Perhaps Bappa had some inkling as to Borda's sources of income, for which his silence was bought with the occasional bribe. Sometimes Borda dipped into his father's pockets when no one was looking, but the heavy price of a thrashing at Samar's hands did not make this a very attractive proposition. So instead, he resorted to a more ingenious business—he became a volunteer to fetch milk bottles from the booth in Kalina in the afternoon. But how did he make money from buying milk when his father always gave him the exact change? There was a trick to this.

Borda would buy toned milk, which was cheaper by a few paise, and paste the blue foil label of full-cream milk on the bottle cap. Apart from the two bottles of milk for his own family, there was additional bonus by way of neighbours requesting him to buy them full-cream milk. So even if there were only four bottles of milk to be bought, he would make a small fortune by the end of the afternoon. On any other errand too, he knew how to wriggle out a few paise by overcharging his mother, father, neighbours, or anybody who sent him; there was no discrimination here. But the milk forgery was finally discovered when Basanti realized that the creamy layer on the boiled milk was no longer as thick as it used to be. Toned milk was devoid of cream. This was followed by closer inspections of the bottle caps that finally blew the lid over Borda's milk scam. The afternoon chore of bringing milk was then inherited by Bappa, much against his wishes.

Another favourite source of Borda's income was the family's piggy bank, an earthen pot called khunti in Bengali or gullak in Hindi that had on it a slit to drop coins into. Borda had devised an ingenious method of disgorging coins from the gullak. Even after months of dropping five- and ten-paisa coins—occasionally a fifty-paisa coin, too, was dropped—when the piggy bank did not get full, it raised questions. On such occasions the needle of suspicion pointed only in one direction—at Borda. A sound thrashing later, he confessed to the truth. After the half-full pot was broken, the change was usually kept with Basanti—with which she bought small household utensils or other *luxury* essentials like a perfume or face cream, 'Afghan Snow' being her favourite. After the failure of the earthen-pot piggy bank, Samar brought a wooden-box piggy bank that he thought could not be tampered with. And sure enough this one became heavy quite soon. And since Puja was round the corner Basanti and the kids decided to break open the bounty, making sure Borda was not around the house. There was always a fear that he would snatch a good part of the booty. But breaking open the box was not an easy task as it had been put together with iron nails. With the help of a winch and pliers when Bappa finally managed to open the box, their jaws fell. What spilled out of the box were not notes and coins but stones and pebbles. Borda had done it again!

With six years separating them there was a certain generational gap between Kalu and Borda. But it was not the years alone that separated them; Borda belonged to a different genre, setting him apart from the rest of his brothers. He went to a different school; he kept different company; while the other brothers had, more or less, common friends. He even ate better than the rest. For breakfast while the others often dipped dry 'chapatis' in a mug of tea and munched them, Borda would insist on scrambled eggs without which he refused eat. For the youngsters his stubborness was a boon, for they too could get a bit of the good food. But sometimes he carried his tantrums a little too far, overturning his plate or flinging it if the food was not to his liking. Basanti was often terrorized by this son, more so because Samar was away at office in the mornings. Sometimes she gave in to his unreasonable demands even if it meant having to borrow eggs or tomatoes from the neighbours. Once in a while, however, his tantrums would be reported to Samar. Those evenings, because his father mostly returned late in the evenings—and sometimes Borda returned even later—he would get the kind of spanking whose chilling memory would keep the younger boys meek and obedient for days on end.

All that Basanti had to do was make big eyes and say, 'Remember *that* beating?'

And the boys would fall in line with her command. After those nocturnal beatings Borda often went off to sleep in a tearful state and without food. No amount of coaxing or coercion from Basanti could make him have his dinner, an attitude he retained even later on in life.

But he didn't always go hungry, as the overnight disappearance of bananas from the house would testify. Samar would bring home bananas virtually every evening, a dozen or half a dozen. Every evening after supper the children were given half a banana to be eaten either by itself or with milk and rice: half and no more. So with six members in the family, three bananas were part of their daily evening ration. The bunch of remaining bananas would hang on the steel wire strung across the walls, which served as a clothes line. These bananas were regularly counted by their father, so there was no question of anyone eating up one without his knowledge. But very often there would be commotion in the house early in the morning, with the discovery of a shortfall in the numbers.

When no one would own up, it would be assumed that Borda had eaten them. Very often the darkened peels would be recovered from underneath his charpoy where he slept all by himself.

Feigning innocence he would say, 'Maybe the rats ate it.'

And Samar would say, 'Yes, you are the rat,' and tweak his ears and pull his hair until he groaned in pain. Somehow, Borda was never ashamed. He would laugh away the pain and insults inflicted on him.

Complaints Galore

Complaints against Borda poured in from strange quarters. Every evening there used to be a man who came to the camp with a trunk loaded with biscuits and goodies on his head, screaming sonorously, 'Biscuit-wallah! Cake-wallah!' Abandoning whatever they might be doing, the boys would rush out of the house to meet him. Other children in the neighbourhood also did the same. There would soon be a crowd around the cake-wallah as he unburdened his tin box, opening it to display an array of biscuits, cookies and even cakes and muffins. Their olfactory senses were assailed by the the sweet smell of baked food. The biscuit-wallah was an irresistible distraction. Most often the boys would buy the small, round white biscuits that cost a paisa each, or the crisp rusk biscuits that they loved to dip in tea and eat; and then there were the long, stick-like 'lathi' biscuits. Once in a while, when their father was in a magnanimous mood, he would buy them muffins that had thin paper cups attached to them. The bills would mostly be paid on the spot. So when, once in every while, the cake-wallah would later come to the house demanding money, Samar would protest vehemently that there was nothing pending. And then the man would roll out his account book, in which he maintained a record—of all the items that Borda had eaten!

The father would refuse to pay, saying, 'I did not ask you to give *him* anything.'

The man would plead, 'But Babuji what can I do, your beta does not let me go until I have given him what he asks for.'

His eyes bloodshot, Samar would have no option but to pay up to the fellow. And then he hunted for his eldest son, who was by now informed of the matter by one of his brothers, and kept a safe distance from the house. But for how long?

Later that evening, even as everyone went about their usual chores, there would be a pregnant air of foreboding and doom. While the three boys carried on with their lessons, their eyes would often be at the door, awaiting Borda's return. On such evenings Borda would invariably be later than usual. Very often he would sneak into the house unseen, tiptoeing through the back door. After this the other boys could overhear their mother chiding him in hushed tones, 'You don't have any shame... Your father will kill you today.'

And as Samar rose to his feet and went into the other room, the children's eyes and thoughts would follow their father as they mechanically read their lessons aloud. Moments later their reading would briefly stop as the air would be rent by cries of, '*O re baba re! Morey gelam re! Aar korbo na re!*' This would continue until Basanti's shrill voice would intervene.

'Enough! Enough! Will you kill the boy?'

In the same breath, she would chide her son, 'You have no shame!'

'Why don't you die... So many children get run over in the streets! Can't you die!'

This was more of a mother's disappointed lament, rather than seriously wishing ill for her son. Tears of pain would course down Basanti's cheeks as she swore at her son. A mother after all, she couldn't bear to see her firstborn beaten so mercilessly. Leaving him groaning, the father, still in a seething rage, would return to his other sons and growl, 'What's the matter!'

And they would resume reading out aloud, marking a return to normalcy.

At the back of their minds, the younger boys were supportive of Borda and sympathized with him. But no one spoke up, because in the small republic of the Biswas family—like in many others of their time—the father had the last word in everything.

The cake-wallah was not alone. Even the 'aam-wallah bhaiyas'—migrants from Uttar Pradesh who bought all the camp's mango trees on contract for the season—would often come complaning to Samar about the misdoings of his eldest son. There was a group of bhaiyas with large moustaches, who wore vests instead of shirts and dhotis instead of trousers, with the red gamchha wrapped around their heads. Their arrival in the camp coincided with the sprouting of mango blossoms whose scent hung heavily in the air, attracting bees and flies. The bhaiyas would inspect the blossoms, based on which they would forecast the harvest, and accordingly bid for the trees. These rustic fellows had a harsh, unkempt and unclean look about them. Among them Lakhhan Bhaiya was particularly robust and fierce-looking, his ferocity accentuated by a tweaked moustache, bulging biceps and a sharp tongue.

By the time the mangoes were green and succulent, these men would roam the camp with long bamboo poles balanced on their shoulders. At the end of these poles there was a sharp twisted knife, around which hung a loose bag-like net. The mangoes they plucked from high branches automatically dropped into the net, saving them from falling on the ground and getting damaged. For the children the bhaiyas were sworn enemies—not because of any old family feud but because they came in between them and their love for mangoes. While mango trees, some of them ancient, grew all over the camp, these bhaiyas took contracts on only the best clusters of trees. The children were free to pluck mangoes from other trees, but it was natural that they eyed the trees chosen by the bhaiyas. The sudden transfer of property rights to the bhaiyas irked the children. Right from the time that the mangoes began emerging from their blossoms and a thick fragrance hung in the air, the boys in the camp started getting excited. But the arrival of the bhaiyas spoiled it all. While they kept a vigil on the trees, the boys in turn had to keep a watch on the bhaiyas so that they could steal the mangoes. To circumvent the bhaiyas, around the time the mangoes were ripening, Kalu would rise early in the mornings even before it was day. In his half-sleep, he would go looking under the trees for ripe mangoes that may have fallen in the wind the night before. Sometimes the search yielded nothing. On lucky days, particularly if the night before had been windy, to his immense delight he would find the ground under the trees littered with ripe mangoes, so many that both the pockets in his pants would not be enough. Then he would use his shirt to cradle home the remaining mangoes.

Borda did not quite share his siblings' enthusiasm for mangoes, but there was something contagious about their excitement. So when his younger brothers asked for his help in stealing mangoes, he could not refuse. No wonder the bhaiyas were often baying for his blood.

Once, while he was atop a tree plucking from a particularly large bunch of mangoes, a friend came panting and informed them, 'Lakhhan Bhaiya is coming!'

Borda slipped down the tree with the dexterity of a monkey, as Kalu gathered the turgid green mangoes scattered on the ground and put them into a bag. But before he was able to escape with the booty, Lakhan arrived in the distance. Kalu ran home as fast as his little feet could carry him. Moments later the door of the house flew open with a bang, Borda dashed in, and bolted the door from inside. He had narrowly escaped, for close on his heels came Lakhhan Bhaiya raving and ranting.

He stood outside the door shouting, 'Come out, you scoundrel! Today I will definitely break your hands and legs, you rascal!'

And Kalu shuddered, fearing that Lakhan would actually break open the door and carry out the threat on both of them. For a long time Kalu and Borda waited like fugitives inside their house; until Basanti, who had gone chatting in the neighbourhood, returned. And then Lakhan directed his tirade at her.

'Behenji, your son is a thief! He stole my mangoes!'

The mother felt stung by the insults hurled. 'Let their father come,' she said bitterly.

'Open the door, Taposh!' she ordered.

'Ask Lakhan Bhaiya to leave first.'

Borda would not open the door until Lakhan Bhaiya was gone a good distance from the house.

That evening called for another memorable round of spanking.

But no amount of thrashing could bring Borda to the straight and narrow path that Samar had in mind for him. He continued to be the cause of his father's bad moods and rising blood pressure. But rescue came soon, in the shape of a new Bengali family that arrived in the neighbourhood—that of Corporal Dhar's. The Dhars were a new couple, just man and wife. And since they were Bengalis like the Biswases, a thick friendship soon developed. Dhar Kaku and Kakima would drop in frequently in the evenings.

'Boudi, can we get some tea?' The man would demand on entering the house.

In the morning when Kaku would be away on duty, Kakima would come to the house and chat with Biswas-di—that is what she called Basanti, being much younger to her. Dhar Kakima was exceptionally fair-complexioned for a Bengali and had a round moon-like face. Every morning when Kaku was gone to the office, she would call out, 'Ai Kalu,' and he would run to her house a few blocks away. Then she would hand him a few coins and he would fetch her a dosa from the MES canteen at the back of her quarters. That was her usual breakfast, of which she gave Kalu a small share. He liked her. Kaku, too, was a jovial person, and most of the time his large teeth were bared in mirth. He had a long face which resembled a horse. It was often said in the Biswas house that Corporal Dhar was a miser, but he once bought the children a packet of toffees, temporarily dispelling this notion. Samar did not like Corporal Dhar much and saw him more as a buffoon who had to be suffered. But the man was deferential towards Samar-da, treating him more like an elder brother.

So when he saw Samar-da lose his happiness over his eldest son, he said, 'Dada, if you give me the permission, I will straighten this crooked son of yours!'

'Are you sure you can straighten him?' he asked, with a rare smile. He knew what Dhar was suggesting was not achievable.

But ever ready to pick up the rod against his sons, Samar was only too happy to give his assent. And soon enough, an opportunity to prove his word came along Dhar Kaku's way. This was when Samar discovered that a one-rupee note was missing from his shirt pocket!

The needle of suspicion automatically pointed at Borda; and mercifully, he also confessed to the theft. But the confession could not save him from a thrashing that more than compensated for the enormity of the crime. When news of the theft reached Dhar Kaku's righteous ears, he was livid with rage. It was a Sunday and as usual he had come over to the Biswases' house for a chat. After listening silently to Samar's story he told himself with greater resolve, 'This boy has to be taught a lesson!'

No one said anything.

'Give me a rope!' he ordered to nobody in particular and everybody in general.

The boys looked at each other but nobody budged from his place to search for a rope. Fearing a reprisal from Borda later, none of the brothers wanted to oblige Dhar Kaku. There was also a tacit agreement among the brothers that Kaku had no business interfering in the affairs of *their* family. Since no one responded to his order, Dhar Kaku himself set out to find a rope. Everyone waited silently as he went about the house looking for a rope.

'I have found one,' he declared finally.

An abandoned charpoy was the source of his claim. He had pulled out the rope that had been used to tighten the choir knitting of the cot.

'Come here!' he ordered Borda with authority, rope in hand.

Borda, of course, stood defiantly like a statue. But there was no stopping Dhar Kaku who grabbed him and began to tie both his hands to the back. After that, he did something for which perhaps even Samar was unprepared. He stripped Borda of his clothes, dragged him out of the house, and tied him to a papaya tree that stood in the open courtyard. Borda didn't yield easily. There was a scuffle of sorts with a lot of kicking, screaming and protesting from Borda and and an equal amount of swearing from Dhar Kaku.

News of the striptease spread like wildfire. Soon the children of the neighbourhood, except the girls, came to see him in hordes and had a good laugh. By the time Borda was released from captivity, all the neighbourhood children had had a look at his pendulum! What incensed the brothers was that the spectators included boys from rival gangs. Even in that early stage of life, they had little rivalries that they took very seriously. Like present-day parliamentarians, boys from one group often crossed over to the other.

The first thing that Borda said on his release after two hours was, 'See if I don't kill Kaku when I grow up!'

Kalu, for one, wished he grew up fast. Somehow the brothers didn't approve of Dhar Kaku's extreme measure. It was a matter of their family honour. They began to hate the man. About three decades later, when they happened to meet a grey-haired Dhar Kaku in another setting, Kalu reminded Borda—himself a middle-aged family man by then—of his promise. And they laughed.

'Best Friend' Ashok

One summer evening during their holidays, while the boys played in the dark outside, Basanti was all alone in the house quietly bent over her sewing machine stitching pillow covers. Suddenly she came rushing out of the house, screaming, 'Snake! Snake! There's a snake!'

None of the boys dared to go inside the house.

'Where, Ma?' the terrified boys asked.

A frightened Basanti pointed to the central part of the tiled roof.

'It was because of the commotion caused by the rats on the roof that I looked up from the sewing machine, and saw the head of the serpent,' she said, fear writ large on her face.

The rest of the snake's body, she said, was in the neighbouring quarter. And soon enough the lady from the next house also came rushing out, reporting the snake's presence. Before long most of the people in the line had left their homes and collected outside Samar's quarter, deciding on the course of action to take. Kalu, in his childhood wisdom, immediately ran up to Ashok's house, which was some distance away in the MES block. Mathew Uncle, Ashok's father, was a hunter and had shot down many a wild creature in the camp, including snakes, with his double-barrel gun.

'Uncle, Uncle...there's a snake in our house,' he reported, panting.

Avid hunter that he was, Mathew Uncle quickly picked up his

gun and followed Kalu. He did not even bother to change his lungi or put on a shirt. Barefoot, bare-chested, wrapped in a loincloth, gun in hand, he came with single-minded aim. His arrival—the only time he came to those airmen's quarters—brought a magic sense of drama to the whole scene. Everyone was looking up to him to lead the way. The snake, it seemed, got wind of the whole affair, and withdrew from the Biswases' house. Then it made an appearance again, and Mathew Uncle, taking aim, let out two booming shots. Both missed their target, as two tiles flew out into the air. The snake seemed to disappear. Much later it was spotted again, this time in the last quarter of the line. And for once Uncle didn't miss his target. The dead snake was finally brought down with the help of a long bamboo pole. It must have measured at least seven feet.

'It's a rat snake!' Ashok's father declared.

That night the Biswases and their neighbours slept wakefully, wrapped in a sheet of fear.

Ashok was Kalu's best friend. They went to the same school. Though Ashok was one class senior to Kalu, the two of them always played together. Their friendship was an enduring one, since unlike other boys who sooner or later went away on postings, Ashok was always there. Being in the MES his father was unlikely to be posted out of the camp; and he was there throughout, until Samar got his posting orders and the Biswases left Bombay. Ashok's house was a mini zoo. There was Jimmy the half-Alsatian. There was Bella the goat, who—tethered to a small tree near the jungle, so that she could feed on grass and fatten her milk udders—got entangled in the rope, choked and died. There were hens and ducks in the large fenced area at the back of their house, and also pigs, besides red-eyed rabbits and a cat. And as though all this were not enough, Ashok's father once had a snake put into a cage. Another time, he had even trapped a wild cat, until one night it escaped, taking with it a couple of fowls. Once he found a baby partridge, but the children were told that it was a pea-chicken. The most exotic pet the family ever had was a deer, but then one day it died suddenly. In the large kitchen garden at the back of the house, there was also a small tank full of red goldfish. A visit to Ashok's house was like a mini wildlife excursion. Once in a while the family was also visited by an uncle who rode a motorcycle. He brought butterfly nets with him, with which the children would go into the jungles and catch butterflies. Ashok told Kalu that his uncle made a living by exporting dead butterflies. He was a rich man, Kalu surmised, considering that he owned a bike. Ordinary people, like his father, rode on bicycles.

Ashok had an older sister whom he called 'kocha', which in Malayalam means sister. Kalu called her Nimmi, an abbreviation of Nirmala. Nimmi was a couple of years older than Ashok but she was more like a friend to both of them and quarrelled often with Kalu. The three often played games that involved mock cooking or bazaars. But very often they came to fist fights, and Nimmi, being bigger, mostly got the better of Kalu. Once, however, he grabbed her by the hair and overpowered her until she cried. After that they did not speak to each other for days on end. It was not that Kalu didn't quarrel with Ashok as well—they did so more often. And then, they too didn't speak to one another for days. But these partings of ways used to be a torment to both the boys, until they started talking again.

The funny part was that even during such a breach in friendship, the two boys still moved around with the same band of friends, whether they were playing cricket or gulli danda. It used to be a large gang of boys mostly their own age, often led by boys who were much older. Not infrequently, younger boys like Kalu and

Ashok were merely spectators, watching the older boys play. Since they were best friends, it used to be very embarrassing for Kalu and Ashok to move in the same group and yet not speak to one another. Often the other boys were not even aware of the rift in their friendship, making the reunion even more difficult in the absence of any mediator. In the beginning, when the fight was fresh in their minds, it was understandable. But over a period of time, when the anger had worn down, they wanted to be friends again. It was an irksome situation—both desperately wanting to resume talking but not knowing who should take the initiative. Avoiding each other's eyes, both felt shy like girls. Each time their eyes would meet, accidentally or otherwise, they would smile coyly at each other, hoping against hope that the other person would say something. It was a pity that there was no peacemaker.

In one such poignant situation the two boys went out of the camp to play a cricket match with the older boys. Ashok was supposed to be playing, but Kalu went along even though his place in the team was not confirmed. The older boys often organized cricket matches with rival teams from outside the camp. The matches were either friendly, in which case there was nothing at stake except their reputations; but very often there were 'bet matches'. For bet matches each player had to pay a sum of money mutually agreed upon by the teams, mostly four annas. The money collected from both teams would be kept with a 'neutral' person who, when the the outcome of the match was known, would hand it over to the winning team. While the losing team went back empty-handed, the winning team players would get back their principal amount. And with the bet money that was won, some sweets or coconuts would be bought and equally distributed among its members. Not just the ones who played but also the hangers-on like Kalu got a share of the pie. They were all part of the larger team. Sharing this booty was great fun, but sometimes there would be quarrels over the unequal distribution of the 'prize'.

The matches were held most often with teams from the PNT colony near Vakola or some team from Kalina. Once in a while, there were matches between rival teams from within the camp itself. These internal matches were played at the camp ground itself, and were often between the youngsters and the older boys. Kalu's role in most of the matches was to sit along with the other boys on the sidelines, legs folded, holding on to the sweaters or watches of the big boys who went in to bat or field. On lucky days, he was granted the privilege of keeping the scores in a notebook. It was a difficult job, considering that you might write down a 'four' but the opposing team might not concede it. Scores taken by the members of both teams often didn't tally. Due to the occasional cheating, the two scorers usually sat next to each another, not as friends but more out of the necessity to keep a check on the opposite team. Once in a while, Kalu actually ended up playing in the matches, either due to an acute scarcity of players or simply because he had succeeded in coaxing out the four annas—the bet amount—from his mother. Basanti had to virtually exhaust all her resources to make sure her children were not deprived of cricket. She never tired of telling them how Tulu Mashi's husband, her Jamai Babu, had played for the Maharaja of Cooch Behar's team.

'You know what? Jamai Babu used to travel in a royal carriage along with the maharaja, whenever they went outside Cooch Behar to play matches,' she would say with the excitement of a schoolgirl.

When the children, visiting Cooch Behar during their summer holidays, put these questions to Tulu Mashi, she was dismissive.

'Your mother is incorrigible...!' she would blush.

For this particular bet match to be played in Kalina on a Sunday morning—when Kalu and Ashok were not on talking terms—

the whole team, along with the extras like Kalu, had set out on foot. Some of the older boys took along their bicycles with them, although they did not ride them. Ashok was there, carrying the stumps, while Kalu carried the batting pads. It was an important day for Ashok, because he had been allowed to play in the match. He was part of the team! The boys took the 'long cut' route through the Kalina gate and past the main road, heading towards the colony in which the ground was located. There was a lot of laughter as Rangan, a clownish fellow, made farting sounds by placing his hands at the back of his knees and paddling his legs.

'See, we have to win this match. Otherwise you will not be able to have the samosas,' the captain of the team, Narayanswamy, kept telling the boys.

It had been decided that each of the players would be given a samosa if they won the match. Soon enough, the playground was visible, and a player from the opposing team came down cycling to welcome them.

'C'mon, hurry up! You are late!' he said.

The players of the opposing team, mostly in whites, were visible in the distance, not far from the bustling road. In their excitement to be there first, some of the boys started running.

Ashok also ran. And before anybody could have realized, a bicyclist with a pillion rider had crashed into him and run over his legs. Ashok lay on the road, writhing in pain. Kalu wanted to soothe him but how could he—he hadn't yet started talking to him! The breach in friendship was so important that it mattered even at a time like this. Then, through the maze of people who had by now gathered around Ashok, Kalu saw that a part of Ashok's leg was contorted, hanging loose. Although there was no external wound, the bone had apparently broken. While some of the boys started to hail a taxi, Kalu impulsively turned on his heels and ran. He ran, ran and ran until he was breathless by the time he reached Ashok's house. Ashok's mother and Nimmi were alone in the house.

Panting heavily, Kalu gulped some air and managed to say, 'Aunty! Aunty! Ashok…'

'What…? What?' the anxious mother demanded.

For a moment, Kalu couldn't speak, numbed by both fatigue and shock.

'Ashok has broken his leg! He has met with an accident,' he finally managed to say.

Aunty's face turned pale as the import of the news sank in.

Just then a taxi arrived, with the boys carrying Ashok inside. His mother became hysterical at the sight, beating her chest with her hands and screaming, '*Mone, mone!* My son! Oh my son!'

Then she collapsed on the road, still beating her chest. Some of the elders in the neighbourhood took charge of the situation and soon the taxi drove away, taking Ashok to the hospital. He was home the same afternoon, with his leg swathed in a plaster. He had to be carried into the house and put into a bed. Several family friends and acquaintances visited Ashok that evening. Kalu was not one of them.

Even though Kalu was dying to see Ashok he couldn't bring himself to go and meet his best friend.

'You must go and see him,' he coaxed his mother the next morning, hoping that she would agree.

Even though their mothers met rarely, there was a special bond between the two women and the families because of the friendship between the children. Kalu's motive in asking his mother to visit Ashok was selfish—so that he could accompany her and have an excuse to be near Ashok, who was confined to bed. Fortunately for Kalu, Basanti readily agreed and mother and son set off for Ashok's house. On reaching the house, however, Kalu's feet got stuck. He would move no further than the threshold.

'Come in, Kalu,' Aunty said, as she saw him lingering at the door.

But Kalu wouldn't go in, despite her repeated pleas.

'Look, he forced me to come, and now he is feeling shy. These boys will quarrel, but also cannot do without one another,' Basanti said.

And both women laughed. Meanwhile, Ashok too started pleading that Kalu come and see him.

'Mummy, Aunty, why is he not coming in?' he demanded.

Even then Kalu did not budge, at which point Ashok began to cry.

Finally Kalu yielded, as Aunty dragged him inside the house. Ashok, looking pallid, lay in bed with his plastered leg placed high on a pillow. On seeing Kalu, he smiled with happiness, despite his tears. Kalu sat down beside him, not looking him in the eye.

'Ask him to talk to me,' Ashok demanded of his mother in Malayali, which Aunty duly translated.

'Let him talk first,' Kalu replied, with his eyes averted.

'How are you?' It was Ashok who spoke first.

'All right,' Kalu said self-effacingly, and both friends laughed with joy, happy to be united. Over the next month Kalu would visit Ashok regularly, while he sat in bed listening to gossip about school and their other friends. When the plaster was a few days old and Ashok was able to move about the house with some help from Kalu, the two boys would play carom. The plaster made the bond between the friends even stronger.

By the time of Ashok's accident Sergeant Biswas's family had moved to Quarter No. 55, one of the two 'special' quarters in the colony. It had two large rooms adjacent to one another. In the front ran a long veranda, covering the width of both the rooms. For the rest of their stay in Bombay, Samar and his family lived in this house. The larger of the two rooms, on the right, was the living—or if you wish—the drawing room. By way of furnishing it contained two coir charpoys that formed a double bed with the help of narrow wooden planks and occupied nearly half of the room, a dressing table with drawers, and an attached mirror so high that Kalu and little Babu had to use a stool to be able to see their faces. The room also had a wobbly high table, on which the sewing machine rested; and a low table, on which the table fan stood. There were also two wooden chairs without arms, with their back-rests wearing green covers embroidered in white, stitched by Basanti. Later, when a radio arrived in the house—one of the first radios in the neighbourhood—the 'machine table' became the 'radio table'. The sewing machine was transferred on to a 'peeda'—a low wooden plank.

It was a large room, about fifteen square feet. To the back were two windows overseeing green shrubs and grass and, at a little distance, a tamarind and a mango tree. Through the gaps in the trees, one could see a block of officers' bungalows. To the front, the larger room had a door and a window that opened on to the veranda, and another door leading to the adjacent room. This room, too, was of similar dimensions, except that to the left a parallel wall a few feet above the ground went right upto the tiled ceiling— somewhat like a long, dark, cavernous chimney. This part of the room was always dark, and the children would often hide there when playing 'ice pice' (I Spy). Putting both legs across the walls on either side, one could drag oneself high up in the chimney. This room had only one window at the back. Near this window was a tap and a cemented area bounded by a two-feet-high wall. This space was used to wash utensils and clothes, and occasionally served as a bathroom for the children's mother. The area next to the tap served as the kitchen, with the floor serving as the dining table. On one side of this kitchen was a little space where pictures of a few gods and goddesses were kept. At this altar every Thursday evening, Basanti—freshly bathed and draped in a wet gamchha— used to read out from the Lokhi Panchali, the Bengali book of prayers that was supposed to usher wealth and happiness. The children would sit around as Basanti read aloud, not understanding a word of what was being recited. There was a certain solemnity to the Thursday evening prayers. Yet the children looked forward to it, because at the end of the recital, after the conch shell was blown three times and they had joined their hands in supplication, prashad would be served—consisting mostly of cut fruits and the occasional peda. Some children from the neighbourhood would also join the prayers. They loved the prashad.

The room also had a single string cot or charpoy, on which Borda slept, while the rest of the family shared the double bed in the other room. The veranda running outside was about thirty feet long and at least six feet wide, its low tiled roof held up by three pillars. The veranda was bare, except for a coir charpoy, which mostly stood on its side against the wall. When it rained heavily, the boys would lie down on the charpoy and watch the copious raindrops forming rippled patterns in the puddles. It never only rained in Bombay. It always poured, slushing down the road to St Mary's in Kalina.

Chivvy Arrives

Soon after the Biswases came to occupy Quarter No. 55, the South Indian family that lived in the adjacent quarter got posted out and left. And then, in an olive green air force truck, arrived the family of Flight Sergeant Verma, a well-built man and black as soot. Hailing from Uttar Pradesh, the family of three daughters and two sons was rustic in their looks and behaviour. Verma 'Unty' would keep bawling and swearing at the children, who went to a Hindi-medium school run by the Kalina municipality. For this reason, despite the fact that Verma Uncle was one rank senior to their father, the Biswases treated the Vermas rather condescendingly. But a friendship soon developed between the families that included all except Samar and his bête noire, Flight Sergeant Verma.

He resented the black man because he once took up issue with him, demanding, 'Why don't you call me "Chiefie"?'

A Flight Sergeant (later rechristened JWO or Junior Warrant Officer) in those days was entitled to be called 'chivvy'—the airmen pronounced it 'chiefie'—by his subordinates. Samar must have hated Verma, because except for his rank he was in every way superior to 'Chivvy'. But it was not just in rank, but also in *group*, that Samar lagged behind. Verma Uncle, being a transport technician, belonged to the First Group whereas Samar, from the logistics trade, was in the Third Group.

In moments of anger even Basanti would say scornfully, 'You

never got your promotion on time; if at least you belonged the First Group, it would be some consolation.'

The lament was not entirely baseless, considering that the First Group people drew considerably better salaries.

Inspite of her acidic tongue, Verma Behenji eventually became a good friend of Basanti.

'Ae Kalu ki Amma,' she would call out to Basanti who would be mostly busy in the kitchen.

They often went out together for evening walks, and spent a considerable part of the day sitting on the charpoy and gossiping with other women. Bespectacled, slightly grey-haired and wrinkled, Verma Behenji chewed paan all day long, and the red-coloured juice often trickled from the corners of her mouth. She talked and looked like a rustic. Under Basanti's tutelage, Verma Behenji soon learnt to dress more like a city woman, even though her boorishness underneath revealed itself from time to time. The two women also went to the cinemas once in a while. Mrs Verma soon started forcing a paan or two on Basanti who, by and by, also got into the habit of chewing the green betel leaf. But then the Vermas were not Bengalis, for which reason the friendship was never quite complete.

Mrs Verma often nagged Basanti, 'Ae Kalu ki Amma, come and sit! What do you do all day long, cooking and cooking?'

'We don't eat dal-roti like you do. We have to have rice, dal, vegetables and fish, otherwise Babuji will not eat his food,' Basanti would retort.

To which Sushila ki Ma—as Mrs Verma was often called— would make a face and thrust a hand in the air, saying, 'Huh, as though we don't eat food!'

Privately Basanti would tell her children, 'These Hindustanis (using a broad term Bengalis apply to all North Indians), do they know to eat like us?'

The discussion around food was often fodder for the two women to quarrel and create a scene. Verma Behenji had quickly developed a reputation in the neighbourhood as a quarrelsome woman, but in her own way, she was a charmer. The Biswases loved to hear her swear at one or more of her five children.

'*Eai Sushila harramjaddi… !*'

Basanti often mimicked Verma Aunty, sending Kalu and his brothers into peals of laughter. That was when Samar was not present in the house.

Another reason for the Biswases' vague sense of superiority was that the Vermas' children, particularly the girls, had taken after their father and were dark-complexioned. No wonder they— particularly the eldest girl, a pugnacious character called Sushila—resented their airs, and the children from the two families often got into quarrels.

'*Kali kaluti baigun looti!*' the Biswas boys teased.

'*Gore gu ke katorey!*' the Verma girls retorted.

Kalu also looked upon them as rivals because Sushila soon collected a group of friends around her, and he obviously didn't like the intrusion into what was *his* domain. Yet they often played together; the tomboy Sushila even playing jhar bandar, normally considered a boys' game. The Vermas also taught the children of the camp a new game called Teelo. The game consisted of two opposing teams. All they needed was a pencil or chalk to make little straight lines like the figure one. The search team would count to a hundred or two hundred, whatever was agreed upon, at the end of which they would shout, 'Teelo!' As a member of the search team began counting loudly, the opposing team would frantically scribble the straight lines, hiding them in obscure locations that were not easily visible, but totalling up to the agreed number. This scribbling could be done with chalk on slabs of stone or tiles or in pencil on walls. After 'Teelo!' was shouted, the search team would set out and unearth the scribbled lines. After the search operation was over, the team that had scribbled the lines would dig out the marks that had *not* been discovered by the search team; and the total of this would be their score. Then it would be the other team's turn to scribble and successfully hide them. The team with the higher score at the end of the game would be declared the winner. The children normally played Teelo in the disused bathroom in front of their house, ingeniously hiding the marked slabs of stones and tiles in strange places, scribbling on the bottom of tiles or on the wooden beams that held the tiled roof.

One afternoon, while Basanti and her boys were asleep (it was compulsory resting time), there was loud knocking on the door. When they opened the door, rubbing their eyes, there stood Sushila beckoning them, 'Come on soon, our Daddy is taking pictures!' Kalu and Bappa quickly jumped out of bed, washed their faces, combed their hair and ran out to get themselves photographed— they could not let go of such a rare opportunity. The Vermas were proud owners of a camera.

Their photos taken, Verma Uncle said, 'Where is your mother? Go and call her too.'

Aunty too added, 'Go son, call your amma. The sun is going to go down soon.'

Basanti came, but reluctantly. She did not like anybody interrupting her afternoon siesta. Half-asleep, and without having tied up her curly flowing hair, she posed for a photo all by herself. A week later when the photos were developed, Basanti looked gorgeous with her flowing hair. She proudly showed the photo to all her friends who came to their house that day. After a long time, she felt flattered. Later that evening when Samar came home, the children rushed up to show him the photo. At first he was happy to see it; but on learning that Flight Sergeant Verma had clicked his wife's picture, his mood became sombre. For a while he seethed inwardly.

'What was the need for you to take pictures?' he thundered at her suddenly.

'What's wrong, why are you feeling jealous!' Basanti fought back.

That was too much for Samar. He caught hold of his wife by the hair and rained a few heavy blows on her. Basanti crouched in a corner and wept bitterly. On seeing their mother cry, Kalu and his younger brother too began to cry. He hated his father at such times, and felt powerless at his inability to protect his mother. It was Bappa who served food to their father that evening. Samar gulped down his food without any remorse. Basanti and the children went to bed without dinner.

An Incompatible Couple

In the photograph taken by Verma Uncle, Basanti, in her flowing hair and simple sari, somehow looked grand. She was not a beautiful woman in the conventional sense, but she was attractive. Light brown-complexioned and slightly built, she had a proportionate figure that any woman would envy. 'You have such beautiful hands and feet,' her friends often complimented her.

She would respond coyly to these compliments without protesting, knowing they were true, not meant just to flatter her.

'Oh, nothing remains after giving birth to four children,' she would protest.

This was an artful way of saying, 'Oh, you should have seen me in my younger days.'

If she had the right audience, she could spend an entire afternoon talking of her glorious youthful days.

'My father was not rich but we belonged to an aristocratic family,' was one of her common refrains.

Basanti had an oval face with arched eyebrows over doe-like eyes. The cheekbones were slightly high and became prominent when she smiled. An outgoing sort, she would rather laugh than smile. The laughter was vibrant, revealing slightly large but even teeth. It was a warm laughter that put people at ease with her. The only shortcomings of her face were a slightly long but blunt chin and a short nose. She had thick curly hair, and told her children tales of how she was admired during her younger days by boys and girls alike. In her own way she was a stylish woman—'up-to-date', as she would say. She groomed herself well, taking care to comb and pleat her hair and tie it into a neat bun. She also propped up her face with powder in the evenings. She insisted that her children too wash and powder their faces and comb their hair before they went out to play in the evenings. When they returned after sundown, they had to wash their feet and hands before settling down on the mat with their books.

In contrast to her husband, Basanti was a gregarious and lively sort, someone who could make friends easily. She was popular with friends and neighbours, but her artlessness and the habit of speaking her mind often led to her friendships being terminated abruptly. The man and the woman were not quite made for each other. If Samar was like bland food, Basanti was all pepper and spice. The relationship between them was not intense; if anything, there was sometimes an element of intense hate. Mutual distaste often manifested itself in verbal duels between husband and wife, with Samar often using foul language to which his wife didn't take very submissively. These fights often ended with the husband grabbing his wife by the hair and beating her up. They were often like two very different people who had been tossed into a forced togetherness; hardly like friends and even less like soul mates. They rarely appeared to share a relationship of love.

'Other husbands sit and talk with their wives for hours together. And your father—till date he has never sat down and chatted with me for ten minutes,' Basanti often lamented to her children.

This complaint would be made within hearing distance of Samar who would not react, provoking her even more, as though her words had been addressed to a wall.

Disgusted and defeated, she would say, 'I hate to see this man!'

To which would Samar would perhaps smile mildly, making Basanti angrier. She would tell him, 'Don't smile. It doesn't quite suit your face!'

And she would mimic a swollen face, mocking her husband. Life dragged along, punctuated by their little quarrels.

Basanti and Samar were mismatched even in their family backgrounds. Samar was the son of a poor and humble farmer who had no other vocation but a talent for acting in jatras that travelled from village to village. Neither of these occupations was much respected in early twentieth-century Bengal, just like even today they are not.

During an exchange of unpleasant words it was common to hear Basanti say, 'After all he is the son of a chaasha, how much better can he be!'

Even in lighter moments she would tell the children, within earshot of their father, 'Your grandfather an actor? Oh, in those stupid jatras!'

Even though the children had never seen their grandfather, they were given to understand—through their mother's exhortations—that he was not a man of consequence, and therefore, not respectable. On the other hand, she told them how she belonged to an 'aristocratic' family—her father and grandfather were lawyers.

She would never miss a chance to tell them about her uncles on her mother's side, 'They were Rai Bahadurs.'

Little did she or the children realize that titles like Rai Bahadur were bestowed by the British, and the carriers of these lofty titles were frowned upon by the nationalists for being sycophants of the Raj.

The children did not know much of all that, but they felt proud to have such 'aristocratic' family antecedents. Basanti also told them of an uncle of hers who was a lawyer in the Supreme Court of India, and another, who was an inspector general of police in Assam. Then there were other uncles who had studied in Canada.

'They were so highly educated that when they came back to India there were no jobs befitting their education,' Basanti once lamented.

Kalu was in awe of these relatives, only heard of but never seen. One of them even had a German wife.

Once, on a summer holiday to Basanti's famed mama bari in Dhubri, Assam, the children were actually introduced to Erica, the German lady, in person. Draped in a sari and sporting the red sindhur on her forehead, she had even learnt to speak in Bengali.

'Speak to her in Bangla,' Basanti had urged the children during an audience.

Later, the awe for the white lady was somewhat diluted.

'She is no German princess,' their father had explained. 'She's the daughter of an ordinary worker, back in Germany.'

The trip to Dhubri was an eye-opener for the children as their mother showed them around the old compound.

'This is where the magnolia tree stood…'

'This is the room where the piano was…'

'This was the outhouse…'

The guided tour of the mama bari of yore was in stark contrast to what the children actually saw. The place was, at the time of their visit, divided into several plots on which the descendants of the great family lived in humble cottages.

But Basanti and her children's arrival had stirred up the entire compound and its residents.

'Aye you are Basonti's son? What's your name?'

'Basonti, your son is so big!' they said when they saw Borda.

The children felt unduly important, with the attention showered on them.

'Did you realize what it was like,' Basanti asked the children towards the end of the trip, swelling with pride.

'And yet, all that was nothing compared to the olden days of glory,' she added, lamenting.

There was another of his mother's favourite stories that inspired Kalu.

'Do you know Johorlal had visited my mama bari…'

'And also Netaji!'

Basanti gave the children graphic accounts of how Netaji Subhas Chandra Bose and Jawaharlal Nehru had come visiting her mama bari in Dhubri. What she never forgot to give the children, however, were the asides of these visits.

According to one such account, when Subhas Bose came visiting her mama's place, the entire village turned up to look at his—hold your breath—excreta!

Obviously, those days the septic lavatory had not yet come to India.

'And did it not stink?' the children wanted to know.

The embarrassed mother never answered.

'Mahatma Gandhi, too, was supposed to come to our mama's house once,' she told the children agog with curiosity.

'But he had laid a condition. He wanted Mama to first relinquish his title of Rai Bahadur.'

'Mama did not agree to that,' she said with pride in her voice; as though the incident had made Gandhiji the poorer.

Basanti knew little about nationalism and politics, neither did she pretend to know much. But there was a certain snobbish attitude about her, inherited, perhaps, from her father who was an educated man but earned little, what with six daughters that he had to bring up and marry off.

'Father was in a poor state, otherwise you think I would have married your father?' she told her children every time she was provoked.

She never tired of telling them how appalled she was when she first came to Samar's home after their marriage.

'I was shocked... Even the servants at our mama bari lived better.'

This reference to servants was never taken kindly by Samar, whose anger was provoked by such comparison.

'And your granny, she made my life even more miserable,' Basanti would continue, as though the incident had taken place just the other day. Her mother-in-law, apparently, was harsh on her upper-class background and never missed shooting a barb at her daughter-in-law.

'"Why didn't your father send along a maid in dowry?" she would ask me sarcastically,' Basanti would tell her sons.

Samar's response to these deprecating remarks about his family was met with deserving silence and contempt; except that once in a while, when Basanti praised her father, he would chip in ironically, 'Yes he was an ukil, but a bot tolar ukil.'

The children did not know what that meant, except that it was a derisive description of their ukil (lawyer) grandpa—a grandfather they had never seen; he had died long before they were born. When they were older and courageous enough to ask their father what it meant, Samar smiled and said, 'A lawyer who sits under the banyan tree and practises law.'

The children realized their maternal grandfather must have been an unsuccessful lawyer. Always ready with a retort, Basanti didn't quite know how to defend that fact.

'At least he was not a chaasha like your father,' was all she managed to say, finally cornered. Calling a person chaasha was tantamount to swearing at that person.

Strangely, despite its long association with communism, the word chaasha in Bengal still carries with it a negative connotation. Unlike chief ministers of North Indian states who proudly claim to be farmers and win political brownie points, chief ministers from West Bengal have made no such claims of belonging to the chaasha fraternity.

In Bengal you still can hear women chide their unruly children, 'Don't behave like a chaasha!'

An Anglo-Indian family

About the same time as the Vermas, there arrived to the Quarter No. 46 a white man who lived all by himself. It was for the first time that the children of the neighbourhood were seeing a white man. Somehow, with his pink colour and bloodshot eyes, Kalu thought the man looked like a monkey. He had an angry scowl, and Kalu and the other boys were afraid of even going close to him. A young Maharashtrian lad called Arun actually thought the man was a monkey. From behind a wall he would poke his face and grimace at him, at which the white man's face would flush to a deeper red, and he would hurl English abuses at Arun. Of course, there was a furlong's distance between the two of them, because of which the boy couldn't hear any of the abuse, and nor could the man catch him. But whenever the man made as though to grab him, Arun would run and disappear into his house. After a little while, he would come back and repeat the pantomime. The stranger's quarter, which was visible from the back of Kalu's house, became a rallying point for Kalu and other kids. The man was a source of great curiosity for the children, on the rare occasions he was seen going in or coming out of his house. The children giggled a great deal whenever they saw him, as though he were some comic creature.

A few days later the Monkey Man's family arrived. His wife was a small brown-skinned woman who wore a skirt and blouse.

Basanti laughed, 'Oh ma, what kind of clothes are these!'

One day the woman in skirts came to their house.

'I'm Mrs Sampio, your new neighbour,' she said.

'You are Anglo-Indians?' Basanti asked.

'Yes,' she said and gave her a summary of their family history. Her name was June.

'Why not July or August?' the boys asked and laughed.

Along with the woman was a big boy—he must have been about twelve years old, while Kalu at this time was about nine— and two girls, both about Kalu's age. All three of them were pink-skinned. Before long the Sampio children became friends with the Biswas boys. The big boy's name was Lui.

'What a funny name,' Kalu and his brothers said.

The older and taller of the girls was called Glanis, and the younger Jennifer. Their father, who the other children were still scared of, was called Sergeant Sampio. Aunty, who was the only brown–skinned person in the house and could speak Hindi, soon became friends with Basanti. She would often drop into the house and chat with Basanti about her relatives in England. Among other things, she taught Basanti how to whip up the white of the egg and make large omelettes from just a single egg. Soon after their arrival Sergeant Sampio made her pregnant, and the pregnancy was visible to all from the shape of her skirt. Mrs Sampio made no attempt to conceal her bulging stomach.

'Don't you feel ashamed?' Basanti once remarked.

'This is the fourth time!' she laughed at the comment, patting her bulge.

Mrs June Sampio was a bubbly, carefree sort. But deep down she was sad and worried, for there was always a shortage of groceries in her house. Her husband would often be drunk and hardly gave her enough money to buy food for the children. If she argued, the man would beat her up.

'What's this?' Basanti had once remarked at the sight of June's bruised hand.

'Oh, nothing. This keeps happening to me. Had a fight with Mr Sampio last night,' she said, as though it was the most natural thing to happen.

And to add to her woes, soon Caroline was born.

'Another mouth to feed,' Basanti commented.

Even before the little girl could crawl her way around, Sampio Aunty's stomach started to bulge again.

A son was born next, whom they named Ashley. Now with five children to feed, there was never enough food in the Sampio household. Every once in a while, Sampio Aunty would come to their house with a utensil and Basanti had to loan out flour or rice to her, all because the man of the house was a drunkard. Of the three older children, Glanis was a good friend of Kalu. Tall, fair-complexioned and blond-haired, Glanis was also soft-spoken and sweet-natured—an angel. Jennifer, who was red-cheeked and freckled, was always digging her nose or her behind. She was also always ready to pick up a fight. Glanis and Kalu would chat together for long hours, and were a bit like baby soulmates.

'How about getting these two married off?' the women who gossiped with Basanti said. And they laughed at the joke.

Lui, the eldest boy, was not too interested in studies or good at it, but he had an exceptional knack for making cardboard models of aircrafts. The children of the neighbourhood were in awe of him. They soon became his assistants, providing him with cardboard, pins and other accessories such as the rubber lids of small medicine bottles, which became the wheels of the aircraft. By and by, the other boys also learned to make these cardboard models. They soon found a 'runway' where they would carry out mock landings and take-offs. The 'runway' was a flat strip of cement that was part of the tank that held all the sewage water from the quarters and even from new multi-storeyed quarters that had come up a little distance away. All the boys under Lui's wing would come here running, aircraft in hand, and 'land' them on the strip of cement. The kind of passionate interest the boys took in modelling and 'flying' their cardboard planes was quite amazing.

His talent for making model planes made Lui a very sought-after fellow among the boys, but then his lack of interest in studies also made him somewhat of a renegade. Lui never went to school. Actually, none of the Sampio children went to school. By any reckoning this was difficult to understand, but since they spoke the Queen's Language no one could think poorly of them. In fact, if anything, Kalu and his brothers felt inferior to them in both colour and tongue.

Burials at St Mary's School

Kalu and his brothers went to St Mary's High School in Kalina, taking the road past the Air India colony. The school had two main gates next to each other, only one of which would stay open. Beyond the gate, to the left, was a very old double-storey building that had a tiled roof and looked quaint, as though it belonged to an era gone by. The building stood precariously, as though it would fall anytime. And indeed, once when heavy rains and a storm raged, the tiled roof was partly blown away and a part of the building caved in. At the end of this building, there was a rickety wooden staircase that led to the upper floor. It also connected with the first floor of a modern three-storeyed building. The third storey of this building was the school hall, in which plays and other cultural events were held from time to time. Adjacent to the modern building was the church, whose spire rose above all other structures in the premises. The church had a large porch held up by square pillars, under which poor people often slept. In fact the school premises served as a thoroughfare for the locals, with the road from the gate going past the church and leading to a village of fishermen and working-class people, most of whom were Christians of Goan descent.

The ground within the school compound was 'littered', every few yards, with slabs of cement. On a closer examination, one realized these were tombstones—the marble tablets paying tribute to the dead. The school compound was also a graveyard, except that the gravestones were not held up vertically. The boys never hesitated or felt guilty about walking over the gravestones. Why, they even played a game called Unchh Neech, in which one had to constantly keep stepping on the gravestones. One was declared 'out' if touched by another player when standing on the ground. To stay 'alive' one had to constantly jump on to the tombstones. Towards the back of the school, next to the church and the other seminary buildings—where the Fathers lived—was a walled compound which was the real graveyard. The children were usually afraid to venture to this part; and on the few occasions that they did go there, they came back with their hearts pounding. Kalu always imagined seeing ghosts in that isolated part of the school. It was a desolate place, full of weeds interspersed with impressive gravestones that often had wooden crosses at the head and quaint little flowerbeds around them. Some of the graves were little mounds of earth with wilted wreaths and withered flowers over them, indicating that someone had been buried very recently. At the back of the new, three-storeyed school building was the playground where older schoolboys often ran around with a football. It was not the usual game of twenty-two players—the whole class of forty boys chased the ball. Kalu often sat in his classroom looking out of the window with rapt attention, little aware of what was going on inside. The wide outside world attracted him.

It was not uncommon for a funeral or a burial to be going on in the school compound at the same time as the classes were on. The children rarely paid heed to these. But Kalu remembered watching one such burial from the classroom. There were a lot of people, crowded next to a Father around mounds of fresh earth, where a new grave had been dug. The very thought that a human being, alive a while ago, could be buried under a mound of earth terrified Kalu. Looking out, he could see the coffin being placed next to the grave and several people kissing it and crossing themselves. Some counted the beads on the rosaries they held in their hands. The mood was silent and sombre. Finally the priest said some prayers, flung some earth into the grave and everyone got ready with ropes to lower the coffin into the ground. At this point two little girls— probably the children of the dead—began to scream and flail their arms, desperately trying to prevent their father (or mother) from being buried in the earth. Kalu could feel their anguish, and lumps rose in his own throat. It was a numbing feeling of helplessness, as if a live person was being interred within the earth and would never be seen or heard for the rest of his life. It left Kalu with a profound sense of loss. How can someone die?—this thought troubled him deeply.

The frequent funerals and burials could never bring Kalu to terms with death. He feared death in a physical sort of way. It saddened his heart every time he saw a grave being dug in the school compound. The prospect of a man or woman lying covered on all sides with earth terrified him; it didn't matter that the person was dead. The thought that ants would slowly be eating the body also gnawed at him. Whenever a fresh grave was dug, remnants of old skulls and bones were often turned out along with the earth. These images affected Kalu in a profound way. At an early age, he had begun to believe in the transience of life. Somehow, he was not quite reconciled to the idea of death.

'What if my mother or father died,' he often wondered, and shuddered alone at the thought. So deep were these fears that he never spoke about them to anyone.

Outside the school compound was a large pond—a lake, rather. It would fill to the brim during the rains, when water hyacinth weeds began to grow and finally clog up the entire lake. Finally, by summer, almost the entire lake dried up, except for a small shrunken patch that remained full throughout the year. During monsoons, the lake became a fascinating place. On their way home after school, some of the boys would spend a long time watching shoals of little fish in the water. Sometimes Kalu and Ashok would remove their shoes and get into the water, and catch the little black baby fish in their cupped palms. But they were unable to hold the water in their palms for long and the fish would often die, making the boys sad. On other days they would remember to bring a bottle from home and carry the fish in it—a source of great distraction on their way back home.

There were two routes that led to the school from their home. One was the shortcut route that they usually took, but it became impossible to navigate because of the slush and mud in the thick of the monsoon, forcing them to take the longer route through the Kalina gate. The shortcut was through the back of the double-line quarters with rows of windows overlooking the path, after which the boys reached the barbed wire fencing of the camp. Somewhere along its length was an illegal opening in the form of a generous parting of the wires, so as to allow people to pass through with ease. One had to bend considerably to pass through the gap in the fencing. Sometimes their shirts, or the schoolbags slung on their backs, would get caught in the barbed wire and it would be a difficult task extricating oneself. Of course, they travelled in groups of seven to ten boys and there were others around to help, but sometimes one could be alone. And then it would be difficult. Just as difficult as getting a torn shirt replaced.

There were other problems in going to school alone. Kalu was mortally afraid of being alone while crossing a particular three-storeyed house. It was an old and eerie-looking house with wooden balconies. The second floor of the house often had two dogs waiting in the balcony. They were large dogs. But Kalu's child's eyes, and his fear, magnified their size. He never saw dogs of that size again. The greyhound-like dogs had sad, black, ponderous eyes and when they barked in their deep and booming voice, Kalu's whole being trembled like the air. His biggest fear was that the dogs, which poked their heads out of the wooden railing, would pounce upon him at the first chance. When in company it wasn't much trouble overcoming the fear—the boys would run away laughing even though they were scared. But when he was alone, going to school or returning, it became a question of life and death—'To go or not to go?' There was always the possibility that the dogs would not be out in the balcony, and Kalu would pray to God that it be so. Since the building was located in the turn of a narrow lane one couldn't see it from a long distance, and one suddenly found oneself facing the dogs. In such a situation there was nothing to do but quietly tiptoe across the turn, as though being quiet would prevent the dogs from seeing him. The other alternative was to retrace his steps and make a detour along a much longer route. Kalu often chose the second option, even though it meant wasting ten more minutes. When hungry and in a hurry to be home, ten minutes was a long time.

The Latecomers

The 'dog-house' was on a shortcut running through Kalina, which passed a lower-middle class locality of Christian families. Their old houses were rather large and quaint single-storeyed structures. The whitewashed walls held tiled roofs that came down very low, about five feet above the ground. From the road one could see the insides of the houses, decorated with artefacts. Virtually every house had an altar, garishly decorated with religious images, with red lamps glowing over a picture of Jesus or of the Virgin Mother and Her Child. The houses with tiny yards were interspersed with shops, but by and large it was a residential area. Hens, ducks and pigs reared by the residents roamed freely around the neighbourhood. One also came across children squatting on the road and relieving themselves. The hens often pecked at the yellow excreta after the children had finished their jobs. The pigs were more aggressive, often beginning to gulp down the fresh refuse even before the frightened children had finished and left. Pigs roamed all over Kalina and could often be seen wallowing in the soggy ground. During the monsoon, the rainwater would stand on the mud road outside the camp which led to Kalina. And soon the entire place would be converted to a ditch—a grazing ground for pigs, no longer fit for human travel, unless they agreed to trudge through ankle-deep sludge, shoes held aloft in their hands.

During the monsoon, the children took the long route to school, which meant travelling all the way to the Kalina Main Gate and then taking the Kurla-Santa Cruz Road. This was longer by a kilometre. Sometimes the boys took another shortcut through the back of the officers' quarters, which took them through a thick forest of mango and cotton trees before leading to another opening in the fencing. This opening was not too far from the one in the original shortcut, but led through a path that was relatively dry even when it rained. Again, this was a route that the boys took only when in a large company. None of them dared to walk it alone, because in one of the cottages located in a wide expanse of green there lived an old white woman who the boys referred to as 'Whitey'. Kalu had never seen Whitey, nor had any other boy. But she was rumoured to have a gun and reportedly shot at people passing by her cottage. Clearly, Whitey was a figment of their childhood imagination, but the fear that Kalu experienced while passing by Whitey's cottage was indeed very real.

The boys never went straight to school. They sauntered around, sometimes aiming stones at a mango or a tamarind tree; sometimes watching someone plucking a honeycomb; sometimes chasing a bird with a broken wing. There was never a dull moment during the roughly two-kilometre-long journey to school. But in their meanderings they often reached school late, by which time the morning assembly was already on. And a school prefect took down the names of children who came in late.

In the morning, before classes began and after the mustachioed khaki-clad maali had rung the 'long bell' that went *ting-tin-tin-tin*, the whole school gathered in an assembly in front of the church, repeating after the principal, a Father in his white cassock:

> *Our Father who art in heaven*
> *Hallowed be thy name*

Thy Kingdom come
Thy will be done
On earth
As it is in heaven
Give us this day
Our daily bread
And forgive us our trespasses
As we forgive those who trespass against us.

Once the prayers were over, Father Sequeira—for that was the principal's name—stood on a high platform holding a long cane in his hand, and gave the assembled students information about the day or the coming week, or warned them not to do this or that, reminded them to come to school clean and properly dressed, and so on. And while this went on, the ranks of latecomers, who stood in a separate row away from the massed assembly, increased in number. The points of discipline and other matters gone over, the latecomers would, one by one, approach the principal, who duly whacked them behind the knees with his cane. In specially deserving cases, like those who regularly came in late, their pants would be pulled down and the cane marks duly registered on their bottoms. The boys squirmed as much in pain as out of shame.

'Show me your buttock... Show me!' the principal said gleefully, as he caned the boys.

While the boys got it on their bottoms, the girls who came in late were whacked on their palms. And while all this was carried out, there would be an impertinent and sadistic grin on the principal's face. It was difficult to understand whether he was angry or took some vicarious delight in caning the students.

Sometimes, perhaps when he had more urgent issues to attend, the principal would let the defaulters go with merely a harsh verbal warning, 'I don't want to see any latecomers next time!'

This reprieve would bring grins of relief on the faces of the latecomers. After the assembly the students would walk, in their respective rows, to their classroom.

Kalu joined the KG class in St Mary's in 1962 and continued till the August of 1969, by when he was in the sixth standard. It was originally a co-educational school, from which girls were being phased out in order to make it a 'boys only' school. The classes of standard six and below were comprised of boys only. Classes at St Mary's were taken in two shifts. The junior shift, up to the fourth standard, went to school in the afternoons from one to four. The senior shift, from the fifth to the tenth standard, had their classes in the morning. The arrangement was fine until first Bappa, and then Ashok, crossed over the threshold of the fifth standard. For a time Kalu felt all alone, yearning for the day when he too would be in the fifth standard and go to school with the 'big boys'.

His First Sketches

Kalu was rather good at studies, having stood third in the second standard, an achievement not attained by any of his siblings. But more than studying, his interest lay in drawing and colouring. He spent a lot of time sketching figures from his textbooks. More advanced art filled him with awe, making him wonder how someone could have actually drawn them. But when he attempted the simpler drawings, like a pair of monkeys hanging from a tree or a peacock perched on a branch, he was impressed with his own abilities. When he proceeded to colour in his sketches with watercolour and a brush, the result was even more impressive.

His drawing book was also full with etchings of Hindu gods and goddesses.

'You made this?' his neighbours in class would ask in disbelief.

'You copied this with tracing paper,' others would accuse him. The accusations hurt Kalu deeply, but he was never good at defending himself.

Bappa, the brother immediately older to him, was a trifle envious of his talent and often challenged him, 'Can you draw this like I can?'

And they would attempt to draw a picture of Netaji or Gandhi.

Bappa's sketching was more skilful, with dark lines and shades. But Kalu's childish renditions were more accurate, resembling the actual picture of reference more closely. And yet it was Bappa who went around bragging about his own sketches, while Kalu kept quiet, feeling like a loser. It was this trait of not being able to assert himself that would one day cost him his choice of career as an artist.

Teachers were mostly affectionate towards Kalu, in the way they usually are towards the 'good boys'. But there were nevertheless a few teachers whom he loathed or rather, feared. One of them was the 'Blanch Teacher'—a severe-looking woman who wore a sari and no make-up. She taught arithmetic in the fourth standard. Stories of her ferocity were passed on to Kalu from Ashok, when she had been Ashok's class teacher. A wrong answer to an arithmetical problem or an arithmetic homework not done meant the Blanch Teacher demanding, 'Show me your hands!'

When an innocent little boy proffered a trembling palm she would shout, 'Not your palms; show me your knuckles!'

And on them she would rap the offending boy with the edge of a foot ruler, until he cried for dear life. So hard did she wield it that, on occasions, the wooden ruler would break into two. In the year that he was taught by her, Kalu never forgot to finish his arithmetic homework. When he got promoted to the fourth standard, one of his persistent prayers to God was that Mrs Blanch should not be his class teacher. That prayer was answered. His class was assigned to Miss Margaret, a dark young lady who wore a frock or skirt-and-blouse, and possessed a sweet disposition, particularly towards Kalu.

'She's black, and so are you. That's why she loves you,' Bappa would tease him.

Somewhat less notorious than Blanch Teacher, but also feared for her cruelty, was 'Glossy Teacher'. She was fair, had short curly hair and was rather beautiful, disguising her ugly side. She taught history in the third standard. Kalu hated the subject particularly because he could not remember the dates of historical events.

'When did the battle of Plassey take place?'

It took him several decades just to discover that the English-sounding 'Plassey' was in fact a small village called Polashi in the backyard of his own native state, West Bengal.

And for every wrong answer, Glossy Teacher would beckon the defaulter in a rather sweet tone, 'Come here, my dear.'

And the moment they were within her reach, she would grab them by their shirt and then pinch them in the stomach, until the little boys doubled up in pain.

When Kalu was in the fourth standard there came a new teacher who, for some unknown reason, went by the name of the 'Karachi Teacher'. She was an old lady who had large flared nostrils and wore huge earrings and too much make-up, giving her face a strange, ashen look. She had great contempt for most Indians and expressed her disgust at watching Indians spitting paan juice on the streets. She spoke English with a strange accent, in which 'No talking' became 'No toking' and chalk became 'choke'. Her strange accent was a source of great mirth for the boys, who mimicked her enthusiastically. It was rumoured that she had come to India from Karachi, a city in Pakistan. She left the school within a year.

Among all the teachers at St Mary's, the one who stood out for her beauty was 'Vicky Teacher'. Tall, fair and beautiful, she had a shock of short black hair on her head. Her beauty was perhaps accentuated by a sweet and delicate disposition. Not once was she rude to the boys, however dull or impertinent they might be. There was always a smile on her face. Vicky Teacher wore tight skirts that revealed fleshy legs, but at that age legs mattered very little to the innocent boys. However, not all boys were that innocent. Some of them devised ingenious ways to take a closer look at Vicky Teacher's 'inner beauty'. One of them was Charlie. He was a 'repeater'—a term that meant that he had failed the previous year. Charlie was the biggest boy in the class and would usually sit in one of the back benches. But during Vicky Teacher's class, he would come up to the front row near the teacher's desk. Once she was seated on her chair and asked the boys to read their lessons while she corrected their copies, Charlie would quietly drop a rubber or a pencil on the floor next to the teacher's desk. And every time he bent down to pick up the rubber or the pencil, he would steal a glance inside Vicky Teacher's skirt.

'She is wearing a red panty today!' he would later inform the boys with aplomb.

These accounts generated a strange stirring sensation in Kalu, but then he was too young to fully understand sex or dwell on it for long. He would not get his first erection until three years later, when in the seventh standard. Nevertheless, at Charlie's behest, he once tried dropping a rubber under Vicky Teacher's table. But while picking it up, he was too petrified to peep under her skirt.

When he got back to his bench, Charlie asked, 'What colour?'

Not wanting to look foolish, he said without conviction, 'Blue.'

'Well done!' Charlie slapped him on the back.

Somehow, the act made Kalu feel guilty. From that day onwards he avoided Charlie's company.

'All humans are my brothers and sisters,' their Moral Science lessons had clearly stated.

So when Steve and Shakuntala, both students of the fourth standard, were caught crouching in a corner of the school hiding and embracing each other, all the boys were scandalized. Kalu—who was in the third standard at that time—thought of them as a bad boy and a bad girl, whom he should never associate with. But however much he tried, he never succeeded in obliterating the tingling feeling under his skin, whenever he thought of them. Perhaps he was starting to shed his innocence, along with his milk teeth.

One day a tooth came off when Kalu was in school. He felt a sense of loss and kept it in his pocket all day, refusing to part with it. Later, back home, he threw it on the tiled roof of his house, hoping that the rats would take it away. This was what his mother had taught him to do.

'If the rats take away your tooth, the new tooth that will grow will be sharp and strong—like those of the rats,' he remembered her telling him once.

There were plenty of rats in the house. The small ones scampered about the house, and the large ones lived among the tiles of the roof and created a ruckus every night. When he was younger, Kalu would be terrified by their rumblings. He used to think they were fighting. But by and by, through keen observation, he realized that the rats were most often copulating, rather than fighting. After that discovery, whenever there was a noise and commotion on the roof he got aroused, even if the rats might actually have been fighting. Pavlovian effect! The result of the commotion on the roof could be seen inside the drawers of the dressing table every few months. Whenever the drawers would be cleaned up, among the bits of torn paper—obviously the work of the rodents—there would be a few pink-coloured baby rats whose eyes had not yet opened. They were beautiful little creatures. Every time his father flung them away into the woods, Kalu could feel his heart wrenched.

Another time his heart beat faster was around the results. The day when their final results would be announced was a time for reckoning at school. It was the day the bright students looked forward to, while the dull-headed ones wished it could be wiped off the calendar. Kalu belonged to the former group, always hoping to be among the first five boys in his class. There used to be an excitement in the air on the day of the results, as parents and guardians accompanied their wards to the school and were allowed inside the school premises, where they crowded into the corridors and stuck out their necks through the classroom windows. There would be unusual commotion as everyone made guesses about who would come first, second or third; other ranks being of little consequence.

'Guess who's going to come first in the class?' was a question that was abuzz in every classroom and corridor.

While every year it was the same kind of excitement, Kalu could never forget the day he got his fourth standard results.

The commotion in the classroom came to a halt as Margaret Teacher walked into the class holding the forty-odd report cards. The report card was a thin booklet, which the boys used to cover with coloured cellophane paper. If the card on the top was red, everyone could tell it was Sujit's. As expected, Miss Margret announced, 'First in the class—Sujit Narayan!'

And a roar of applause rent the classroom.

Then she paused for a while and everyone, including Kalu, shouted, 'Leo! Leo!'

They rooted for Leo because he was the next best boy in the class.

But just then the teacher announced, 'Second in the class… Kalu Biswas!'

It could not be true. Kalu thought he had misheard his name.

But before he could verify with someone, everything was drowned in the loud clapping and cheering.

'Congratulations, Kalu!' he vaguely heard the boys cheering him.

He was delirious with joy and could not hear anything after that. He was on cloud nine! It was the closest he had come to being the first boy in any class.

Basanti was immensely proud of her third son.

'Learn to be like him,' she told Babu and Bappa.

'Congrats!' even Borda shook his hands.

'Let me see your report card,' his father asked, incredulous.

A Live-in Tutor

It was not by fluke that Kalu stood second in the fourth standard. Earlier that year, one evening, a stern, mustachioed man had accompanied their father to the house. After he was served tea and biscuits, Samar introduced him to the boys, 'This is Roy Kaku. From today he will be master moshai—your tutor.'

It was not known what prompted Samar to get the children a tutor. But after that evening, by the time the boys returned from play and washed themselves, Roy Kaku would often be there in attendance. He would come to the house and head straight for the 'radio table', which was now converted to a study table, and around which the three brothers sat. Of course, Borda was not part of this tutorial scheme. Some evenings the boys returned from play to find their teacher waiting for them—seething in rage, they thought. On such evenings they would rush straight to the table with their school-bags, furtively eyeing the man. Roy Kaku was the silent sort, speaking only when absolutely necessary. For a teacher, he spoke very little. More than actually teaching, it was just his presence that ensured the boys did their lessons. Even when they failed to finish allotted tasks, the tutor would not upbraid them verbally. His angry eyes did most of the speaking, and he silently tweaked their ears till they winced in pain.

While he taught the boys, Basanti would bring him a cup of tea and sometimes sweets she had prepared. Even these he accepted without exchanging a word with her.

'Strange man he is,' she would later tell the boys.

The fear of Roy Kaku was inversely proportional to the children's age. Babu, the youngest one, was in class one then and was the most terrified of him. Once he felt sick but dared not say so to Kaku, who would think it was an excuse to evade studies. That evening, little Babu threw up on the study table. But Bappa and Kalu continued with their lessons; such was the fear of the tutor.

Once, when the lights went off, a candle was lit and in its dim orange light Roy Kaku narrated a ghost story that had the brothers, particularly little Babu, trembling with fear. The story went thus:

A man and his wife were travelling to their ancient village home in a horse-drawn cart. It was a long journey on a lonely road. When it was dusk, they were not even halfway through the journey. Soon the dusk gave way to a dark and silent night. All that the travellers could hear was the clicking of the horse's hooves, as it galloped to a steady rhythm. Slowly, the moon came up in the sky, and as its light permeated through the canopy of trees, it cast dark shadows on the road. Some of the shadows were like ghosts.

The travellers were afraid, but neither of them spoke about their fear. Then suddenly, one of the cart's wheels came off and it came to a crashing halt. Luckily, no one was hurt.

'Babuji, it will take me some time to repair the cart. If you walk down a little further, you can find another cart,' the horseman said.

So the couple began to walk away, afraid of waiting further in the dark, silent night. Just then a voice called from behind, 'Babuji, won't you pay me something?'

It was the tanga-wallah. It was a strange voice, pleading at one level, commanding at another. In a strange sort of way, there was something forbidding and frightful about the tanga-wallah's demeanour. He had not spoken a word throughout the journey.

The man wanted to protest, but something told him not to get into an argument in the middle of nowhere. With his wife around, he wanted to take no chances and decided to pay.

While he fumbled with his pocket looking for money, the tanga-wallah lit a lamp. When he found a coin he gave it to the tanga-wallah, without particularly looking at it. The man and his wife were about to leave when the tanga-wallah said, 'Is this all?'

Then he extended his hand and moved the lamp close to the coin.

The coin lay in a hairy animal-like hand that had claws instead of nails.

'Bhoooot... !' The man's scream quivered as he ran, dragging his wife along.

They ran and ran along the road, until they were out of breath. Finally, after what seemed like an eternity, they saw a flicker of lights and it gave them hope. When they came close, they realized there were some horse carts, just as they had been told. They quickly boarded one of them, giving the name of the village they wanted to go to, not even bothering to check the price. When they were gone a little way along the dark road, the cartman—he appeared to be a more communicative sort—asked, 'Babuji, what is the matter, you appear to be troubled?'

The man recounted his experience from earlier that night. Just then, the cart came to a creaking halt and the horseman lit up a lamp. The couple was happy. The light made their fears seem distant. But the next moment, the man moved the lamp towards his free hand and asked, 'Babuji, were his hands like this?'

It was the same ghost hand!

The man and his wife fainted.

The children remembered the story, narrated in the dark, for the rest of their lives.

Roy Kaku was a 'living-in'—which meant that he was a bachelor and lived in the billets at the other end of the camp, and ate food from the airmen's mess. Which is why, under Samar's instructions, he was often served dinner, so that he did not miss home food. The Biswases had an open house and many a living-in 'kaku' ate there with relish. There was one common factor uniting these men—they were all Bengalis and young bachelors. One such regular visitor was Choudhury Kaku. A tall and loquacious character, this uncle would stay up in the house till late in the evenings, chatting with the boys and their mother. Much younger to Samar, he spoke little in his presence and was deferential towards him. One late night when the mosquito net had been tied and the brothers had retired to bed, Choudhury Kaku announced to their Mummy and Daddy, 'There is something I want to tell you today.'

The children, on hearing that, quickly picked up their ears and poked their faces out of the mosquito net. At which Choudhury Kaku began laughing with embarrassment, and Samar scolded his children, 'Don't lend your ears when elders are talking!'

The boys quickly withdrew their heads back inside the mosquito net, but kept their ears wide open. After much fussing Kaku finally disclosed, 'I want your permission...'

Impatient to hear more Basanti snapped, 'For what?'

Kaku laughed and said, 'It's not so important...'

'I want to call you kaku-kakima.'

He wanted to address Samar and Basanti as 'kaku' and 'kakima' rather than as 'dada' and 'boudi'.

Basanti began to laugh uncontrollably.

'O ma go, I thought you had something more important to tell!' she said.

Samar, on whom such decisions rested, was happy to give his assent.

From that day, Choudhury Kaku became Choudhury-da for the boys.

It was funny to hear Kalu and Babu call a grown-up man Choudhury-da. Bappa and Borda were quite comfortable calling him dada.

Choudhury-da got posted out soon.

He was soon replaced by Burman Kaku, another living-in, whom the family treated like their own as he hailed from an area close to their own native place in Chakdaha.

Burman Kaku soon became a courier of sorts for Samar, who would load him with currency notes and other goodies, to be handed over to his mother, whenever he went on leave.

When he returned from his holidays he would bring back a pile of things with him—achaars, boris, kashundi, tea leaves, etc.—which were return gifts from their granny.

Most of the kakus were like migratory birds. They were around only for short periods—ranging from a year to three years—during which they came to their house quite often. And then, suddenly, they vanished from the Biswases' lives, gone on posting.

Sarkar Kaku

An exception among the 'migratory birds' was Sarkar Kaku, who was a resident of Miltry Camp even before the Biswases came, and remained there even after they left Bombay. Sarkar Kaku was a Corporal, one rank junior to Samar, but there his subordinate status ended. Sarkar Kaku had wealth surpassing even that of officers. He owned a car and a scooter, in those days when owning a car was very uncommon, even among officers. (And officers, Kalu thought, were the richest people in the world.) Sarkar Kaku's house was full of expensive things, including a pedestal fan, a high-technology radio, a gramophone record player and a ladies' bicycle that his Anglo-Indian wife used to ride. Kaku was extremely suave and handsome, though not very tall. He had a copper complexion, the kind that is the result of good eating and drinking, and a face that was very cosmopolitan. His curly hair was black and brushed back, forming a little puff that fell on to his forehead in the way of film stars of the sixties. His eyes were always half-shut and dreamy and a smile seemed to play at the corner of his parted lips, which mostly held a cigarette between them. His chain-smoking had rendered a dark tinge to his lips. Unlike the other uncles, Sarkar Kaku was always well dressed and never without a tie. His clothes, the aura of wealth, and a pleasant disposition made him something of an enigma to the children. They were flattered whenever he came to their house, which was at least once a day. The children particularly liked him because he often brought them goodies in the form of chocolates, cakes and cookies. Sometimes he smoked cigars and pipes, and the children watched him with awe and admiration. He kept with him a fancy black-and-gold cigarette box that Kalu often held in his hands and sniffed. Even Kaku had that heady smell of tobacco about him. Every time he held Kalu between his legs while he sat on a chair, or seated him on his lap, Kalu took in the sweet aroma of roasted tobacco.

Sarkar Kaku lived a short distance away from them, in the double-line quarters, and the children often visited him. Exchanging samples of cooked food was a common practice between the two families. And the Biswas boys particularly looked forward to the mutton fried in pepper that Sarkar Aunty sent in often. Aunty was a tall woman with short hair like the teachers at school, and like them she also wore skirts and frocks and spoke English. She was a bony woman and had large eyes set deep in their sockets. She wasn't beautiful but there was an air of superiority about her, attributed to the fact that she worked at an office as a 'steno' and brought home a pay packet fatter than Kaku's. But Kaku earned more from his 'side business'—which was collecting rum bottles from the military canteen or mess and selling them outside the camp to civilians for a premium. Even as children, Kalu and his brothers vaguely knew that this was something illegal and that some day he would be nabbed. In fact the children were faintly aware that Kaku's disproportionate wealth was a source of heartburn for several people, who were on the lookout to have him caught. That vague knowledge, however, did not detract from his popularity with the Biswas family. In fact they were indebted to Kaku, because he had introduced Samar to his 'side business' as well, which he carried out on a much smaller scale. Nonetheless, it brought him some extra money, so that the children could eat well and go to a good school. Every evening Samar would secure the bottom of his trousers with a clip so that it did not get greased by getting caught in the bicycle chain. He would then mount his bicycle, his office bag bulging with the bottles, and ride away. The bottles were sold at a premium to his fixed clients, among them one Mr Gomes of Air India. When he returned home late in the evening his bags, hanging from the cycle handle, would be full of vegetables, fish and fruits. The Biswases ate late. And they ate well.

Whenever Sarkar Kaku had to draw his wife's attention, he would call out, 'Darling!'

And strangely, this would make Kalu and his brothers feel scandalized. The atmosphere and choice of words in their own home was, by comparison, greatly stiff and staid. Basanti and Samar never addressed each other by name. That was the tradition. It was 'paap' for a woman to utter her husband's name. But even men rarely addressed their wives by the name.

'O go shuncho!' was the accepted way for husbands and wives to draw each other's attention.

But just because he called her darling, it would be a travesty of the truth to suggest that the Sarkars' conjugal life was full of bliss. Kalu often witnessed Sarkar Kaku and Sarkar Aunty quarrelling violently. Once, in the course of a tiff, Aunty smashed china plates on the floor and Kaku was so charged up that Kalu thought he would kill her. But all he did was to glare at her with bloodshot eyes. The fights often ended in fisticuffs with Aunty taking on the more aggressive role. She also abused Kaku freely, once calling him a 'bloody bastard' to Kalu's utter shock.

The boy was more used to violence perpetrated by men to which women, like his own mother, meekly submitted. This was so different. While he was too young to understand the reasons behind these regular fights, it seemed that Kaku's drinking habit was one of the causes. And he also kept late hours, making Aunty suspicious. One night when Kaku did not come home till late, Aunty came running to their house, half hysterical and on the verge of tears.

'Your uncle has not returned home since yesterday,' she cried.

But Samar was not at home and there was little the boys could do.

'Do you know if anybody has a phone?' she asked tearfully.

The boys were not aware of anybody having a phone, even though there was a telephone exchange at the far end of the camp. But Kalina would be closer.

'Accompany your aunty to the Kalina market,' Basanti directed Bappa and Kalu.

It was the same road that they took for school, and yet by night, in the dim focus of the torchlight, the place looked so eerie. They finally found a shop that had a telephone and Aunty made frantic calls to all possible places where Sarkar Kaku could be found, but to no avail. By the time they returned late in the night, her children had gone to sleep. Aunty began to sob, her entire body shaking in the silent night. Much later there was a knock on the door, and when an eager Aunty opened it, Kaku stepped into the house. He was drunk and stumbled in on unsteady feet. The woman who had been so anxious a while back pounced upon him with such rage as Kalu had never seen. Kaku quietly submitted to her violence. She must have loved him a lot.

The Sarkars had three children, all of whom were more 'Anglo' than Bengali. The eldest one was a girl a little younger than Kalu, called Becky. Her face resembled her father's but she was mentally retarded, and her lopsided walk and slurred speech made her look rather funny. The next was a boy called Babason, who was rather disconcertingly quiet just like his sister was garrulous. The youngest child was a boy who was normal, naughty and funny. In retrospect, Kalu would realize that there was always something pensive about Sarkar Kaku's face. The disabilities of his first two must have weighed heavily on him. Maybe, in the Biswases he found what he missed in his own children and family—a simple Bengali home. For despite all his sahib-like pretentions Kaku belonged to a very humble lower-middle class Bengali background, rooted in the village. And he was nothing more than a plain and simple MTD, which in simple parlance was a driver, but in the air force jargon a Mechanical Transport Driver. But it was strange, the boys had never seen Kaku in uniform. Yet, whatever his calling, there was something regal about the man. However humble his job, in a certain sense you could call him a prince.

One evening Sarkar Kaku actually took the Biswases out for a royal treat. On the assigned day, just before sunset, he arrived at their house in his car. All the children, with the exception of Borda, had dressed up for the occasion and trooped into the cream-coloured Hillman. It was a red letter day—their first ride in a car! The boys looked at one another and giggled as if to say, 'Is this real?' Even Basanti could not suppress her excitement, as much as she would have liked to conceal it.

'We used to have a car in our mama bari,' she reiterated to the boys, who could read her feelings.

Leaving the camp, going past Santa Cruz and Bandra, they went winding up and up along the Malabar Hill Road until Kalu thought that the car would slide back along the slope. The fact that it did not was a surprise to him. After the ride to Pali Hill—where, Samar explained, all the film stars lived—they went to Marine Drive. Here, in an open-air restaurant facing the sea, they sat down and a waiter thrust a book at them. When the boys looked askance, Kaku smilingly explained that this was a menu card. Basanti began to giggle at the fanciful idea of having to read through a menu for ordering food. Seeing embarrassment writ large on their faces, Kaku hailed the waiter and ordered something. The waiter disappeared, only to return after a long time with a tray full of biryani. The plates were laid and they did not know what to do with the white pieces of cloth. Again Kaku came to their rescue, showing the children how to place the napkins on their laps. Basanti could not suppress her sense of amusement and giggled all the time till Samar chided her. But even he was in a rather happy mood, a rare thing for the children to see. The biryani, covered with silver foil, was delicious, but much of the taste was lost because they were too self-conscious to be eating in the presence of so many people. Moreover, the Biswases were ill at ease about belonging to a class lower than most of the other guests in the restaurant. As the supper was getting over, the waiters brought in little bowls of water with pieces of lime floating in them.

Basanti began to giggle again, saying, 'Na baba, I can't drink this!'

'My stomach is full too,' each of the boys protested.

Kaku smiled indulgently at their ignorance, explaining that the water was meant to clean their greasy fingers, and then he proceeded to show them how. They followed suit, greatly impressed by Kaku's savvy and familiarity with the manners of the rich. After the waiter brought the bill there was a little argument between Kaku and Samar over the right to pay the bill. Finally it was Kaku who paid up. Samar, despite his protests, must have felt relieved, for the bill was sure to been hefty.

Later that evening, loitering around Marine drive, Sarkar Kaku took the family to yet another expensive restaurant where he ordered ice creams. And they were surprised to be served ice creams on plates in the form of bricks. Till then Kalu and his brothers had known ice creams only as something mounted on stick or scooped up from paper cups. After the sweet finale to the grand meal, they started homewards. Bombay looked beautiful as the lights flashed by.

Suddenly, looking at his watch, Samar announced, 'Arre Sarkar, it's past eleven!'

'My God...!' Basanti exclaimed.

They all started feeling guilty for having stayed out so late into the night. Soon, the roads were virtually empty and Kaku drove fast. By the time they reached the camp the children were already drowsy and Basanti was constantly chiding them, 'Don't go to sleep, we'll be home soon.'

But Kalu dozed off. When he came to, his mother was rudely shaking him, 'Get up! Get up!'

He rubbed his eyes and realized they were waiting at the road near the double-line quarters. It took him some time to realize that Kaku was already being accosted by Aunty and a heated exchange was going on between them. Aunty had apparently intercepted the car. She had been waiting for long on the dark road for the car to return. Obviously Samar and Basanti were not very comfortable at the scene. They beat a hasty retreat, the family walking back the remaining distance to their home in the dark night. From the hushed conversation between their parents, the children surmised all was not well.

Next morning Kalu's fears came true when Sarkar Aunty came calling. He was all alone in the house.

'Where's your mother?' she demanded.

There was nothing unusual about that, except that the tone of her voice and the fire in her eyes left Kalu with a feeling of foreboding. She left the house muttering something and Kalu, knowing her temperament, could sense an impending disaster. He shut the door behind Aunty, leaving a little chink through which he could watch her, without her noticing him. She went across to the line opposite theirs, shouting obscenities. Kalu guessed the profanities were aimed at his family, though he could not hear the exact words. Aunty's venomous outpourings attracted one or two women of the line, who left their household work and came to her. Before long she had gathered a crowd of women. From a distance, Kalu could see Aunty gesticulating to the women and pointing towards their house, her eyes so large he thought they would pop out of their sockets. Kalu, little child that he was, was scared for his mother's safety. He wondered what would happen if Basanti, chatting obliviously somewhere in the neighbourhood, were to come out and be accosted by Aunty. Sarkar Aunty narrated her story to the women for a long time, spitting several times with vengeance in the direction of their house. When she finally left, Kalu felt relieved. When Basanti came back to the house Kalu narrated the incident to her. She was lost in thought for a moment, and then angrily marched out of the house to find out what had transpired. That incident haunted Kalu for a long time. It never occurred to him to wonder why Sarkar Aunty should be so angry and jealous of his mother, just because her husband had shown their family some favour. The black mood did not last long. The Pujas were round the corner.

The Pujas—A Time to Celebrate

Every year around August, a bespectacled man in white pyjama-kurta, with a cloth bag slung over his shoulders, visited the house of the Biswases on a Sunday morning. For the children, his arrival signalled the arrival of the Pujas. While he chatted with Samar in Bengali over tea, the harbinger of the Pujas would finally pull out a pamphlet with the picture of Ma Durga printed on it. The pamphlet gave details of the five-day Puja programme. While the family was absorbed in the pamphlet, the man would fish out a receipt book and write out a sum, over which Samar invariably haggled. But he always ended up paying the money, generally a ten-rupee note. The moment he had collected his 'chanda' towards the community Durga Puja Committee of Santa Cruz East, the man would rise to leave. Mounting his bicycle, he would take instructions from Samar about the homes of other Bengalis who may have arrived in the quarters recently.

The arrival of the Pujas was an exciting time for the children. After the damp long-drawn monsoon, there was a dry windiness in the air. The sun shone brightly through white clouds floating in a blue sky. Leaves in the bushes glistened as they trembled in the gentle breeze. The children could sense that the Pujas were around the corner. Then on a Sunday morning, Samar would summon the children to help him clear the cobwebs from the corners of the walls in the house. For a change, the children did not mind being asked to work at all. It was also a time to keep the parents in good humour, so that they could ask for some pocket money, or an extra set of clothes. This was one time of the year—the only time—when they were all bought new clothes. And pocket money, unlike the other times of the year, was not always outside the realm of possibility.

A lot of excitement and planning preceded the Puja shopping. The children were excited about what they would buy, even though they knew it was their father's view alone that finally prevailed. That did not prevent them from dreaming of this Terylene shirt or that Terycotton pant. Even Basanti would be looking forward to the saris she planned to buy. After long drawn plans, the entire family, sans Borda, would go to the market one evening and return with bags full of shopping. Among them would be a sari or two for Basanti, ready-made pants and shirts for the brothers, leather slippers for Basanti and sometimes shoes for the boys. Very often Samar would buy a long sheet of fabric, so that the pieces could be cut out from it for all the three brothers. In the event, the brothers had identical clothes and even though they did not look much alike, anybody could guess they belonged to the same family. As the oldest among the three, Bappa hated sharing shirts and pants of the same print with his younger brothers, but his protests could achieve little. When he grew older, Bappa would buy a shirt-piece or two for himself with the money he made from tuitions—he would show these to all of his friends before going to the tailor. Kalu and Babu would look at his acquisitions longingly. They secretly hoped that one day they, too, would be able to give tuitions.

Borda, of course, was not included in this Puja-shopping list. Rather, he refused to meekly accept whatever was handed down to him by Samar. Unlike his other siblings, he found his father's choice of clothes too downmarket and simple for his exalted tastes.

So Samar would give him a reasonable amount of money, with which he would buy clothes of his own choice. This amount was obviously inadequate for Borda's sartorial tastes, and he would supplement the money from his own undeclared sources. With them he would stitch tight pants and fancy shirts. Often his tight pants would get under the skin of their father, who would thrash him soundly for his 'vulgar' style. Unlike his younger brothers who wore half-pants, Borda wore drain-pipes that—in keeping with the fashion of the times—were skin-tight. So tight were his trousers that every time he returned home late in the evening, he had to be helped to get out of them. And who else but Kalu had to do this job ever so often! Taking off the trousers was quite a technical job. Borda would sit on a chair and stretch out his leg. Kalu would then insert a piece of paper, smeared with talcum powder, at the back of his heel, to reduce friction between skin and trouser. Once the talcum paper was in place, Kalu would pull the trousers with a swift stroke. Then it was the next leg. It was a dexterous job, and success did not come easily. But the younger brothers did not mind the chore, because Borda was also generous—for their pains he would tip his brothers a few paise from time to time. On any given day, he was a better source of money than their father. In a way, they adored him.

The final build-up to Durga Puja was the night before the *Mahalaya* programme would be aired on the radio. Samar would sleep with the alarm clock—borrowed from a neighbour—beside his head. It used to still be dark when the alarm would go off, and the boys would be groggy with sleep when their father woke them up. Meanwhile, he struggled to tune the radio and catch the right Kolkata frequency from where *Mahalaya* was transmitted. Finally, after much tuning, the radio would intermittently come to life.

Through the heavy static interference the celestial voice of

Birendra Krishna Bhadra would invade the morning air: *'Ya Devi sarvabhuteshu, shakti rupe…narayani namastute, namastute.'*

This divine narration was interspersed with songs in praise of Ma Durga—*'Jaago, maaa tumi jago… jago Durga jago…', 'Rupang dehi jayang dehi…'*

These early morning renderings in Sanskrit and Bangla stirred in them a strange kind of spiritualism. The voice of God, transmitted all the way from AIR Calcutta would come in sporadically, the radio unable to hold on to the frequency for a long time. Those days, communication satellites were not yet part of everyday life. By the time the poorly tuned version of spiritual songs and hymns were over, the first ray of daylight would appear. It was a very special morning for them, as it marked the seven-day countdown for the Pujas. The Goddess had begun her journey to the earth, for the salvation of humanity. Meanwhile, the clothes from the tailors would arrive and would be neatly tucked away. And every time one of the neighbours dropped by, Basanti would display their new acquisitions and her shining saris which were folded like precious trophies, even though in reality they were very ordinary clothes. The Pujas and the clothes bought a certain renewal to their lives. They often lived from one Puja to the next Puja.

On Shoshthi—the first day of celebrations—Basanti would wake up the children earlier than usual and order them to take their baths. Ordinarily they would have protested, but it being Puja time they excitedly bathed, put on new clothes and sat down on the cot in the veranda. It gave them a feeling of purity, which was a necessary accessory for the days of the Pujas. Then the entire family—even Borda was not exempted—would troop out to the Kalina bus stop, from where they took a bus for Santa Cruz. On reaching the Puja pandal, full of young and old people dressed in new clothes, there would be an air of expectancy as if something would happen. Nothing spectacular happened, except that the family went straight to the hallowed enclosure where the clay deities stood. The centrepiece of the pandal was the ten-armed Goddess Durga, who stood majestically astride a tiger angrily thrusting a spear through the chest of the wicked but muscular and handsome demon, Asura. Durga was flanked on one side by Laxmi, the goddess of wealth, and on another Saraswati, the goddess of education and wisdom. On the outsides would be Lord Kartika and the elephant-headed Ganesh. Next to Ganesh there would be a banana tree draped in a sari.

When Kalu asked his mother why a sari was wrapped around a tree, Basanti promptly replied, 'That's no ordinary tree—it is Lord Ganesh's wife.'

She did not narrate to him the mythological story behind it, for in all probability she did not know much about it herself. Basanti wasn't a religious sort, never being initiated in the scriptures. Neither was she too deferential towards what she obviously considered ludicrous stories. Her children inherited much of her general lack of veneration for sacred institutions or even fellow humans beings.

The Puja pandal would be full of the sweet smoke of burning incense, mixed with the fragrance of perfume worn by men, women and children. This was the unmistakable fragrance of the Pujas. The faithfuls, who had fasted overnight, crowded together to offer onjoli prayers. It included repeating slokas in unison after the priest. Most of the prayers, being in Sanskrit, were incomprehensible to Kalu, his brothers and his parents as well, but they religiously repeated every word after the pujari, 'Namoh, Chandi, namo Chandi…aesh sochondono, billo patra.. pushpanjali Duragaboli namoh!'

At the end of it everybody flung fistfuls of flowers at the goddess and knelt in supplication. Every year after onjoli Kalu repeated his own personal prayer, 'Oh Ma Durga, be kind to my father and mother and see that I do well in studies.'

He was never more demanding.

After onjoli they ate proshad, which included sliced fruits, a fragment of sandesh and some sweet bundias served in cups made of leaves. The boys ate with relish, after which they dragged their father to the makeshift canteen that sold Bengali sweets. For once Samar would generously buy the white, spongy rassogollas and soft black golapjams. As the morning wore off, smoke arose from the nearby kitchen-tent where the community bhog was being cooked. Children played in little circles of their own. The Biswas boys mostly kept to themselves, often comparing their clothes with those of other children. What they saw did not boost their self-esteem. Basanti felt the same way but she still managed to carry herself well, even striking conversations with old acquaintances she had met at the earlier Pujas.

As noon approached the rows of chairs facing the elevated stage would be rearranged in two long lines. One line of chairs was meant for sitting, while the chairs in the opposite line served individual tables. People, particularly children, would rush to occupy these chairs, after which leaf-plates would be placed on the makeshift tables. Then plastic glasses would arrive, followed by little heaps of salt and a piece of lime on each plate. This would be followed by a group of young men gustily serving piping hot khichudi and labda—a mixed vegetable preparation—followed by tomato chutney and finally payesh, a sweet and fragrant porridge of rice and milk. After eating the bhog the family would rush back home in the BEST bus for a brief nap. Rejuvenated and fresh in the evening, they would return to the Puja pandal for the cultural programme. These often included a magic show or enthralling performances by starlets from the Bombay film industry. Very often there would be a 'variety programme'. In between these performances, they would have a dinner of snacks from the makeshift stalls that sold a variety of non-vegetarian foods. When they returned home late at night, the entire family would be tired from exertion. The same routine was followed for four days. On Dashami, the fifth and final day, it would be time for Bisarjan or immersion of the Goddess in the evening. Their hearts would be heavy as this was the last day of the Pujas—time to say goodbye to celebrations. The idols of gods and goddesses were mounted on trucks. To the accompaniment of beating dhaks, the people walked the convoy to the Juhu Beach, shouting, 'Bolo, bolo Durga mai ki jai!'

At the beach the idols would be disembarked and immersed into the Arabian Sea. And the faithful shouted for one last time, 'Bolo, bolo Durga mai ki jai.' Bisarjan over, 'shanti jal' would be sprinkled on the people. After the immersion ceremony they returned home, as if to an empty world.

While the Biswases patronized the Puja at Santa Cruz East alone, they went all over town wherever a Puja was being held. That mainly included Santa Cruz West, Khar, Shivaji Park and Bandra. These visits to the other Puja pandals were mostly in the evenings and were dictated by the quality and popularity of the cultural event being held there. They did not always travel by the BEST buses. Sometimes an air force coach or a truck would be arranged by the Bengali airmen from the camp. This was good fun, as all the Bengali families got to travel in a group. One evening when the Biswases emerged from their home, all dressed up to go out in the coach, they found to their shock and dismay that it had already left.

'Baba, Baba, the coach has left!' It was Babu who broke the news.

Kalu and Bappa felt cheated, Basanti felt wronged, and Samar's face was clouded with anger and disappointment. But it was Puja time and they *had* to go out. Gulping down their anger, the family walked down to Kalina and took the bus for Santa Cruz. After that they went to Khar, and then to Bandra. It was late in the night when they came out of a pandal to catch the bus back home, when suddenly they came upon 'their' air force coach. Legitimately, they could have taken the coach back home, and it would've been much simpler to do so. But then the insult of the evening was too fresh in their minds. They wanted to have nothing to do with the coach. But just then, they ran into a couple of families from their neighbourhood.

The lady, the wife of a senior flight sergeant, was obviously trying to be patronizing when she said to them, 'Why don't you come along in our coach?'

Basanti, who was by this time seething with rage, replied acidly, 'Since when did it become *your* coach? And as for us returning home, we can afford to take a bus; thank you for your kindness.'

And they left the scene in a huff, leaving the other Bengalis flustered and guilty. The children supported their mother's sense of pride, even though—while they walked back home from the Kalina bus stand tired—they cursed and blamed her for their plight. The other Bengalis were comfortably snoring in their beds by the time the Biswases reached home.

The added charm of the Pujas came from the fact that during those four to five days, Samar did not once bother the children with studies, and they even skipped school without being reprimanded for it. Sometimes the boys went to the Puja pandal all by themselves because Samar or Basanti did not quite feel up to it. In such situations, Bappa used to lead his younger siblings. Borda, being too absorbed with his older friends, would not condescend to accompany them. On the rare occasions when he did, it was only for a short time; after which he disappeared with his own friends and the three brothers felt abandoned. They did not know many people at the Puja pandal and huddled together on their own, often feeling foolish. Sometimes they felt ignored by the few well-dressed children present there, who played only among themselves. Particularly there were one well-dressed boy and his sister, who strutted about the pandal with authority and were frequently coddled and enquired after by the adults. These two were the children of the Puja committee president, one Mr Ganguli who came to the pandal dressed in a dhuti-panjabi and riding a car. Kalu and his brothers watched these children with a mixture of awe and envy. Being unaccompanied by their mother or father also gave them a sense of freedom.

On one such independent journey, as the bus in which they were travelling waited at a stand, the sweet smell of jalebis invaded their olfactory senses. Sniffing hard, the boys looked hungrily in the direction of the shop that had a crowd of people demanding or hogging jalebis. 'Like to eat some?' asked Bappa, reading the minds of his younger siblings, as they longingly gazed out of the bus window.

'Yes, yes!' Kalu said, his face lighting up with a grin.

'Me too,' Babu agreed.

But before the boys could decide to get off the bus, it started moving. In any case, they barely had any pocket money given to them, just the bus fare. As they moved away from the hot jalebis, the aroma lingered on. By the time they reached Santa Cruz, Bappa had hit upon a plan.

'See, if we can walk down back home, each of us will be saving ten paise on the bus fare. With that money we can buy the jalebis.'

Kalu and Babu readily agreed. That afternoon, after eating bhog, the three brothers set off on foot for their six-kilometre journey home. There was a spring in their step until they reached the sweet shop. The shopkeeper gave them a large quantity of jalebis in exchange of twenty paise. The boys were delighted as they bit into the soft syrupy sweet. But by the time they languidly reached home, it was quite late and their parents were anxious.

'Why have you been so late?' Basanti demanded to know.

'The bhog was served very late and we did not get a chance to sit till the third batch was over,' Bappa lied. They did not reveal the secret of the jalebis to their mother until well after the Pujas were over.

Admitted to the Hospital

During the years when his health steadily deteriorated, Samar would promise to the man who came to collect chanda that he would donate an extra ten rupees to the Puja fund if 'Ma' granted him life to see the next Puja. He slowly went down with mounting problems of blood pressure and a weakening heart. One day, he didn't return home on the afternoon truck that brought back all the airmen from the office in Cottongreen. The anxious children ran to the uncles who knew their father, but nobody could tell them anything.

They only assured them, 'Don't worry. He may come a little late.'

But Basanti and the boys were worried, afraid that he may have met with an accident or some other mishap. Later that afternoon, an army ambulance pulled up near the house and a uniformed airman delivered Basanti a letter from the officer commanding. The boys read it and explained to their mother that Samar had taken ill, and that he had been put on the DI List. The 'DI' in the list actually stood for 'dangerously ill', but the children interpreted it to be the 'death list' and they began to cry. Basanti too was weeping. The airman who came to deliver the letter was awkward at their breakdown and tried his best to convince the children that their father was all right—that he had come to take them to see him in the hospital.

'Please don't cry, he will be fine,' he assured.

But Kalu was sure this was the last time he would be seeing his father alive.

On the way to the Ashwini Naval Hospital in Colaba, the airman explained that Samar had been at his desk in the afternoon when he suddenly began to have pain in his chest. He also began sweating profusely. Luckily for him, a taxi was soon hailed and he was driven to the hospital on a supply of oxygen from the local Medical Inspection Room.

'It was a heart attack.'

It was the first of a series that would follow later.

Samar was asleep when his family was allowed to see him in the ICU. A red bulb glowed outside the ICU and they had to take off their shoes before entering. At the sight of tubes and pipes stuck to her husband's nose and arms, Basanti immediately began to cry. The nurses had to show them out, with whispered assurances that he would be all right soon. That evening the family returned home, without having spoken to Samar since he continued to be under sedation. At home all was quiet, as they silently went about their chores. They went to bed early, after eating a sparse meal. Early the next morning, Basanti and the boys returned to Colaba in the military ambulance that travelled regularly from the camp, ferrying serious patients to the hospital. Samar recovered after a few days, and for a while after that all was well again. But the family got worried each time he was late to return home; and true to their fears, every now and then he would land up in the hospital bed, instead of coming back home from office. Once he woke up in the middle of the night, complaining of a pain in his chest. The rest of the family slept on, but Basanti and Kalu were awakened. She massaged his chest until Samar felt better. Kalu had nothing to do, but he could not go back to sleep that night, fearing that his father would die. To add to his fears, Samar spoke to him as though bequeathing a responsibility.

'My son,' he said, 'you must do well in your studies, so that you can earn a living and take care of your mother.'

Kalu kept wondering why his father was saying all this to him, when Samar added, 'I will not live for long… You must be a good boy.'

He looked at his father sitting next to him in the bed, vaguely visible in the darkness. And soon his father would be dead. Kalu felt lonely and terrified. He wept silently. From that day, Kalu was in constant fear of losing his father. In his prayers to God, he always begged for Samar's life. God must have answered the little boy's prayers, for Samar lived to be seventy, even though for the last three years of his life he remained in a vegetative state of coma. He had suffered a cerebral stroke.

One evening in 1968, Borda did not return home at all. Late at night on the next day he made a quiet appearance at the back of the house. By then the younger brothers had finished their studies and supper. Borda, hiding from their father, came to the window and said something in hushed tones to Basanti—about someone having died in a certain Cyril's family, which was the reason for his staying out. In the darkness outside, they saw the silhouette of this Cyril, who had come along with Borda but wouldn't come in.

When the news was conveyed to Samar, perhaps because of the news of death, he said no more about his eldest son than, 'I will not allow him into my house!'

Moreover, he had to catch the early morning train the next day, for he was going on his annual sojourn to meet his mother at their village in Chakdaha, some sixty kilometres from Calcutta. Samar stuck to his threat. That night Borda and Cyril slept outside the house in a charpoy. His brothers quietly sneaked out a rug and a bedsheet for them. The acts of kindness were prompted as much by affection as out of fear of reprisals in the future. The two were also hungry, but Samar had issued orders that they were not to be given any food. Since Basanti could not have pumped up the noisy Primus stove without bringing it to Samar's attention, she wondered if she could get something cooked at a neighbour's house. But then it was too late in the night, and if the Vermas found out the reason, their family would be brought into disrepute. So Borda came to the kitchen window and his brothers smuggled out to him whatever was left over of their dinner. All of this happened with their mother's tacit support, Samar having no inkling of what was going on behind his back. Kalu went to bed that night feeling sorry for Borda. At the same time he envied his eldest brother for the freedom of sleeping outside the confines of home, under the open sky.

A Larceny and A Gift

Next morning, after Samar left early to catch his train, Borda swaggered into the house with authority. A sumptuous breakfast of scrambled eggs and parathas was arranged for him and Cyril, who lived in the MES quarters at the other end of the camp. After that they were held up in the living room for quite some time, until the younger brothers' curiosity wore off and they went away to play in the neighbourhood. When they returned a while later, Borda and Cyril were missing from the house. Their mother, who was visting other women in the neighbourhood, was informed. Suspecting something, she came home running and headed straight for her trunk.

Finding it without the padlock she let out a scream, 'Oh ma!'

She began frantically rummaging through the contents of the trunk. The boys did not know what she was searching for, but at the end of it she let out a desperate and resigned cry, 'My jhumka!' The children knew then that her large gold earrings had been stolen. As a last resort, she came to the window and shouted desperately, 'Taposh! Taposh!'

By then the two young men were nowhere within hearing distance. Basanti was in tears—the earrings were among her only valuables, bequeathed by her parents during her wedding. And to think of it, they were five sisters in all. The jhumkas were a precious part of the dowry she had brought years ago.

For the next two days there was no trace of Borda. A heavy silence hung in the air of the house as they waited for him to return. But then adversity they say never comes alone but in pairs. On the third day of Borda's absence, Kalu came back from school feeling ill and with a watery boil on his belly. The women of the neighbourhood, who inspected his body, pronounced that it was chicken pox. Basanti immediately took him to the doctor who lived in the officers' bungalows. He confirmed the suspicion. The next day Basanti took Kalu to the MI Room (medical inspection), from where they were taken in an ambulance to the other end of Bombay. It was an exciting journey sitting in the military ambulance as they drove along the Marine Drive and finally entered the sedate precincts of the Ashwini Naval Hospital in Colaba, where Samar had earlier been admitted. Here Kalu was examined by another doctor who looked stern, wore white shorts and sported a beard. A sailor who was also an attendant at the hospital finally escorted him to the Isolation Ward, which was at a remote corner of the hospital complex, facing the sea. By now a lot many boils had appeared on his body and he felt weak and feverish.

With Samar on holiday, Borda absconding and Kalu in the hospital, Basanti felt lonely at home with only Babu and Bappa for company. Kalu also felt very lonely at the hospital, despite the fact that the ward was full of soldiers from the navy, army and air force wearing striped shirts and pyjamas—the patients' dress. He was the only child inmate of the ward, and since the hospital uniform would not fit him, he was allowed to wear his own shorts and shirt. A couple of uncles—Bengali seamen—became friendly with him, but they were soon discharged. Two nurses in white flitted about the ward during most of the day. One of them, a cheerful South Indian lady, came up to him after the first night and asked, 'Who is Bai?'

Apparently, as often happens with chicken pox patients, Kalu had started hallucinating the previous night and called out for help to the Bai—the maid who scrubbed utentils at their home.

In the mornings, after the doctor's round, Kalu would sit near the gate of the ward compound beyond which they were not supposed to venture, being patients of the Isolation Ward. He would watch the long black road leading from there, waiting for his mother to come. At around eleven she would appear—a small speck in the distance, carrying a bag in which she brought him home-cooked food and other goodies. Sometimes Babu or Bappa came along with her. Basanti would stay for about a couple of hours, after which it would be time for the ambulance to return to the camp in Kalina. In the evenings when most of the patients' families visited for a second time, Kalu felt lonely and sad as his mother could not come. He would go and sit on the wall facing the sea, watching the ships pass by in the distant horizon.

One morning, Kalu woke up to find a brown-coloured packet on the small table next to his hospital bed. At first he thought somebody had left it there by mistake.

But the patient in the next bed said, 'Somebody had come to see you last night; you had gone to sleep by then.'

Nobody was able to say who it was. Kalu tore open the packet, and to his delight found it full of black grapes, bananas, oranges, biscuits, 'chickies' and also a new shirt. But more than delighted, the gifts intrigued him. He just could not understand who the 'Santa Claus' was. When his mother came to visit him the next morning, the mystery of the packet was unravelled.

'Your Borda has come back; he had come to see you last night,' she said.

Kalu's adoration for his Borda grew even more.

Another morning, as Kalu gazed at the road waiting for his

mother, it was his father who appeared instead. Samar had returned from his holiday. Among the things he brought for Kalu was a small bottle of wood apple pickle, which his grandmother had especially sent for him. The incarceration in the hospital lasted for twenty-one days. At the end of it Kalu felt like a free bird, but he was also sad to leave behind the few friends he had made in the ward. The 'sisters' were particularly sorry at his departure. It was Samar who accompanied him home in the ambulance.

Everything seemed to have changed when Kalu went back to the camp. Even their house looked different. A Bengali family had arrived on posting from Kanpur and settled down in the neighbourhood, with three sons about the same age as Kalu and his brothers. On reaching home, one of the first things Kalu did was to go to the back of the quarters and inspect the ber tree which was in fruit at that time of the year. To his not-so-pleasant surprise, he found a strange young lad gathering the ripe ber from under the tree. Kalu had never seen him before and soon realized that he must be one of the new Bengali boys who had arrived. He reacted with anger at this young stranger. His anger was incited from the fact that the boy looked back at him with an air of defiance, as though Kalu, and not he, were the intruder. He felt threatened. The Biswas boys believed that all trees within the camp, particularly the ones near their house, belonged to them. Anybody plucking or picking fruits without paying some kind of obeisance to them was resented, particularly when it was a stranger as in this case. Kalu glared at the boy and nearly came to blows with him. He had recovered fully from chicken pox.

Another stranger had arrived in the neighbourhood. He was an artist, the brother-in-law of one Sergeant James, who lived in the blocks opposite their house. Kalu was very intrigued by the appearance of this man and was very curious to see his paintings.

The only other artist he knew and admired was a boy called David, his elder brother Bappa's classmate in the eighth standard, who he thought painted exceeding well though he was mostly interested in designs. Even in that early stage of life, Kalu vaguely nurtured the ambition to be an artist. So when an artist came to stay with the James family, Kalu felt very excited. The problem, however, was that their family was barely acquainted with the Jameses. Only Basanti had occasionally spoken to James Aunty, who hailed from Madras and barely understood Hindi.

'Ma, please go and tell Aunty that I want to see the paintings,' Kalu pleaded with his mother.

The lady was more than happy to give permission.

'Come sonny, what are you ashamed of?' she welcomed him in.

The artist himself was an aloof sort, but he was impressed by the little boy's curiosity.

'Do you paint, son?' he asked kindly, to which Kalu nodded.

The paintings were beautiful. But even though he fell in love with the paintings, Kalu was disturbed to see the artist from close quarters. He was a sickly man, a bundle of bones who was coughing all the time. It was rumoured he was suffering from TB. Apparently he was also poor and had come to live off his sister. After a brief anonymous stay, marked by violent coughing, the artist departed. Soon news came that he died of TB.

After learning of his death, Kalu's romanticism about becoming an artist was somewhat dampened. He imagined that if he became an artist, he too would never have enough money to eat and die of TB. Perhaps his father was right in chiding him when he said, 'Don't waste your time painting; it will not give you food.'

'Bombay the Last'

There came a time when the Biswas children were tired of living in Miltry Camp, particularly after Ashok and Nimmi moved out to another part of the camp, far away from where they lived. After that Major Xavier was posted out, taking with him Peter and Benny, the only officers' children whom they played with. Over the years other close friends of their father were also transferred, and at times Kalu too wished he had gone away to another town, another school, new friends. By now they were among the oldest residents of the camp, but with so many newcomers they sometimes felt like strangers. One afternoon, the lady of a newly arrived family hailed Kalu when he was on his way to fetch milk. 'Arre bhai, how much do you charge for a month?' she said churlishly.

She had mistaken Kalu for one of the several boys from Kalina who would fetch milk from the booth for a small monthly premium. Outraged at the insult, Kalu just measured her up with a cold gaze and moved on.

Later the lady apologized to his mother. 'Sorry Behenji, I did not mean to hurt the child,' she pleaded. The incident convinced Kalu that he was indeed a lowly-looking fellow. His brothers actually laughed at Kalu when he recounted the incident. Adding insult to injury, Bappa said, 'Poor lady, I don't blame her. You look just like that, after all!'

The opportunity to leave Bombay finally came.

One afternoon, after coming back from office, taking his usual bath and sitting down to his meal on the floor, Samar announced to his wife, 'I have been posted to Allahabad.'

A news as momentous as this was conveyed without betraying any emotion.

Basanti said incredulously, 'Really? You must be joking.'

When there was no response from her husband, she knew it was true. Samar was not someone used to banter or frivolity. Not when eating, at least. Eating was a solemn affair for Samar, who, bent over his plate, his left hand resting under his right armpit, hungrily gulped down his food. Eating was too serious a business to be interrupted by talking. If Basanti happened to ask a question while he was eating, he would only grunt a monosyllabic 'Yes' or 'No'.

When Basanti broke the news to her children, they were delighted. Soon they had spread the news to all and sundry in the quarters. Suddenly their friends in the neighbourhood became solicitous and the boys from rival gangs became less belligerent. Overnight the children's little rivalries and petty politics seemed irrelevant. All of a sudden they felt marginalized—as though they had no stake in the future of what had been their neighbourhood since birth. When it was his last day in school, Kalu's class teacher announced his departure to the entire class. She gave a moving speech, regretting the departure of such a nice boy. She actually chided some of the more naughty boys, saying to no one in particular, 'I wish some of you had gone away instead of him, poor boy. We'll miss you.'

The entire class clapped their hands. Everybody came up to Kalu and shook his hands. By the end of the day, there were tears in his eyes at the thought of leaving all his friends from St Mary's. Walking away that day, he looked back at his school building for one last time and felt weak in the knees for the rest of his journey home.

As the days wore on, the departure bore down heavier on the children. Earlier, they had not quite realized that they would have to leave forever the house they lived in, the neighbourhood, the trees and the fun. The entire camp was their playground. And, to think of it, they had one of the two biggest houses—the envy of the neighbours. The moment it became known that Sergeant Biswas was posted out, there was a flurry of lobbying among the flight sergeants and warrant officers to lay their hands on Quarter No. 55. Meanwhile, the women in the neighbourhood turned all their attention to Basanti.

They would tell her, 'Arre Behenji, what will we do when you are gone?'

The pretended concern made Basanti more bitter: 'I know it's all lies, behind our backs they all want us to leave. They were all jealous of the quarter we had.'

But many of their neighbours were genuinely saddened by the news of the Biswases' impending departure. As their days at the camp neared their end, every day one or the other of the neighbours would invite them over for lunch, dinner or high tea.

For the children it became a guessing game, 'Guess who will invite us tomorrow.'

But soon they ran out of invitations. And to think of it, there were still two days left to go. With most of the household goods and utensils been packed away beforehand, Basanti did not quite know how she would rustle up a meal. She had hoped that some of the neighbours would feed the family on the last two days. That was the norm. But there was still hope. The two Bengali families there were yet to invite them. Even though they were not the closest of family friends, they were Bengalis after all. 'You mark my word, they'll invite us this evening,' Basanti told her doubting sons. Perhaps it was an oversight, they thought. The mother and three sons—for Borda was in Banglore by then, training as a catering assistant for the air force—would talk among themselves, 'What a shame, our own people have betrayed us.'

Yet at the back of their minds, they were sure that sooner or later the call for lunch or dinner would come.

It didn't.

With just hours left for their departure, it was Rajan Aunty, the wife of the master warrant officer, who saved their day. Basanti, smarting under the insult from her Bengali friends, was very reluctant to accept the invitation. But Rajan Aunty would hear none of her feigned protestations. She pampered the Biswases with a breakfast of idlis, dosas and vadas, apologizing for not being able to organize a proper lunch.

And she confessed to Basanti, 'If only I knew about it... I thought your Bengali friends would be organizing lunch.'

There was no bitterness or sarcasm in her lament. It was just that people from your own state naturally took care of such things. The Biswases' love for their own community, never quite overflowing, had evaporated, turning into hostility.

'Did you see, these Bengalis, our own people, have cut our nose,' Basanti said.

Samar, never much of a socializer, silenced her with, 'Will you shut up!'

Some time in the future, at leisure, a post-mortem of this lapse on the part of the Bengali neighbours would be done.

But the Biswases, particularly Basanti, could never really fathom why this had happened; nor could they get over the insult for a long time.

But when it was time to leave, all the bitterness was forgotten. By the time the posting truck that was to take them to the railway station arrived, a big crowd of men, women and children from the quarters had assembled around it. Ashok, Nimmi and their mother had also come over from the other end of the camp. Bappa's friend David and Gilbert had come all the way from Kalina. Even their Bengali neighbours turned up, somewhat self-conscious with their guilt. Some of the women from the neighbourhood began to weep openly. Basanti, too, was crying. Kalu and Babu could barely hold back their tears. In the melee of hugging and parting words Kalu and Babu ran back to their vacant house, looked at the bare walls, and wondered if they were leaving for good. All this time it had not quite dawned on them. Then they scribbled their names on the wall and the date.

It was 17 August 1969.

When the posting truck revved its engine, they waved frantically to the waiting crowd. Some of their young friends ran behind the posting truck for a distance. David was the last to trail the truck on his bicycle. Soon he, too, disappeared. There were no more known faces behind them. It was evening by the time the train rolled out of the VT station. There was hardly any room in the third-class compartment, every nook and corner taken up by their wooden boxes and steel trunks, the bed-holders and sacks of knickknacks—the worldly belongings of the Biswases.

When the glittering lights of the city were finally behind them, the children waved their hands to the city, 'Bombay, the last… Bombay the last!'

Their tryst with Bombay was over.

Part II
Allahabad

A Place Called Sulem Sarai

The Biswases reached the Allahabad station in the wee hours of the morning. As they stepped out of the station followed by their coolies, a bunch of strange-looking tempo drivers vied with each other to take them to their destination. 'Bauji, bauji…This way, this way…' there were at least a dozen tempo-wallahs tugging at Samar's sleeves. Samar began to haggle with them but it was soon discovered that the wooden packing boxes were too large for the cramped tempos, which ran on three wheels and had a snout-like bonnet that covered the engine and the front wheel. Once the tempo drivers receded the tanga-wallahs took over, frantically beckoning to the family. Samar finally settled for two of the tangas that quoted the lowest price. The tanga was a horse-drawn carriage. They fascinated Kalu and his brothers, who had seen tangas before but only in films. Even Basanti kept giggling at the idea of having to board a tanga. After much huffing and puffing, the entire luggage was loaded on to two tangas they had hired.

'But where do we sit?' Basanti asked, giggling along with her children. The tanga-wallahs had a difficult time accommodating the entire family into the two carriages. After everybody had found a place, the tanga-wallahs lashed out at the horses with both their tongues and their whips. The animals made a strained effort to move, as the load was too heavy. Another lash, another kick, and finally the carriages creaked forward.

'Oh ma, I'm falling,' Basanti squealed.

But soon the unsure trot turned into a steady ride. The children and their mother were laughing at the novel experience. It was only their father who betrayed no emotions. With the steady rhythmic clicking of hooves and the crunching of wheels they were soon on the G. T. Road, passing by the cantonment. Before they were ready for the ride to be over, they had reached Sulem Sarai, a typical North Indian mohalla on the outskirts of Allahabad.

The day had not yet broken fully, and one could see plumes of white smoke rising from homes.

'The morning chullha is being lighted, most people here cook on coal fires,' Samar explained to his wife and children.

'You will have to learn how to light a chullha,' he told his wife, who made a face at the very thought of a coal oven.

Soon the tanga turned into a lane and took another turn, before Samar ordered the tanga-wallah, 'Ruko, ruko… Stop!'

The horses heaved a sigh of relief. The children jumped out of their seats as the horse carriage turned and squeaked to a halt. Their mother squealed with a mixture of alarm and excitement, 'Arre, someone take my hand!'

Finally it was Samar who helped his wife out of the tanga. The day was just breaking. In the faint twilight of the night-morning Samar knocked at the door of a brick house that had not been plastered. After a while a big, dark man emerged, rubbing his eyes.

'Arre, you have turned up rather early,' he said and quickly disappeared indoors, returning with the keys of what would be their home for the next few months. Jangi Lal—for that was the name of the landlord—was a pleasant-mannered man despite his tall, harsh appearance. He helped the family unload their luggage from the tanga, and soon the Biswases were in their new home.

Before the children could gauge the dimensions of their house, their mother asked tersely, 'Is this all?'

To which Samar responded, 'What were you expecting—a palace?'

And then he added, 'You know how much it costs? Thirty-five rupees a month!'

Basanti made an expression that said, 'I'm not going to live here!'

The house had two rooms—one eight by ten feet, another eight by twelve. Each room had a wooden bed, taking up most of the space in it. There was no separate kitchen—the larger of the two rooms also had to serve the purpose of cooking. One of the rooms opened out to a small courtyard. At one end of the courtyard was a lavatory, and adjacent to it was a bathroom. Both the bathroom and the lavatory consisted of three bare walls and had no roof. The family was just about coming to terms with their new surroundings when a dark girl appeared holding a tray with steaming cups of tea, followed closely by Jangi Lal. 'This is my daughter,' he introduced. Both Basanti and the children were happy to find tea in the cold morning. But just after she had taken a sip, the mother spat out the liquid.

'Baba, is this tea!' she exclaimed and refused to have another sip.

Fortunately the girl had left by then.

'Get the stove out,' she ordered, and Bappa unpacked one of the trunks and whisked out the Primus stove. Soon a bottle of kerosene, as if materializing from nowhere, was poured into the stove and Basanti made her own tea and rotis. The hungry children dipped the roti into the hot tea and had their first breakfast in Allahabad. Tired from the journey, they dozed off soon after. When they woke up, it was sunny and there was bunch of curious neighbours peering at them.

The Biswas children found these new people strange and rustic. They were dressed poorly and spoke Hindi with a rural accent. It took the children a while to realize that they had come to live in a village in North India—many things here would be different from their previous life. For instance, water for daily use had to be brought from a nearby community well. Initially the children were happy with the novelty of drawing water from a well, but sometimes they were embarrassed by the idea of bathing in the open. Moreover, while initially the neighbourhood came forward eagerly to help them draw water, gradually they realized that the help was not spontaneously forthcoming. It hurt their pride. Coming from Bombay gave the children a sense of superiority. They expected help from these rustics without asking for it. The boys condescendingly answered the neighbours' queries:

'Is Bombay a big city?'

'How long did the train journey take?'

'Do they, Bombay people, speak only in Angrezi?'

There were many questions to be answered.

One of the first visitors to their new home was Thakurain, a plump woman in her late thirties, her head covered with the pallu of her sari and a big bindi adorning the middle of her forehead. She struck a quick rapport with Basanti and started calling her Didi. She also chewed paan and brought Basanti a sheaf of betel leaves, instantly winning her goodwill. More of her confidence was gained when Thakurain organized the chuna, jarda and other paraphernalia that go with the betel-chewing habit. Within a matter of hours, Thakurain became a regular feature of the new Biswas household. She soon became Basanti's confidant and the source of juicy gossip from the mohalla. Thakurain's popularity with Basanti was in direct proportion to the envy she generated among other women of the mohalla. They hated her proximity to the new neighbour from

Bombay, whom every other woman wanted to befriend. Basanti made no attempt to tone down her air of superiority. It was manifest in her stories from Bombay, which the women listened to in rapt attention, asking her eager questions from time to time. After lunch, the women would drop by one by one and crowd around the charpoy at the Biswas house in the afternoon sun, most of them mechanically knitting away as they gossiped. Basanti presided over these afternoon sessions. She became a leader of sorts.

Even Jangi Lal's wife, the landlady, came to these afternoon rendezvous. She was a slightly built and demure woman, also pregnant at this time. Kalu, who was just about awakening to the secrets of life, was vaguely—but only vaguely—aware that this woman's pregnancy was a result of coitus with Jangi Lal. 'How could she take on the weight of such a big man like Jangi Lal?' it made him wonder. And something mildly stirred in his groins. He didn't realize it was an erection, one of his first.

Soon, they also learnt that Thakurain had a 'sauten'—a co-wife. And the son who lived with her was actually a stepson from her husband's other wife.

'Thakurain is a "baanj"—a barren woman—which is why her husband had to marry again,' Mrs Jangi Lal once explained to Basanti, whose curious sons were all ears.

Later, Kalu would be very surprised when he met Thakurain's husband for the first time. He had expected to see a superman who could handle two wives, but here was a regular middle-aged man who usually wore khaki trousers and shirts, and worked as a guard at a government office.

There was another man in the neighbourhood that caught the children's attention. This man, whom they called Gupta Uncle, worked in the railways and was also an artist. Kalu became a frequent visitor to his house, fascinated by the paintings of gods and goddesses that Guptaji made. Often, he would be absorbed in watching the man paint. It would inspire him in turn to make his own sketches and paintings, which he showed to Gupta Uncle, allowing the man to become his guide and critic. To be honest, it was the atmosphere of shared interest that Kalu found more valuable than Guptaji's actual work, which he found rather ordinary.

Guptaji was an austere sort of man who had two grown-up sons. The older son was married and lived separately from his parents. Gobind, the younger son, was rather quiet and went to the Allahabad University for his master's in Hindi. He was in awe of the new neighbour's children who spoke such 'farretedar' English.

While Gupta Uncle painted, he would often shout out to his wife, 'Gobind ki Amma!'

At this his wife—a bent woman—would demurely appear with a glass of water or cups of tea, as was ordered. The bent Guptain, with her head hardly three feet high, was an object of comedy for the Biswas boys and even their mother. They would often mimic her gait and have a good laugh until Samar shouted, 'What is the matter!'

And all would be silent again.

The gay abandon of their arrival in Sulem Sarai—minus school and the rigour of studies, and with all the novelties of language and culture and the wonderful succulent guavas—did not last very long.

One afternoon Samar came home and announced, 'Your admissions have been done!'

'It has cost me a fortune and I expect you to study hard. This is a good school,' he added.

Bappa got admission into the eighth standard of their new school, Kalu to the sixth and Babu to the third. The next day their father did not go to office.

'Get ready, I'm taking you to school,' he commanded Kalu. The boy, taken aback by the privilege, took a quick bath, oiled his hair and put on a set of clothes that had been pulled out of the iron trunk. He also wore his old school shoes and socks. Dressed for the occasion, he mounted the bicycle rod and rode away with his father. It took them half an hour to arrive upon a magnificent cluster of red brick buildings. His father turned left under the arch of an imposing gate, on which was written St Joseph's Collegiate. The desolate street following from the school gate was lined with a row of neatly trimmed hedges and tall trees. When Kalu dismounted from the bicycle, which his father parked under a tamarind tree, he was overwhelmed by the size and grandeur of the buildings. Suddenly he felt acutely conscious of being poor. A senior schoolboy zipped past them on a fancy bicycle, which he parked at some distance from them. The boy was fair-complexioned and wore an expensive jacket. The look of him made Kalu feel very inferior.

'This is a rich people's school, na?' he whispered to his father, who nodded assent.

The atmosphere was so quiet and forbidding that even his father avoided speaking.

Tucked underneath the huge arches, invisible to outsiders, was the school's bookstore. Unlike the desolate scene outside, the cavernous bookstore was a beehive of activity. Well-dressed children and parents were pestering the shopkeeper, 'Bhargavaji give me Dudley Stamp... Bhargavaji do you have Macmillan's Grammar... Bhargavaji please give me this...that...'

The queries flowed one after the other as Mr Bhargava and his helpers ran back and forth from customer to shelf and shelf to customer. Very hesitantly, Kalu's father gave out a list to Mr Bhargava and soon they had a pile of books laid in front of them.

When Bhargavaji gave them the bill for the books, Samar looked faint. He searched all his pockets and counted all the money he had—he was far short of Mr Bhargava's bill. Kalu felt ashamed. He wished he could dissolve into thin air. It was Mr Bhargava who came to their rescue.

'No money, sir... Never mind, sir. I keep the books for you. Come tomorrow, sir, with money,' Mr Bhargava was a decent sort of man and made light of their predicament.

'Happen sir,' he told Samar reassuringly.

Later that afternoon when Kalu recounted the story to his mother and brothers, she chastized her husband in Bengali, 'What was the need to put them in such a big school? *Bamon hoye chaande haat!*' Literally translated, the phrase meant that dwarfs should not aspire to touch the moon.

Over the next few days the women in the neighbourhood were subjected to Basanti's staple lament of 'O what a big school these children have to go to! You know how much their fee is?'

When no one bothered to ask, she volunteered, 'Fifteen rupees a month!'

Fifteen rupees was indeed a princely sum in 1970, at least by the standards of Samar's income.

In the same breath Basanti would ask her neighbours, 'Which schools do your children go to?'

To which the women answered lamely, naming some vague Hindi-medium schools. Kalu and his snobbish brothers would laugh at even the names of these schools, one of which was Mahila Gram Inter Kallege.

The Life of a Coat

Once the admissions were over, the Biswas household spent the next few days planning for the children's winter uniforms. Unlike Bombay, winters in Allahabad were cold. It was compulsory for the students of St Joseph's Collegiate School to have either full-sleeved pullovers or blazers, navy-blue in colour and displaying the school crest. Buying ready-made sweaters, which were also sold at Mr Bhargava's store, was an expensive proposition that Samar rejected summarily. Instead, one evening he came home with a batch of cheap wool balls.

'But these are white in colour,' the children protested.

They were silenced once their father unwrapped a piece of paper containing shining granules of blue dye. The dye was dissolved into warm water, added with salt and the wool immersed into it all night. The next morning the wool was appropriately navy-blue in colour, and within a couple of weeks Kalu and Babu had their high-neck pullovers ready. It made Kalu particularly happy, for he had never imagined he could own a sweater. Much of the knitting had been done by Thakurain and Basanti's other sahelis in the neighbourhood. On her own Basanti could never have accomplished the job before winter was over and gone. Having lived in Bombay, the need for knitting had not arisen before.

Bappa, now the eldest of the three, had a blazer coat instead of a pullover. It was a secondhand coat bequeathed to him by Sarkar

Kaku. The issue of an impending cold winter had come up in a discussion before they had left Bombay for Allahabad, when Sarkar Kaku had told Bappa, 'Why don't you take this coat of mine, I have no use for it in Bombay.'

Bappa had protested at first, but quickly yielded to Sarkar Kaku's suggestion when he realized that he would be shivering in the Allahabad winter otherwise. Now as he took out the coat and put it on, there arose another problem—the coat was far too large for Bappa's frame and hung loosely on him.

'You're looking like a scarecrow,' Kalu and Babu told him.

Later that evening Bappa went along with his father to Shanker Tailors on the main G. T. Road. A much sought-after man, the proprietor of Shankar Tailors was reluctant to take up an 'altering' job. However, Bappa prevailed upon him and he agreed to alter the coat. Even the cost for alteration seemed exorbitant, nearly as much as stitching a new coat. But once it was done, Bappa was so proud of his coat that he could not stop checking himself out in the small mirror that hung on the wall at home. Since the six-inch-by-six-inch mirror gave him only a partial view, it was Babu and Kalu who had to answer his constant query, 'Is it looking good?'

The younger boys envied his fortune. But after a few years at school, the coat's colour had faded so much that Bappa was upbraided by his class teacher, Mr D'cruz.

'This colour won't do!' he was told.

When he put forth the problem to their father, Samar promptly brought another packet of blue colour and the coat was dyed. When Bappa outgrew the coat, it was handed down to Kalu. By then the coat had developed a few holes, and it was still a little too big for Kalu, yet it remained a family treasure.

But in the winter of 1971, when war with Pakistan broke out, the coat took on an entirely unforeseen role. During the war evenings were a time for 'blackouts'. As darkness fell over the city, an ominous wailing siren would rend the air. Often a jeep with a blaring mike would travel down the streets, warning the people that no light should be visible outside their homes. By now the Biswases had shifted to a two-storeyed house overlooking the main road, and Samar and the boys had neatly pasted black carbon paper on the glass windowpanes to take sure that not a single ray of light escaped the house. Even so, Kalu was terrified by the siren and would crouch under the bed with Babu, imagining that the Pakistani planes had arrived and would shower bombs on them.

Long after the sirens became silent and the dreaded bombs did not fall, the two of them would quietly sneak into the terrace and watch the darkened street below with a mixed feeling of fear and excitement. There was something primordial about the dark streets then, as though they had gone back in space and time and hid many unspoken secrets. On one such blackout evening, the two brothers descended from the terrace and ventured out into the street to buy peanuts. Their mother had given them a ten-paisa coin. To keep out the cold, Kalu put on his old school coat, digging his hands deep inside the pockets.

'*Mungfali dena!*' the boys pleaded with the hawker.

It appeared to fall on deaf ears as the mungfali-wallah catered to the swelling crowd of customers around his pushcart. In winters, North Indians love eating peanuts and other assorted dry fruits.

Waiting impatiently for their turn, Kalu suddenly realized that his coat pocket was at the same height as the pile of peanuts on the cart. He discreetly fingered the peanuts and a few of them fell straight into his coat pocket. He repeated the process and some more nuts tumbled into his pocket. He felt emboldened. Because of the blackout, the mungfali-wallah did not notice the pilferage.

By the time the mungfali-wallah handed them a paper packet of peanuts worth ten paise, both of Kalu's coat pockets were full. On the way back, when Kalu showed the booty to Babu, his younger brother's eyes popped out, incredulous. The success of this foray delighted the boys, as they savoured the spoils of the evening with Basanti, who had no idea of the theft.

As long as the war lasted, every evening after blackout the two brothers would swoop in on the mungfali-wallah like owls in the dark preyed on lesser animals. With a five-paisa coin they would approach the hawker just around the time when he had a crowd of customers to deal with. Then Kalu's dexterous fingers would quietly fill his pockets, until the mungfali-wallah had found time to listen to their demand. Sometimes, when the mungfali-wallah was too preoccupied with other customers, the boys would grumble at the delay and leave. By then, of course, the coat pockets would be full; and they would even have saved the five paise. When the war was over in less than a fortnight, putting an end to the blackouts, Kalu and Babu were hugely disappointed. Their evenings became aimless. The coat, which had suddenly become an accomplice in crime, lost its newfound relevance. It hung from a nail in one corner of the house. With the end of winter, it was completely out of use.

Then one evening in early summer, the lights went off again. As the hurricane lamps were lit around the neighbourhood, the two brothers looked at each other briefly and the same thought crossed their mind.

'Let's go to the mungfali-wallah,' they spoke almost simultaneously.

Coaxing out five paise from their mother was not easy.

'Why don't you understand, I get no money from your father,' she wailed. But, as usual, with a little more cajoling the money appeared. Kalu put on the forgotten coat.

In the warm weather the coat looked incongruous, but the boys ran fast to the mungfali-wallah demanding peanuts for five paise. Happily for them, the hawker was busy trying to fix his gas lamp and could not attend to them immediately, even though there was no crowd. Kalu was having a field day filling his pockets, when suddenly the lights came back. Under the golden glare of the streetlamp above them, the mungfali-wallah caught him in the act, red-handed. For a moment the two stared at each other transfixed, both in shock. When the boys finally realized they had been caught, they turned tail and fled. Behind them they could hear the mungfali-wallah shout, 'Saale haramzade…illicit sons of illicit fathers!'

They were panting hard for breath when they reached home, feeling like fugitives. Kalu in his oversized coat was also looking like one.

'God, we were nearly caught!' he said breathlessly to Babu, adding, 'Don't tell Mother.'

That was the last occasion when the coat was worn. Finally it was given away to another hawker who took old clothes in exchange for steel utensils. The coat yielded a small steel tumbler.

'Is that all!' Basanti exclaimed and snatched back the coat.

Finally, the hawker, realizing the value of the coat, bartered it for a large stainless steel pan.

'Not a bad deal,' Basanti told herself.

The coat was passed on to a third owner.

First Day at School

After days and weeks of preparation, the first day at school was finally upon them. The new school had more novelties than one. Unlike St Mary's in Bombay, the boys had to carry lunch to their new school, for the school hours were long, from 8 a.m. to 4 p.m.

The night before, the children were very excited about what lunch they would take to school. They wondered what rich children ate for lunch, and to be equal to them, after much deliberation, ordered their mother to make samosas.

'You can make them, Ma?'

Poor Basanti had never prepared samosas before. But she did not want to let down her boys who, she was aware, were going to attend 'a very big school'.

'Don't worry, I'll make nice samosas,' she put up a brave front.

Preparing a lunch box was going to be a novel experience for all of them. So they went to bed early, to be ready for their next morning's experiment. When the alarm went off they were all up abruptly, rubbing their eyes reluctantly, but excited. They were shocked that it was still dark and there were bright stars visible in the morning sky. Basant lit the stove, pumping it to full flame until it roared like an engine. While the boys brushed their teeth and washed their faces, their mother prepared tea and parathas for breakfast. They ate by the side of the stove, warming themselves as they dipped the parathas in hot tea. By the time the boys had put on their new school uniforms, their samosas for lunch had been deep fried—in mustard oil!

'Let's taste one, Ma,' the boys pleaded.

'I've made only nine of them, three for each of you. Whoever eats one now will have only two during his lunch break,' their mother warned. So the tasting was put off.

The lunch box was put into Bappa's school-bag and Basanti instructed them to meet up and eat together during their lunch break.

The bicycle ride to school was a long and tiring one for Bappa. He had a hard time pedalling through the weight of his two brothers, with Babu sitting on the front bar and Kalu on the rear carrier. By the time they reached school, Bappa was hot and panting for air. But more than Bappa, it was Kalu who squirmed with embarrassment every time they were passed by a car carrying one or more of their school-fellows. Some of the boys even waved at them—mocking, Kalu thought. The brothers felt poor, miserable and out of place. None of the boys at St Mary's in Bombay came to school in a car. St Joseph's gave them an inferiority complex.

Moreover, it was a strange feeling going to a school where they did not know anybody. The brothers moved together in a huddle. Everyone looked askance at them. After depositing their bicycle at the stand, they left for the junior building across a huge playground. It was a massive four-storeyed, brick-coloured building. They finally found Class III A, where they left Babu. Bappa then saw off Kalu to Class VI C, and left to discover his own ninth-standard classroom.

The new faces in their classrooms made all three brothers uncomfortable. Babu actually began weeping soon after Bappa and Kalu had left—he thought he would never see his brothers again. In his own class, Kalu felt as though everyone was staring at him as if he were some strange lowly object.

'What's your name, are you new?' he was pleasantly taken aback when a boy in the neighbouring bench spoke to him.

'Yes, I've come from St Mary's in Bombay,' he said.

'Bombay!' the boy was impressed.

He quickly struck a friendship with the boy who, Kalu presumed, was very rich. And then the boy asked him the dreaded question, 'What does your father do?'

Kalu had anticipated this question before and had rehearsed the answer several times. But when the time came, he couldn't bring himself to tell a lie.

'He's a sergeant in the air force,' he said timidly.

Luckily, the boy misheard his answer. 'Oh, surgeon … a doctor!' he said, impressed.

Kalu did not correct him, and felt a stab of guilt for letting the lie prevail. But in the course of the day, he found himself lying once again about his father.

'What does your father do?' yet another new friend in the class had asked.

'He's in the air force,' Kalu said, evading a direct answer.

'A pilot!' the new friend asked excitedly.

'No, he's a warrant officer,' Kalu replied, his voice trembling with the burden of another lie. And to pre-empt further questions he asked the boy in turn, 'What does *your* father do?'

'He's a contractor,' said the boy. 'He makes buildings. Did you see the block of four-storey buildings near the railway flyover? My father built it.'

'You mean he built the entire building!' Kalu was aghast.

Aziz, for that was the name of the boy, nodded in the affirmative. Kalu kept wondering how one man could have built such a large building himself, not realizing that Aziz's father was only a contractor and not the owner. Kalu knew little about owning houses—he had never known a house of his own. He remembered how his father had made grand plans to build a two-room house after he received his retirement money. At last, they would have a house they could call their own.

Kalu was in awe through most of that first morning in school, wondering just how rich his classmates were. Unlike at St Mary's in Bombay, where most of the children came from poor or lower-middle class homes, the new school made him acutely conscious of being poor. Finally, the recess bell rang and the other children ran out with their lunch boxes, or went to meet their servants (the politically correct term domestic help had still not been invented) who had brought them lunch from home. Kalu slipped out of the class unnoticed and waited under the large neem tree for Bappa to come. After a long wait, Bappa finally appeared with their tiffin box in hand.

'How is your new class? I've already made a few friends,' Kalu said.

'They've started calling me Bambaia ... But most of them speak in Hindi,' Bappa said. The last comment was more of a lament.

The two of them strode towards the junior-school building, exchanging notes on their first day.

Little Babu was sitting in his classroom, a little bewildered, and was reassured when he saw his older brothers. Then the three of them came out into the football ground, where the other boys were playing in groups or eating out of their tiffin boxes. Kalu's singular concern was that nobody should see them eating.

'The rich boys would laugh at our food,' he said to himself.

Finally, they retired to an isolated corner of the football ground away from prying eyes.

Making sure no one was looking, Bappa opened the tiffin

box and distributed the samosas equally among his brothers. The samosas had gone cold, but the boys were hungry and devoured their first samosa soon. While they were eating a football rolled by close to them and Kalu quickly shut the tiffin box, lest someone coming after the ball discovered what they were eating. Just then a largish boy came panting and grabbed a samosa from Bappa's hand.

'Tasty, man!' he said biting into the samosa and disappearing into the distance with the ball.

'He's my classmate,' Bappa informed his brothers proudly.

Kalu was surprised that even a rich boy could like what their mother had cooked. In the subsequent days he discovered, to his surprise, that most of the boys brought rotis and parathas for lunch just like them, and not sandwiches, cakes and pastries as he had imagined. He soon realized how unnecessarily foolish he had been. Gradually the brothers overcame the shame of eating in front of the others. Soon they were not only eating and sharing their food; they were also joining other classmates in stealing the tiffin boxes of boys who had brought something special. After the first few days the brothers were on their own, bringing their individual tiffin boxes. Having made new friends from their classes, they no longer met up to eat lunch together. Yet, from time to time, Kalu would go to the junior building to check on his little brother.

Lunchtime at St Joseph's had a particular aroma that Kalu could not resist, especially as he passed by the Crafts Room. At lunchtime, this room was transformed into a dining hall. The large hall became a beehive of activity, with liveried servants, mostly from the Allahabad High Court, attending to the brats and their taste buds. When Kalu passed by the Crafts Room, his olfactory senses were invaded by a sweet and inscrutable smell. It was a distinct scent, separate from the smells of the various cooked foods; but despite his irrepressible curiosity, Kalu could never lay a finger on what exactly it was. What did those children eat? Was it the smell of cakes…was it pastries?

It took Kalu nearly two decades to solve the mystery. By then a married man with his own house, one day he was overpowered by the same mysterious scent of food that he remembered from school. Overcome with nostalgia, he tried to track the source of the scent and was taken aback when he discovered it. It was the smell of ripe bananas lying on the dining table! He remembered then, most of the servants brought bananas for the 'baba logs', which they would peel and force down the throats of their masters' scions.

'It's strange,' he thought, 'I've always loved bananas. How come I didn't recognize their fragrance at school?'

Classmates Give Kalu a Complex

Over the days and weeks, school became a place to look forward to. Kalu had many friends. Most of their fathers were either from the Allahabad University or the High Court. There were others from the cantonment—sons of officers from the army or air force. From these boys Kalu kept a safe distance, fearing the secret of his father's low rank would be revealed among them. One of his close friends was called Tanmay Vachaspati, whose father was the head of the Department of Physics and mother, a reader at Allahabad University. Vivek Mushran's father was the head of the Chemistry Department. Siddharth Sahi, who always came first in the class, said that his father was the head of the Maths Department in the university. There was also Navroz Dhondy, who was a Parsi and nearly as 'gora' as an Englishman. Navroz's father came on a motorbike to drop off his two sons, including Darius, the younger. Kalu was initially in awe of all these classmates, but once they became familiar it made no difference what backgrounds they came from. But then one day he saw Tanmay's mother dropping him off in an Ambassador car, and he was overcome with awe. He thought of his own mother and said to himself, 'How backward we are.'

Even the thought of Basanti driving a car was enough to make him laugh. Tanmay went a few notches higher in his esteem. But bigger surprises lay in store.

In this crowd of the children of heads of departments, colonels and bank managers, Kalu felt lost—somewhat like a second-class ticket-holder on a train, who had barged into a first-class compartment. He yearned to meet someone whose father was an ordinary person, a clerk or even a chaprasi, someone who belonged to his class, and someone with whom he could share his feelings of awe. Finally his wish came true in the shape of Ahmed Saidullah. Like him, Ahmed too was a new entrant in Class VI. And, like Kalu, he too was dark and short, with unkempt, dry brownish hair. He had large watery eyes, like those of a beggar Kalu had seen in a painting. And he had a very short neck, giving him the nickname 'the Neckless Gunk'. And finally, like Kalu he too wore a crumpled cotton uniform that marked him out to be a poor man's son.

'He's like us,' Kalu told himself, and an unspoken empathy developed.

The best part was that Ahmed spoke English and no other language. In that sense Kalu too was a 'sahib', since he spoke chaste English. At last, he thought, there was someone who would understand him and share his class feelings. Kalu even felt sorry for Ahmed—for the fellow, with his large doleful eyes and crumpled uniform, looked even poorer than him. He began to patronize the boy, not that Ahmed cared particularly. There was something disdainful about Ahmed, as though he scorned the boys who could not speak the Queen's Language properly. Ahmed was proud of his English.

But Kalu continued to feel sorry for him. And then one day Sunil Tandan, whose father was a chief engineer with the Electricity Board said, 'Arre, Ahmed, you're here! Your mother's been looking for you. She's brought your lunch.'

Kalu, who was within earshot, felt more than sorry for Ahmed.

'Poor fellow, how will he meet his poor mother in front of these rich children,' he told himself.

Quietly, he followed Ahmed from a distance towards the school gate. What he saw near the gate left him aghast—a woman with short hair and wearing sunglasses got out of a car, and Ahmed ran into her arms. After a while, he returned with a tiffin box and the woman drove away. Kalu was incredulous.

'Who was that?' he nearly confronted Ahmed.

'My mom. Why?' Ahmed asked.

'No, I was just wondering…' Kalu trailed off.

He felt betrayed.

'Here was one guy who I thought was like us, and he also turns out to be like the rest.'

Later, at an opportune moment, Kalu asked Ahmed rather timidly, 'What does your father do?'

'He's the DM of Pratapgarh,' Ahmed said, without even deigning to look at him.

Not wanting to look silly in front of Ahmed, Kalu found out from another classmate that DM stood for District Magistrate. From that day, Ahmed became to him a sort of a taunting symbol of the upper classes. Kalu felt a strange discomfort in his presence. One day, in his usual tomfoolery, Kalu poked a pencil at Ahmed's back. Irritated, he turned around and gave Kalu a disgusted look as though saying, 'Don't let your class show!'

After that Kalu kept a safe distance from Ahmed the Neckless Gunk, even though the two of them moved around in the same English-speaking gang, despising the boys who spoke only Hindi.

Kalu was never truly part of the English-speaking gang. He hovered on its periphery—a low-caste pretending to be a Brahmin; or more appropriately, a soldier's son trying to mix with officers' children. The gang mostly consisted of defence officers' children. There was Reginald Varadrjulu, a polite and studious sort of boy, whose father was a major, an army doctor. Then there was Keith, an Anglo-Indian, whose father was a colonel. The bespectacled Bob Taylor looked like an Englishman, and his father was a group captain, an air force pilot. Ranbir Singh Sanhotra was a 'sardarji' who never spoke a word of Hindi, and again the son of a colonel. Kalu, with his habit of laughing at people, named him the 'Angrez Sardar', something that the gang didn't consider funny but the other boys in the class found immensely rib-tickling. And as if there weren't enough officers' children in the class already, they had a newcomer one day by the name of Mukul Sharma. His father was a squadron leader in the air force. Even his mother, who joined their school as a teacher, taught—what else but—English! But thankfully, Mukul did speak Hindi as and when the need arose. And warming some hearts like Kalu's, Mukul's mother, too, spoke Hindi without the 'chhi chhi' accent of Anglo-Indian teachers. The only civilians in the English-speaking gang were Navroz and Ahmed, and a boy called Zaheer Babar, whose father was a Professor of English at—where else—Allahabad University. And along with these children of illustrious families, there was Kalu.

He was more tolerated than accepted as an insider of the gang. There were reasons. The gang members exchanged comics and fat novels. They went to English 'flicks' and listened to English music, none of which Kalu did. Half the time he could not comprehend their discussions about a movie watched the week before or a novel that most of them had read. On one or two occasions when he had gone to watch an English movie, he came back disappointed because he could not comprehend a word of the accented English. It was true that he spoke English, and it gave him a passport, however half-hearted, into the gang; but he did not have the added privileges that would make him one of them. He remained an outsider. But his stock in the gang fell particularly after Mukul's arrival. Since Mukul's father was in the air force, he knew precisely what Kalu's father's position was. The knowledge was transferred to the other boys when Kalu picked up a fight with Mukul one day. The fight originated in the arts class. Kalu got the highest marks in the class for drawing a house. It was a house with a tiled roof.

'How did you manage to draw those tiles?' the gang, appreciating his painting, asked.

And pat came Mukul's jealous barb, 'How else—he lives in one of those "kutcha" houses with tiled roofs! His father is a sergeant.'

Kalu's face flushed with embarrassment and he began to hate Mukul.

There was no respite from humiliation, even though most of it was self-inflicted. Ever since they had grown too old to be carried on Bappa's bicycle, Kalu and Babu would wait along with two other boys at Sulem Sarai for the city bus to take them to school. While they waited for the bus, Kalu felt embarrassed to see the other schoolboys whizzing past in their cars. Whenever the bus was late, which happened very often, they would run into Mukul and his two sisters being driven to school in their Fiat car by their mother. Mukul's family lived further down the G. T. Road, near Bamrauli Airport. To complete the humiliation, Mukul always waved to Kalu and Babu as he passed them by.

To avoid running into Mukul, Kalu and Babu often hid behind a waiting truck or a lamp post whenever they saw Mukul's car approaching, emerging from their hideout only after the car had gone out of sight. One day, Mukul's mother—whom some of the boys in school had christened 'Jhabri Billi' because of her short, unkempt hair—stopped the car and gave a lift to Kalu and Babu. But Mukul's sisters did not speak to them, and Kalu felt extremely affronted. He vowed never to accept a lift again from Mukul's mother; even though, to be fair to her, she was quite an affectionate sort of woman.

Surprises in Sulem Sarai

Meanwhile, life in Sulem Sarai, though uneventful, brought with it its own little surprises. On evenings when the boys accompanied their father to the 'sabzi mandi', they were enchanted by the sights, smells and sounds of a village market. The market had different sections for vegetables and grains. Their father spent hours haggling over the prices of rice and vegetables despite the commodities being dirt cheap compared to Bombay. The fish market was at a distance from the sabzi mandi, isolated in the outskirts of the village. Most locals, who were pure vegetarians, looked down upon the purveyors of fish and other non-vegetarian delights. After their purchases were made, usually Bappa would carry the heavy burden of rice and wheat on his shoulders, the younger siblings carrying the bags of vegetables. Nevertheless, the boys looked forward to the market days, because it also meant being bought the occasional goodies. They hung around the four-wheeled pushcarts and trolleys, which were stacked with peanuts, cakes made of bajra and other delicacies made of sugar or jaggery. The carts would be thronged with flies, honeybees and even wasps and hornets, attracted by the sugary fare. But more than the eatables, it was the rustic language and attitude that the boys enjoyed most. The Hindi they spoke in Bombay was very different from what they heard here. And they learned the hard way, that the Bambaia Hindi they spoke was actually guttural. It was a shopkeeper who made them realize this.

In the middle of her cooking one evening, Basanti found there was no salt in the house and Babu and Kalu were dispatched to the grocer.

'*Ek Namak ka packet dena be!*' Babu ordered, reaching the shop.

The middle-aged shopkeeper turned around, irritated, to look at his young customer, and Babu snapped again, '*Abbe, namak dena!*'

That was too much to take.

'*Jhakki ho kya?*' the shopkeeper scolded.

Kalu, fitting into the role of elder brother, came quickly to Babu's defence. '*Gali mat dena,*' he admonished the man behind the counter.

As he was to learn later, 'jhakki' was not so much an abuse—it meant mad. The shopkeeper had only wondered if the little boy was mad.

Meanwhile, a small crowd had gathered to watch the spectacle. One of the men in the crowd pulled the two brothers away and asked them in English, 'Where have you come from?'

'Bombay,' Kalu replied proudly.

'That's the problem,' the man declared, and proceeded to explain to them the nuances of 'tum', 'aap' and 'abbe'... The language had a bureaucracy. Unlike the universal 'you' in English, in Hindi one had to use one set of words to address one's elders or superiors, another for equals and yet another for those beneath one.

Their first lesson in proper Hindi learnt, the children returned home empty-handed, the shopkeeper firmly refusing to sell them any of his wares. On their mother's orders the two got a mild thrashing from their father. It was Thakurain who finally sent them some salt from her kitchen. It was religiously returned the next day.

'Never keep a person's salt,' Basanti explained to her children.

'One becomes a "namak haraam" by eating another person's salt.'

It was a literal explanation of who was a 'namak haraam'—a thankless bastard.

One evening their father returned home later than usual. But he appeared pleased with himself, his usual scowl replaced by a half-smile.

'I met Suren-da,' he informed Basanti.

The boys quickly surrounded their parents and learnt that Suren-da—Suren Jethu as the boys would address him—was their father's older cousin.

'He is a very learned man,' their mother informed the boys. Actually, Suren Jethu was a journalist and a subeditor with the *Northern India Patrika*.

'Just one rank below the editor,' the boys surmised from their limited understanding. Of course, they did not quite know what an editor did, even though Kalu had once aspired to become a journalist. The boys listened eagerly how Suren Jethu's family had received their father with great warmth.

'Boudi told me, "Akaloo, there is no need to live in a rented house,"' Samar recounted.

Then he described Suren-da's house to his wife, which to the boys sounded like an enormous two-storeyed building.

'She's told me that we must move in with them before the month is over. She wants me to save the rent—you see how thoughtful that is!'

Basanti was happy that at last they would have a decent place to live in.

But she was also sceptical, 'I don't know baba… It's not a good thing to freeload off one's relatives.'

Nevertheless, a few days later, the Biswases packed their luggage once again and headed for Alopy Bagh—very close to the famed

Sangam, the confluence of the rivers Ganga, Yamuna and Saraswati. Soon they ensconced themselves in Suren Jethu's comfortable house. It was a decent two-storeyed house—grand, by their standards—with the front wall covered with pink bougainvilleas. They had the entire upper floor to themselves—two large rooms, a huge balcony and a kitchen. Alopy Bagh was a middle-class colony of retired government officials, who had put their life's savings into building the houses they lived in.

First Lessons in Journalism

Suren Jethu had some six or seven children, but they were all grown up and behaved like adults with Kalu, Babu and Bappa. Kalu was greatly impressed to find that he had such distinguished cousins. Nantu-da, whom they rarely got to see, was a leading footballer in the UP state team. He would return late in the evenings after practice and would be out of town most of the time playing for his state. Then there was Nomi-di, who studied law at Allahabad University and was a university topper. For most of the days she would pace up and down the first floor terrace, reading aloud from her law books. She appeared to be in a perpetual examination mode. Then there was Gita-di, a dark, muscular girl who wore skirts and was the university captain in volleyball. Kalu, who vaguely understood 'university' to be the universe, could never stop marvelling how his cousins topped its class or captained its team. He was completely overwhelmed by them.

'University topper..., university captain! *Baap re!*'

There was also Nana-di, a fierce young woman who was a postgraduate and taught at a school. Tapan-da, the least distinguished of the siblings, worked at a government office, chewed paan and returned home late in the night. Everyone in the house would know the time of his return, because Suren Jethu—who was hard of hearing—would have removed his earplugs by then, and Tapan-da had to shout to him to make himself audible. Tapan-da also often came up to the first floor and demanded a paan from his Basanti Kakima. Basanti felt flattered that nephews from such a distinguished family could be so humble as to ask her for a paan— she never enjoyed making a paan more. The eldest of Suren Jethu's children was Pinto-da, whom the boys never got to see. Everyone spoke of him in hushed tones of respect, mentioning that he was an IAS officer. But Kalu was not impressed when he learnt that his cousin was a secretary in a certain ministry.

'Secretary, what a thing to be!' he told himself.

It was much later in life that he learned that 'secretary' was the pinnacle of a career in the Indian bureaucracy.

Suren Jethu was a dark-complexioned man in his late sixties (he must have been horny in his youth, to have produced so many, it occurred to Kalu). He was hard of hearing and wore a pair of thick glasses that made his eyes appear much larger and fiercer than usual. He also had a perennially leaking nose, into which he kept stuffing snuff. Once, the boy stole his snuffbox and went into paroxysms of sneezing after inhaling the brown pungent powder. Suren Jethu wore a dhoti kurta and carried a stick with him. Babu, particularly, would be terrified of him. And Basanti would cover her head with the pallu of her sari whenever he appeared before her. Sometimes he would appear from nowhere demanding, 'Bouma, give me a cup of tea.'

Demurely, Basanti would make the tea and send it with one of the boys.

'Oh, I feel ashamed going in front of him,' she would plead with them.

Kalu was in awe of Jethu because he still wrote occasionally for the *Northern India Patrika*.

'How does one become a journalist, Jethu?' he once asked him.

He soon realized what a big mistake that had been. Jethu would now often call out for him and dictate articles that he had to scribble down on a notepad. The articles were often about gods and mythology that made little sense to Kalu. Though both of them were reclusive by nature, Samar and Suren-da gossiped a great deal about life in Pabna in Bangladesh, where they had grown up. They mostly spoke of relatives.

'Do you know so and so died... Do you know where X is...? Y's son went to London...' There was a lot to cover.

The children did not notice at first that Jethima never came to their floor when Suren Jethu was around. Jethima was a severe, grey-haired, wrinkled woman, and was always scolding someone or the other. Basanti, who was forced to be respectful towards her since she was an elder, was often her unwitting target.

'Don't break the coal with so much vigour, the building will collapse!' she would come and tell Basanti, who had been compelled to replace her Primus stove for cooking with a coal stove.

Though itching to retort to such outlandish barbs, Basanti would hold back in fear of her husband. Later, she told her children, 'The old hag has always been like that. She doesn't even speak to her husband. They haven't spoken for the last five years. God knows what kind of a witch she is.'

Of course, all this was said out of her husband's hearing range. Samar would never forgive her for such uncharitable remarks about his kin. But soon he too realized that his Boudi was becoming a little too overbearing for comfort.

At the brink of a potential conflict, the relationship between the two families warmed up all of a sudden. Samar had brought news of a very good match for Suren Jethu's dark-skinned daughter, Gita. Several previous attempts at getting Gita married off had proved futile, her dark complexion always turning out to be the hurdle.

With Samar coming up with a prospective groom, the attitude of Jethu's family towards them suddenly turned benevolent. Every now and then there would be calls from the ground floor.

'Arre Akaloo, why don't you come down here,' Jethima would call out.

And to keep his wife pleased she would add, 'Arre Basanti, why don't you also join us?'

And as everyone discussed the prospective match, hot cups of tea would be served. The excited conversations went on for several days, and the boys were also sometimes allowed to join in. The prospective groom, they discovered, was an engineer from Nagpur who belonged to an equally distinguished family.

'Own house…father retired government officer…another brother doctor… What more can one ask for?' Jethima said. 'And the best part is that she will have no mother-in-law to trouble her.' The groom's mother had passed away a few years ago.

Sometimes, the talks were so engrossing that the two families ate together, so that Samar and Basanti did not have to return upstairs for their meal. It was no wonder, for Samar was playing the crucial contact between the two families. He wrote the letters, negotiated the dowry and even decided what the menu for the wedding would be. He was the fulcrum on which the marriage hinged.

After a few days the prospective groom and his family came all the way from Nagpur to take a look at Gita-di. The day they came to visit, tension hung in the air of the house. Each of the prospective bride's siblings had been assigned specific roles in taking care of the guests. It was important to ensure the groom's party did not feel too let down by Gita's dark complexion, carefully camouflaged with rouge and talcum powder. So each one had a duty to keep the guests pampered and 'engaged' so that undue attention was diverted from the prospective bride's appearance.

Only Suren Jethu, father of the prospective bride, seemed detached from the entire proceedings, taking little part in what was going on around him. His role in the matchmaking exercise was completely taken over by Samar. On the day the groom's family arrived, even Jethima seemed to become servile towards Samar— she had to get her daughter married at any cost. An unmarried girl in the house was like a load on her chest. Her humility and enforced good manner paid off. The match was fixed. When they departed, the groom's family shook Samar's hand firmly and assured that Gita would soon be their bouma.

It was a coup of sorts, with every member of the household eating out of Samar's hand in the days and weeks that followed. He was consulted on virtually everything—the sari that Gita would wear on the wedding night, the menu for the 'bor jatri', the jamai's suit, the guests to be invited… In those days, there was a call from downstairs every evening.

'Samar can you come down please…?'

'Samar we have to discuss the dowry.'

'Samar, please, can you bring Basanti downstairs…'

'Nebu Kaka'—for that was what the cousins called Samar—'Ma is calling you downstairs for a cup of tea.'

The Biswas boys were happy with the attention their father was getting. For once, even Basanti was impressed with the influence her husband wielded. As was her nature, she expressed it in one of her taunts, 'Go, go… Your Boudi is calling you!'

And Samar, with a smile playing in the corner of his lips, would go downstairs obediently, as though on some noble mission.

But once the match was fixed, the days of influence appeared to wane quickly. Soon the calls from downstairs became less frequent, and Samar himself returned to his former reserve. Sometimes, he even made excuses to avoid going downstairs.

'These days they are talking directly to Nagpur. There's no further need for you, now that the wedding has been fixed,' Basanti taunted her husband.

Even the boys understood vaguely that they were no longer relevant to the wedding that was to take place, though no one was quite sure what exactly had happened. On the evening before the wedding, Jethima finally called from downstairs, 'Basanti, come downstairs with the bothi, the vegetables have to be cut.'

Basanti, her pride partially restored, just about shifted in her seat, when Samar ordered his wife, 'No, you will not go downstairs!'

It was then that the children guessed that something had seriously gone wrong between Jethu's family and them. The next day—the day of the wedding—there were guests in the house from early in the morning, but their father went to the office as usual. Basanti and the children were expecting that they would be called downstairs for lunch, since that was the normal practice— relatives of the bride never cooked in their own house on the day of the wedding.

But no call came. Finally Jethima came upstairs and told Basanti, 'You all must come for the reception in the evening.'

The invitation was extended very perfunctorily, and Basanti hissed behind Jethima, 'Huh…as though we don't get food in our house!'

That evening was most humiliating for the children. They expected to be cajoled into going downstairs to partake in the rich feast that had been prepared, much of its fragrance pervading the air. Even Basanti was half-prepared to go downstairs, which was apparent to the children from the fact that she had not cooked supper. Basanti, Samar and the three boys waited in the fond hope that Jethima would finally appear upstairs and persuade them into coming downstairs for the marriage feast. But nothing like that happened. Many of the guests who had finished their meals came upstairs for a quiet smoke and peered into their room.

'Oh, you are tenants,' they said and went away.

Finally Basanti cooked a meal of rice and boiled potatoes. The family ate in silence, the smell of good food still lingering in their nostrils. In less than a week's time, they moved away from Suren Jethu's house. In a little more than a month they also learned, much to their vicarious satisfaction, that Gita had been sent back home, disowned and discarded by the groom's family. 'Serves them right! God has taught them a lesson,' Basanti remarked self-righteously.

Afzal's Home

After the brief honeymoon at Suren Jethu's house, the family returned, like homing birds, to Sulem Sarai. This time, their house was right on the G. T. Road, a few furlongs ahead of the lane that led to Jangi Lal's house. It was closer to the market square and the weekly mandi could be seen from the rooftop, at the back of the house. The yellow-coloured, two-storeyed building was called Afzal's Home. There was a bit of history stuck to its peeling walls. It had once belonged to a prosperous Muslim family, who fled to Pakistan in the wake of the Partition that gave birth to the Muslim nation. The building was so large that it was difficult to find a single buyer. But this was a time of great tensions between the Hindus and Muslims of India. News of riots and butchering, trickling in daily, were only adding to people's fears. The Muslims in Sulem Sarai, like elsewhere in the country, were in a rush to migrate. So instead of waiting around for the right price Afzal hurriedly found two buyers who were interested in the building. The two were refugee 'lalas' who had just migrated to India from the same village in the Punjab now in Pakistan. Without much haggling the building was sold to the two lalas, going by the names of Chawla and Dewan. A vertical wall was erected, dividing the building into two identical halves. But the new buyers neglected to get rid of the old name—Afzal's Home—which remained painted in white on the yellow front balcony.

The Biswases came to live in the part of the building that belonged to the Dewans. To be more precise, they came to occupy two rooms on the first floor of Dewan Chand's portion of the house. Unlike Inderjeet Chawla, Dewan Chandji did not live in the house he bought. He converted the ground-floor rooms facing the road into grocery shops. At the back of the shops were storerooms stacked with jute bags full of rice, wheat and other grocery items. Behind the godowns lived his other tenants, petty officials in the Geep Flash Light factory that was a short distance outside Sulem Sarai.

The first floor of the house had just three rooms, two of which were taken on rent by Samar. To enter the house one had to get into a narrow lane with naked brick walls on either side. So narrow was the lane that the children learnt to scale the walls rising vertically, keeping one foot on each wall. The wall on the right side was the huge wall of Dewan Chand's house. There were doors in this wall that opened into dark cavernous storerooms. Just before the door to one such storeroom, a spiral staircase led to the first floor of the house and then the terrace. On the landing of the first floor, one door opened to a kitchen with tiled roof. Two steps above was a narrow room eight feet wide and twenty feet long. Why such a narrow room? Well this particular room was divided into half as a result of the partitioning of Afzal's home, of which the other half had gone to the Chawlas. The end of the narrow room had a window facing a courtyard-like balcony overlooking the G. T. Road. The other door on the landing led to another room, which also served as a common passage to the toilets for the tenant who lived in the third room on the floor. A barred door between the rooms divided the tenants, and had several gaping holes in it.

The toilets included one lavatory at the far end and two adjacent bathrooms, each having a water tap. The 'beehive' walls in the toilets not only provided a view of open fields behind the house, they also served as niches to keep the soap and other toiletries. The slanting earthen-tiled roof of the toilet leaked during the rains. The dry latrine consisted of a long pipe, and every time one shat it produced a splattering sound from the ground floor below. This was also accompanied by the loud buzz of flies that were stirred by the falling excreta. If one day the sweeper—a girl with pockmarks called Asha—did not clean up the mound of shit that collected below, using the latrine could become a hellish experience, particularly for Basanti. She would bribe Asha with tea, parathas and other inducements, just to make sure that she cleaned the latrine everyday. Asha, a brazen, carefree sort of woman, would come to the first-floor landing every morning around ten and demand tea and food from Basanti before she got on to her dirty job.

There was a separate cup for her, with a broken handle, which Asha would retrieve from a niche in the wall. Basanti would pour her the tea from a height, lest a direct connection with the woman defiled her. Similarly, the rotis, too, would be dropped into Asha's open palm from a height, like manna from heaven. Sometimes Asha would lunge forward as though to touch Basanti, who would retreat screaming for her life. And Asha would double up, going into peals of laughter revealing her pink gums. The element of untouchability between them was not laced with any rancour. In fact, Basanti and Asha were even friends of sorts. They would sit and chat, even though they did not quite comprehend each other's language. Kalu, who sometimes shared their company, realized the conversation occasionally bordered on the ludicrous.

'*Bur bolo… bur bolo*,' Asha would occasionally urge Basanti, and laugh.

'Bur', Kalu knew meant cunt. Somehow, he even started to find this older girl sexy. The thought that she carried human excreta on her head made him recoil, but he could not help stealing a glance whenever—and it happened often—the girl let her dupatta fall, revealing ample breasts.

The kitchen and the 'passage room' overlooked a hollow courtyard downstairs that had been equally divided between Dewan Chand and Chawla. It also afforded a full view of the first floor of the Chawla household, which was adjacent to the courtyard. Recently renovated, their rooms looked new and slick. The Chawla grandchildren were nearly the same age as Babu, Kalu and Bappa. Sitting in the kitchen, Kalu would observe the Chawla household with envy. He discovered that the Chawlas cooked on a gas oven, had a refrigerator and even a wall-clock that went 'tong-tong' every hour. The boys Lucky and Pappu wore expensive clothes, and the eldest, Sunil, went to boarding school. But Kalu also found, to his surprise, that these well-dressed boys could not speak English. So at one level, he and his brothers felt superior to them. Basanti too initially refused to feel inferior to the Chawlas.

'Kalu ki mummy, you are kiraidars, na? How much rent do you pay?' Lucky's mother once asked her.

To which Basanti replied, 'Yes, but I don't know how much the rent is.'

Actually, even the children knew that the rent was thirty-five rupees, but it would be humiliating to admit it. To counter the implied insult, Basanti would ask in her turn, 'Lucky ki mummy, which school do your children go to?'

And when she had heard the answer she would smugly reply, 'Oh, good. These convents my children go to are so expensive!'

But despite the pretence, it was clear to all who the better-off family was. The feeling of inferiority never quite left Basanti and her children.

A Bird's-Eye View

The view from the roof of Afzal's Home, overlooking the G. T. Road of Sulem Sarai, was interesting. The highway was always busy with the traffic of trucks that ran between Calcutta and Delhi. Occasionally, there was even a jam. Right in front of the house was a mosque. On its ground floor, there was a mutton shop owned by a short Muslim man whom everyone called 'Natte'. In front of the mosque there was a perpetual cluster of ekkas and tangas, waiting for passengers while their horses fed and relieved themselves at the same time. There was something heady about the smell that emanated from that mix of horse urine and dung. Some of the ekkas had a shroud, in order to provide purdah for the Muslim women who travelled in them.

Next-door to the mosque were a flour mill and a jewellery shop owned by a pleasant-looking Hindu fellow called Chhedi Lal. His wife was perpetually pregnant. The man was apparently a great fan of Indira Gandhi. Once, when the prime minister of India came to Allahabad by road, Chhedi Lal made sure that she stopped by at his house and accepted a garland from him. Indira Gandhi was coming on a tumultuous visit to Allahabad—her childhood home—following one of those landslide victories in the elections. The entire road, on either side, was barricaded to hold back swarms of admirers waiting to get a glimpse of the prime minister. In that brief melee when Chhedi Lal garlanded her, Kalu managed to fleetingly touch Indira Gandhi.

'Her hand was so soft,' he recounted to his mother.

On a regular day, Chhedi Lal was a pleasant man with a ready smile on his face. But there was one time he got into a tiff with a neighbouring shop-owner, and then he was like a man possessed. Both the men brought out their guns, aiming at each other, and were ready to kill. They even shot a few rounds in the air, sending shock waves in the neighbourhood. Kalu was so gripped by fear that he crouched behind the wall of the roof overlooking the road, emerging only well after the guns had fallen silent.

The G. T. Road was hemmed with shops and houses on both sides. The two or three-storeyed houses dominated the skyline. The others, like Chhedi Lal's house, were single-storeyed and had sloping tiled roofs. Right across the road from Afzal's Home was a two-storeyed mud-and-brick house, in which a blind beggar lived.

'Does he have a wife… Does he have children?' Kalu often wondered. All he had to do was saunter across the road and find out, but he never did so in all of the eight years that they lived in Afzal's Home. The beggar was impossible to miss, because every night he would return home pounding the road with the iron rod that served as his walking stick. He was a punctual man. On hearing the metallic sound through the silence of the night, Kalu and Babu would say, 'It must be ten o'clock!' Rising from their studies, they would run to the roof and follow the beggar till they could hear his last steps fade into the two-storeyed hovel.

It was on one such rush to the roof that Kalu observed something else that left him baffled. On the dark first-floor terrace of Chawla's house, he noticed a violent scuffle-like movement on a bed. Not realizing at first what was happening, he rubbed his eyes and focused his attention at the sight. In the half-light, he felt a surge of sensual passion at what he saw. Lucky's father, stark naked, was pounding away at the bed over his prostrated wife. The *violence* must have lasted a few minutes, after which there was quiet. Minutes later Aunty stirred out of the bed, and tying her pyjama strings, returned indoors. Uncle, after a quick wash, went off to sleep. It was a revelation for Kalu—something so scandalous he did not share it with anyone.

But the scene began to haunt him all day and he felt a tingling sensation all over, particularly around the groins. Soon the nocturnal visit to the terrace became an addiction. When everyone else in the house would be occupied with the nine o'clock news and other pre-dinner activities, Kalu would quietly sneak to the terrace in search of the real action. Mostly he was early. Sometimes the bed on the terrace would be empty. So he would move towards the hollow courtyard of the building. From there he would watch Harish Chawla Uncle, immersed in a book in a brightly lit room, scratching his dark scrotum and fondling his erect penis as he read some lurid novel.

Aunty, of course, would be busy finishing the post-dinner cleaning and washing. When the dishwashing and cleaning was nearing its end, Harish Uncle would instinctively move on to the charpoy on the front terrace. There he would feverishly turn and toss in his bed and crane his neck, watching out for his wife to come. Once she appeared he would pin her down to the bed, and the rapid-fire banging action would start without any preliminaries. Soon after lifting her petticoat, he would quickly penetrate his wife until she groaned in delightful pain. The action lasted no more than five minutes. The pantomime over, the woman would tie the lace of her petticoat and return to her bed indoors. And the man would return to his sleep, following a quick wash in a corner of the terrace. The scene would leave Kalu hot and tingling with passion.

The secret 'scandal' of Harish Uncle 'fornicating' with Aunty was unleashed one day, to none other than their son Lucky. As usual Kalu and Lucky got into a fight over a kite that flew over their terrace. When he couldn't overpower Lucky, who had snatched the kite, he blurted out what he had meant to keep a secret. 'You know what your father does? He screws your mother,' he told Lucky.

Unfazed, the boy countered, 'And what does your father do to your mother?'

For a moment Kalu pondered, but he had to let the realization pass by. The very thought of his own father and mother in the act was so revolting that he closed his mind to the very idea, more so because he thought it might be true. Till then, Kalu had just vaguely known of the relationship between husband and wife. He was in the eighth standard then—still an innocent boy.

That year their biology teacher Ms D'Costa began to teach them about reproduction and reproductive organs. Ms D'Costa had large, heaving breasts. For once the boys in the class were all attention, unevenly divided between the lesson and her mammary glands. When it came to the description of the male and female reproductive organs the boys were taut with excitement. While some were sniggering, the more daring ones were staring meaningfully into Ms D'Costa's you-know-where.

'Look at my face, and stop looking elsewhere!' flustered by the attention, she reprimanded the boys. When the class was over, Rathore, a dark lanky boy who had become a close friend, nudged Kalu, 'What were you looking at?'

And with a wink in his eye, he added, 'Real big boobs, aren't they?'

Soon they graduated to biology 'practicals' as Ms D'Costa taught them to dissect frogs. When it came to displaying the reproductive organs, there was a huge crowd of inquisitive boys around her table. As Ms D'Costa bent over the dissected frog most of the boys were not looking at the frog—their eyes were penetrating deep into her cleavage and their nostrils were taking in the heady perfume of her body. Once the practicals were over, most of the boys got into heated discussion over the dimensions of their teacher's mammary glands.

'I touched it with my elbow, it was soft like rubber,' Rathore confessed.

Half a dozen other boys too made the same claim.

Thanks to the 'mammarian' diversions the heavy load of the curriculum—particularly of physics, chemistry and mathematics—felt a little bearable. Some even shifted their allegiance from PCM to biology!

Who Wrote that Essay?

Ever since the art classes had abruptly ended after the sixth standard—leaving a void in his life—it was the literature and English composition class that Kalu mostly looked forward to. *Macbeth* by Shakespeare, *The Crucible* by Arthur Miller, *The Mayor of Casterbridge* and *Far From the Madding Crowd* by Thomas Hardy—Kalu loved them all. He would get under the skins of the characters and literally live through their joys and sorrows, particularly their sorrows. Somehow he thrived on tragedy. So when Fanny Robin died in *Far From the Madding Crowd*, he wept for her. Similarly, he cried for the mayor of Casterbridge in his final days. Given a choice between *Macbeth* and *Twelfth Night*, he would pick the dark tragedy. Even the short stories of Premchand touched him deeply, though he was not very comfortable with reading or writing in Hindi. But Kalu's reading did not go much beyond course books. When Ahmed or Navroz would exchange novels with other members of the English-speaking gang, Kalu would stare at them with a mixed sense of awe and inferiority.

'How do they manage to finish those thick novels?' he would ask himself.

What intrigued him more were the authors—he failed to fathom who wrote those big fat novels. And yet, he was among the highest scorers in the essay-writing class. Getting four or five out of ten was a rare score only select boys got. Kalu was invariably among them. Why, sometimes he even scored better than Ahmed!

The essay-writing classes made him feel smart and worthy. He was not a bad student in general. It was just that physics, chemistry and maths made him feel wretched and no better than the duffers. The English language classes redeemed his self-esteem, even though he could not quite figure out the logic behind the high scores he got at essay-writing. Like the rest of the English-speaking gang, he too was content to believe it was by fluke. And then one day, Mrs Hopkins, who taught them English, announced Kalu's marks before returning the corrected essay copies:

'Six out of ten!'

It was the highest in the class. As Kalu collected his copybook from Mrs Hopkins, she asked coldly, 'Where did you copy that essay from?'

Taken aback by the question, Kalu fumbled for a reply. He was never quick on his feet when it came to thinking or rebutting.

'No ma'am…but I did not copy…' he finally managed to blabber.

Back to his bench, he was smarting from the insult. But eventually a voice inside him said, 'Buddy, you write well. That's why the teacher thinks you've copied the essay from somewhere.'

It was the first left-handed compliment he had received for his writing abilities. He began to believe in himself.

But the English-speaking gang could never quite accept anyone getting more marks than them, at least at essay-writing. One day when Father Rego, the headmaster, was taking the class instead of Mrs Hopkins, who was on leave, the English-speaking gang decided they would confront Father as to how some boys who always spoke in Hindi could score more marks than them in English. It was Keith Menezes who stood up and articulated the question on behalf of the gang, 'Father, how's it possible that boys who cannot even speak proper English get more marks than us?'

A murmur of approval rose from the other gang members, urging for an answer. Their target was not Kalu but one Akhil Gupta, who also consistently scored good marks at essay-writing. The conflict had arisen because Akhil rarely spoke in English. Faced with this serious question, Father Rego's scowl gradually melted into a cynical smile. He caressed his unkempt grey stubble, wiped his glasses and said in a patronizing tone, 'My son, I see your point...'

At this point the English-speaking gang got excited and there was a murmur of approval.

'But speaking English, you must remember, is not quite the same as writing English,' the headmaster added.

'In speaking you can get away with guttural, slang language. In writing, you have to be refined. Good writing only comes through when you have internalized a language, when you learn to *think* in that language.'

'By the way, how many marks did you score, Keith?' he finally asked.

'Two,' a crest-fallen Keith answered.

Now the rest of the class sniggered. The English-speaking gang quietly swallowed its pride, resenting Father Rego, whom they had expected to take their side.

But Father Rego—the spirit behind St Joseph's Collegiate School— also had laid down strict instructions that the boys of St Joseph's would speak only in English within the school premises. When he realized that very few boys were following his diktat of their own volition, he appointed a band of boys from the senior classes to regulate the matter. These boys were produced before the morning assembly on the next day.

'From now on, whoever is found conversing in Hindi inside

the school compound will be fined ten paise. I'm appointing these boys for the task,' Father Rego announced. As Father discussed other matters of discipline, there was sudden silence.

'Billy Goooat!' just then some old boys jeered from the main road, just outside the school compound. 'Billy Goat' was Father Rego's accepted nickname among the boys, in recognition of his short beard. But that moniker was used only in hushed private conversation.

A murmur of protest rose from the assembled students, but soon it died down. A part of the murmur was in approval of whoever had shouted Billy Goat, as no one inside school could openly dare to call him 'Billy Goat'. Just like no one could question his decision to 'enforce' English.

One day when Kalu was caught speaking in Hindi by Debasish Mitra, a boy from the tenth standard, and asked to pay up, he refused.

'It's my national language, and this is my country,' he said.

'That's true,' his friends murmured.

A small rebellion brewed over the matter and Kalu was finally reported to Father Rego. A few weeks later, once again at the morning assembly, Father announced a repeal of the order.

'I understand many that of you are upset, since Hindi is your national language. I understand your nationalistic sentiments,' he said.

A murmur of approval rose from the assembly, and above the din he added, 'My purpose in imposing the rule was to make sure that you learnt English. That's why your parents send you to this school.'

A lot of the boys rallied around Kalu and he became the day's hero.

Just then someone shouted. 'Thanks, Billy Goat!'

This time, the shout had come from someone within the assembly. It was followed by a stunned silence. Soon a hurried announcement was made—unless the culprit owned up, the whole school would be punished.

Finally, when no one came forward, the assembly was dissolved. All the boys were sent back to their classrooms, apart from the tenth-standard students. They were made to stand in the sun for a full hour. It was Mr Joe Shankar who presided over the punishment.

When Kalu Became a Hero

There was another occasion when Kalu was hailed a hero. This time, the boys had even hoisted him on their shoulders. The incident happened during the time of their third quarterly exams.

For weeks and days before the beginning of the exams, two boys from the senior class would regularly interrupt classes and announce: 'Your kind attention, please! This announcement is from the Principal. All are requested to pay their pending fees before the third quarterly exams commence. Those who fail to do so will be debarred from appearing in the exams.'

These announcements had a strange intimidating effect on Kalu. Somehow he felt the warnings were being personally addressed to him, as he had frequently defaulted in paying his fees on time. At one level he took the warnings nonchalantly, believing the threats would not actually be carried out. Yet he dutifully conveyed the warnings to his father.

'Baba, I'll not be allowed to sit for the exams if I am late with the fees,' he reminded.

'Tomorrow,' his father assured him, but he always forgot.

Samar was so preoccupied with making ends meet that Kalu often felt that the fees were a burden he was unnecessarily inflicting on his father. So he did not remind his father too forcefully. When the exams arrived he went to appear for them, without having paid the school fees. Fortunately, no one seemed to mind. Like the rest of the boys, Kalu too was supplied with the question paper and sheets to write his answer. Soon he was immersed in his writing.

'Good!' The invigilator actually bent over his paper, observed him and patted him on the back. He was appreciating the boy's handwriting. Happily, Kalu was halfway through his paper, when Mr Joe Shankar entered the classroom. At first, the boys barely took notice of him.

Mr Shankar was tall and well-built, a man who always managed to look stern with his bushy, brownish-red moustache and large, angry eyes that seemed ready to pop out. His large, ruddy face—accentuated by a bald pate—had a permanent scowl that sent down shivers of fear in the hearts of even the most impertinent boys. Usually Mr Shankar taught geometry in the ninth standard, but when matters of discipline had to be imposed it was he who was always called in.

'Is there anyone in this class who has not paid his fees?' Mr Shankar went over to the blackboard and shouted.

Kalu's heart missed a beat. It then began pounding so hard he was afraid everyone would hear his heartbeat. He pretended to concentrate hard on his question paper, not even daring to look up lest his face betray his fear. For a few moments there was silence and he was relieved, thinking the worst was over.

But then Mr Shankar, peering at a sheet, asked, 'Who's Kalu Choudhury, from Class VIII C?'

All the boys looked in his direction and Kalu had no option but to stand up. Mr Shankar charged in his direction and, without any ado, grabbed his answer sheet.

'I'm sorry sir, I'll bring it tomorrow,' Kalu pleaded. 'Please sir… please,' he begged.

'Nothing doing,' Mr Shankar replied and ordered him to leave the classroom.

Having failed to impress upon Mr Shankar his situation, Kalu pleaded with the invigilator, Mr Sharma, who had minutes ago appreciated his handwriting. 'Please sir, why don't you tell him?'

Mr Sharma shrugged helplessly.

Kalu ran after Mr Shankar, who had walked out of the classroom taking the boy's answer sheet with him. There was a small scuffle in the corridor, Kalu trying to snatch back his answer sheet. But Mr Shankar was far too tall and strong for him. When he had lost the battle with Mr Shankar, there were tears rolling down his eyes.

In his imbecile rage, Kalu cursed under his breath, 'Bloody bastard!'

Mr Shankar, who had walked a few paces away, turned back.

'What did you say... What did you say?'

Before Kalu could say anything he spun under the impact of a heavy slap. More slaps rained down one after the other, as Mr Shankar towered over him, his eyes bloodshot, his mouth frothing, demanding, 'Come again! Come again... Repeat what you said!'

His hair dishevelled, Kalu had no time to regain his composure.

But soon, wiping his tears he stood up defiantly and said, 'I told you nothing!'

More slapping followed.

'I did not tell *you* anything,' Kalu stood his ground firmly.

By then the commotion in the corridor had distracted the invigilators, who opened their classroom doors and made concerned enquiries. With the invigilators outside, the boys who did not know their answers had a field day with ten uninterrupted minutes of copying off their neigbours. When the invigilators returned to their classrooms, Mr Shankar dragged Kalu to Father Rego's office.

'You will be dismissed from the school!' Mr Shankar threatened, as the two walked down the silent corridors, past the quietly busy classrooms.

Mr Shankar walked into the headmaster's office alone, with Kalu standing outside and feeling like a convict. A while later Father Rego emerged from his office, Mr Shankar in tow.

'What is this I hear?' he asked.

By then Kalu had contrived an answer. Putting on his most innocent expression he said, 'Father, you know me. Can you believe I would say something like this?'

Moved by the boy's face, Father Rego replied, 'But you are not implying that Mr Shankar is lying?'

'No, Father… But it may be possible that he is only imagining that I said things…'

The questioning lasted for about five minutes, after which Father Rego ordered, 'Go back to your classroom now. I will have to get to the bottom of this matter.'

Kalu ran back through the silent school and stood outside the classroom, relieved that he had been spared dismissal from school. At least for the time being.

When the school bell rang and the boys burst out of the classrooms, Kalu was surprised that his friends and even those with who he had only a nodding acquaintance came up to him and shook his hands.

'Congratulations yaar, he *is* a bastard!'

Kalu did not know how to react. He had certainly not bargained for becoming infamous. The news had spread to other eighth-standard classrooms as well. Many of the boys came up to Kalu and slapped him on the back. Others watched him admiringly from a distance. Kalu began to enjoy the attention—the difference in taste between fame and infamy was not very great, he realized. Soon his own friends—Rathore and members of the English-speaking gang—scooped him up on their shoulders. He was heralded like a hero.

'He deserves a treat!' someone said, and they took him to the ice cream seller. Kalu did not even relish the taste of the ice cream as much as he relished the first taste of being recognized.

When Mr Khan, their physics teacher, was passing by the ice cream vendor and saw the boys, he remarked sarcastically to Kalu, '*Neta ban gaye ho!*'

The incident had become known to the other teachers as well. News travelled fast inside the school compound. Particularly when it was bad.

But the euphoria of being recognized did not last long. The fear of being dismissed from school returned soon to haunt Kalu. The thought of his father getting to know about the incident bothered him more than anything else.

'My father will kill me,' he thought aloud.

'Don't worry yaar, we're there!' his friends comforted him.

A bunch of them even went to Father Rego and pleaded his case. In the end it was Sharma Aunty—Mukul's mother—who said she would put in a word for Kalu with Mr Shankar.

Two days later she informed Kalu, 'I've spoken to Joe. Go and apologize to him.'

The next day, after school hours Kalu posted himself outside the staffroom, hoping to catch Mr Joe Shankar before he left the premises. It was already dusk. The bus he took to go home would also have left. But Kalu waited outside the door of the staffroom like a sentry. Many teachers walked in and out, but there was no sign of Joe Shankar. Finally when he saw Ms D'Costa coming out, Kalu approached her and said, 'Miss, could you please tell Mr Joe Shankar that I'm waiting for him?'

Miss D'Costa looked surprised.

'Joe? He must be at home,' she said.

Kalu melted away from the door of the staffroom. It was getting dark and he quickened his steps towards the bus stand, but then a voice inside him said, 'Why don't you sort out the problem before you go home today?'

He remembered the famous doha by Kabir Das taught in his Hindi class, '*Kal kare so aaj…*'

So instead of going home, he headed for the enclosure across the road where many of the Christian teachers lived. Joe Shankar was a bachelor and lived all by himself. The rumour was that his wife had passed away soon after marriage. When Kalu knocked at the huge wooden door, for a while there was no response. He was about to leave when the door creaked open, framing the huge silhouette of Mr Shankar.

'Oh, it's you!' he muttered with a slur.

'Come in…come in,' he added with a smile.

This was a different man from the stern Mr Shankar Kalu had known at school. There was a gay abandon about him. Kalu quickly realized that his geometry teacher had been on a high, nursing a drink too many.

'So you do not want to be dismissed from school!' Mr Shankar said, and laughed wickedly.

'No sir, I have come to apologize…' Kalu said meekly.

Mr Shankar took his trembling face between his warm hands and held it steady. He said in an unusually affectionate, voice, 'Don't worry, my dear boy.'

And then his wet fleshy lips kissed Kalu full in the mouth, the moustache tickling him.

Despite the deep discomfort caused by the kiss, Kalu was happy that Mr Shankar had forgiven him, and above all, saved him from being dismissed from the school.

'Thank you, sir,' he said and made to leave.

That's when Mr Shankar grabbed him by the hand and drew

him to his chest. His breath was reeking of liquor. Kalu recoiled at the smell. It was as if that involuntary act of defiance made him more attractive to Joe Shankar, for he pinned Kalu down to his bed and began kissing him violently, his wet mouth sucking at the boy's lips till they hurt. In the next few minutes he peeled off his clothes and began heaving himself maniacally on the little boy, his body stark naked. After what seemed like an eternity, Mr Shankar sagged on him with all his weight, leaving his thighs wet with a sticky fluid. For a few seconds, Mr Shankar lay limp over him, and Kalu was too terrified to move. Finally, he heaved himself up from the bed.

Kalu wanted to bolt immediately, but Mr Shankar grabbed him again. This time he stared him in the face and uttered in his half-drunk voice, 'If you talk about this to anybody, you'll be thrown out of the school! Understand?'

Desperate to get away, Kalu replied, 'Yes sir.'

He rushed out into the cold dark night, trembling with fear. The events of that dark evening remained buried in his heart. Whenever he ran into Mr Shankar after that, he averted his eyes and a strange feeling of fear and awe gripped him. He felt entirely under the man's power as though hypnotized. In a strange dark way the man held the boy in his thrall.

Adult Encounters

Homosexuality was no stranger to St Joseph's Collegiate School. Mr Khan, the physics teacher, was said to have laid Neeraj Saxena when the class went for an overnight picnic outside Allahabad. Since it had been a paid picnic, Kalu could not go, but he heard the story from other friends. Apparently, Mr Khan and Neeraj had slept under the same quilt, and the next morning Neeraj had marks all over his fair cheeks. After that incident, the boys nicknamed Neeraj 'Rajai'—the word for quilt. The encounters were not confined to the teacher-student relationships. They took place even among the students. The most conspicuous example of this was a boy called Amit Bose. A big burly bespectacled fellow, Amit looked no different from any other student.

Actually the specs made him look intelligent and above average. He had traces of a moustache that made him look older than the other boys. Despite his intelligent looks most teachers called him a 'duffer' and a 'jackass'. To ensure that the children had imbibed what was taught in the previous class, the beginning of every period would see teachers asking questions from the previous lesson taught in the class.

'Yes sir, yes sir...'

A crowd of hands from the front benches would go up in the air, eager to show their knowledge. It was strange; the teachers ignored the hands dying to answer. They scanned for the hands that had not gone up.

And somehow it was always Amit who would be singled out for answering a question.

Whether it was from the history sir: 'Amit, what was the year 1857 famous for?' or the biology teacher: 'How many bones does the human body have?' Amit never had an answer.

Whenever a question was asked he would stand up and look blankly in the air, not even pretending to make an effort. Actually many of the boys who knew the correct answer were eager to prompt, but Amit never appeared interested to answer. Somehow it appeared as though Amit was more than willing to stand through the classes rather than take the trouble of answering a question. Despite his large build, Amit must have been made to suffer a very low self-esteem thanks to the teachers. He was forced to feel like a buffoon. So he devised his own ways of getting back at the school system. He would seek sexual gratification from students who were good at studies. One day after the morning assembly, Kalu found Amit standing right behind him. It was all very fine until the boy realized that Amit was rubbing his crotch against his bottom. He was even feeling up his buttocks with his hands. Kalu did not protest. But after a while there was something hard that Amit was trying to shove behind him. It was an erection he was trying to placate! The matter ended without much ado.

Since they were both Bengalis, there was already a certain affinity between the two. Then one day when Kalu's bench-partner was absent, Amit came and sat beside him. While Mrs Daniel carried on with the geography class, Amit suddenly put his hands inside Kalu's shorts and began fiddling with his organ. It enlarged, giving him a happy feeling. Meanwhile, Amit opened his fly and began displaying his erect penis. It was large. And as the geography class progressed, Kalu felt compelled to hold it in his hands. This exercise was repeated every time Kalu's bench-mate was absent.

Then one day, towards the end of the day's classes, Amit told Kalu in a conspiratorial tone, 'Wait for me after class. I'll show you something!'

He gave Kalu a clean sheet of paper to hold. The paper baffled Kalu.

'Is he going to do some kind of magic trick?' he wondered.

When he asked Amit what the paper was for, all he could get out of him was, 'Just wait!'

When all the boys had left for the day the two boys tiptoed to the upper floor, Kalu holding the paper like a magic wand. After inspecting the classrooms and making sure no one was around, Amit suddenly caught hold of Kalu and began shoving at him from the back. Taken aback by the sudden assault, Kalu tried to flee. But Amit gripped him firmly between his arms and thighs, banging away consistently at his behind. When Kalu finally wriggled out of his grip, Amit restrained him with one hand. With the other he flicked out his erect penis and began stroking it vigourously.

'Give me the paper… give me the paper!' he said with urgency.

He snatched the paper from Kalu, and just in time, a thick creamy fluid flowed into it.

Kalu was terrified at the sight. Despite the attentively devoured biology lessons on reproduction, it did not register to him immediately that what he was looking at was semen.

'You want to try it?' Amit asked.

Kalu ran down the stairs and escaped.

Nevertheless, Amit was the first friend to teach him the pleasures of masturbation. Later, masturbation became a distraction whenever he was alone. The first few times, when he would reach the peak of his gratification, his penis would twitch at the climax. Then one day, the rich, creamy fluid poured out, and Kalu was terrified again. But by this time his fear was tempered by the knowledge that it was semen—that he had attained puberty. He was in sync with the biology lessons.

His first encounter with the opposite sex took place a few months later, with a woman much older—the maid. Bimla Devi would come to their house every morning to scrub the utensils and sweep the floors. A young woman in her twenties, she had pouting lips and a supple body that was neatly wrapped in a sari. She wore a large bindi—indicating that she was married—and laughed a great deal—indicating that she could be fun. Kalu had never considered her with any sexual intent, though occasionally he had stolen looks at her bared cleavage. Then one morning, when Basanti went for a visit to the doctor, she left the house in charge of Kalu.

'Make sure that Bimla cleans the house properly,' she instructed him.

When she had left, Bimla came to do the washing and cleaning.

'You are alone in the house?' she asked with disbelief.

Getting an answer in the affirmative, she repeated, 'All alone?'

'Yes.'

Kalu confirmed, after which Bimla Devi quickly went off to attend to the utensils. Then she took out a bucket of water and began to mop the floor in the room he was in. Kalu was reading a newspaper. As she worked away, she repeated her question, 'You are all alone?'

This time Kalu was irritated. He lowered his newspaper and was about to lash out at her when he was stunned into silence by what he saw.

From his perch on the chair he could see Bimla's large white breasts as she bent forward to wipe the floor. A current ran through his body and suddenly he felt a throbbing sensation between his legs. His ears became hot but he pretended to continue reading the newspaper, too afraid to look at her directly. When he stole a look again, Bimla was laughing at him, her breasts bobbing up and down with her laughter. Then she began scratching her breasts, wriggling one of them out of her blouse, revealing a dark taut nipple.

With her wicked smile, she asked again, 'You are all alone?'

Kalu had run out of words. Burning with desire, his eyes did the speaking on his behalf. But even he was not prepared for what followed.

Without any ado, Bimla rose from her squat position on the floor and thrust her soft breasts at his face. Moments later, she had untangled herself from her saree and was standing with only her petticoat on. Kalu could not believe the luscious sight her sari had concealed. His jaw dropped in amazement. Then Bimla's mouth clamped itself on his and she began sucking his lips. He pushed her away, but she came back. As her tongue rolled inside his mouth, he realized that he enjoyed the sensation. He let himself submit to her. Once his guard had fallen, he began sucking her lips with equal fervour. By now both were feverish with passion, oblivious of the world around. When Kalu disengaged himself briefly, Bimla lifted her breast to his mouth. At first, he pumped them with his untrained hands, relishing their soft suppleness. Not fully satisfied, he kneaded them harder, until she pulled back accusingly, 'It's hurting!'

Soon she was burying his face in her breasts again. The she lifted one of her orbs to his mouth and ordered, 'Suck it…!'

He sucked the nipples and the flesh. Groaning in delight, the woman wrapped herself more tightly around him. By now Kalu was in command, his hands groping the wet sticky delight between her thighs. As his fingers pressed against the soft juicy inside of her organ, it become too much for Bimla to restrain herself. She grabbed hold of his body and strode on him like a man. She wanted him inside her. The hard throbbing flesh found little resistance entering her. The hot and wet sensation was pure joy. He went deeper and deeper inside. Bimla began to heave herself up and down upon him. The up-strokes and down-strokes made Kalu delirious. He had never known such pure physical joy. Unable to hold back, the joy overflowed, squirting semen—the seeds of life—inside her. When they were done, Bimla reproached the boy as she put her clothes on, '*Hai Raam!* What have you done?'

Kalu felt miserable with guilt of the 'sin' he had committed. But soon it wore off and he hungered for that woman, for that raw unadulterated pleasure she had given him. But Bimla never came back to their house again.

Borda Picks Kalu's Pocket

Borda came home to Allahabad on his annual leave from the Air Force Training Centre in Belgaum. Though he had not cleared his matriculation examination, Samar, through the good offices of one Flight Sergeant Paul—a fellow Bengali who worked at the Air Force Recruitment Office in Bombay—was able to get Borda admitted into the air force. His trade was that of a 'catering assistant', which meant he would procure and provide food at the air force messes wherever he was posted. His trade was in the Fifth Group, a notch below the drivers, who were in the Fourth Group.

'It's a good trade,' Flight Sergeant Paul had said when Samar went to thank him with a box full of the choicest sweets.

'He can always make some extra money,' Flight Sergeant Paul had added.

That 'extra money' could be made setting aside a part of the ration meant for airmen or officers and selling it in the market. Even on this trip, Borda had brought with him some 'surplus' ration that was 'adjusted' from his mess.

His arrival in Sulem Sarai was not exactly a pleasant one. He was shocked by the size of their rented house.

'Where will I sleep?' he demanded, looking at the room.

His query was not entirely unreasonable. The long room had just one big charpoy that could hold two occupants. The two wooden boxes near the window served as a sofa by the day and were used as a bed at night by the boys' father. Occasionally when Samar was on guard-duty for the night, the boys got a chance to sleep on the 'sofa'. On regular days Kalu and their mother slept on the floor, with a mosquito net over them.

Borda decided he would sleep in the room that served as a common passage for the bathrooms. Soon after his arrival, Borda gathered the three younger brothers around him, opened his suitcase and begun to take out the clothes and other goodies he had bought for all of them. Finally, he pulled out a silk sari he had bought for Basanti.

Smiling from ear to ear, their mother responded typically, 'Huh, all my life your father has given me sack-like saris to wear! Now in my old age, I have no use for this.'

But she could barely suppress her happiness. It was her first pure-silk sari after marriage. After all, she was supposedly only thirty-six years old.

Actually, Basanti remained thirty-six for quite a few years, until her sons had started poking fun at her, 'Ma, how many more years will you remain thirty-six?'

At that, she would rush to hit them.

Borda also brought a large tin of coffee and several cans of butter, all 'adjusted' from the airmen's mess, where he now worked as the second-in-command of the kitchen. Stealing was a dirty word in the armed forces, so they devised the euphemism 'adjustment'. Stealing from the government was not quite the same as robbing an individual—they conveniently 'adjusted' to the relativity of stealing.

Borda was on a sixty days' annual leave, but soon he did not know how he would spend the time. For the first few days, he would cook exotic meats and chicken—and even custards and cakes—recipes he had learned at the air force mess. When he ran out of new dishes he fretted and went away to Kanpur, where Basanti had recently discovered that her long-lost first cousin lived. In Kanpur Borda became popular with the girls—his cousins and their friends. Kalu and his brothers envied their unseen Kanpur cousins, as Borda would splurge on them. When he ran out of money, he came back home and began pestering Basanti to return him the money he had given her upon arrival.

'Why don't you go back to your "Kanpur Mama" and ask him for money?' Samar demanded to know when he got wind of it all.

Seeing him reduced to penury, at one point Kalu felt sorry for Borda and thought of helping him, but luckily his better sense prevailed. He had with him a small, secret fortune built copiously by suppressing the desire to spend on himself. He decided it should remain a secret from Borda.

Over the weeks and months Kalu had assiduously built his own little 'bank balance' of some sixteen rupees. Virtually all of this fortune was built by dodging the conductor of the city bus that took them to school. Usually, Kalu and Babu had their monthly passes for the city bus. But when the pass expired, they had to take money for the bus fares from their mother. Being the older of the two, the money would be handed over to Kalu. But he never bought the tickets.

Like every other day, the conductor would ask, 'Ticket?'

And Kalu, without batting an eyelid, though his heart would be in his mouth, would reply, 'Pass!'

The conductor would never bother to check their expired passes. This larceny went on till their father had renewed their pass. But the ill-gotten wealth thus gathered was rarely wasted on trifles such as ice cream or kurmure. Since the money was in loose change, Kalu would first amass the coins in his school-bag. When the change became too large and conspicuous to handle, he got it converted to currency notes at their landlord's shop, Durga Das. The paper notes, mostly of five-rupee denominations, were much easy to hoard. In all he had saved up sixteen rupees.

Kalu had stashed away his money in his thick geography book, hidden from the rest of his family and the world. Though Babu did have some inkling that his older brother was cheating with the bus fare and making money, he had no idea that the fortune was concealed in the geography book. Being a pragmatic person, Kalu did not keep all the notes in one page. They were distributed over three or four pages, so that if someone chanced upon one note, at least the others would be saved. It was like having a number of bank accounts. Little did he know that for all smart people, there are always a few who are smarter. Every few days he would come back to his geography book and turn its pages making sure the money was safe. Then one day he made a silly mistake.

He asked Borda, 'If I gave you the money, would you have returned it?'

Borda replied with a smile and a twinkle in his eye, 'You have money?'

At once on guard, his younger brother replied, 'No, no…I was just asking.'

Little did Kalu suspect that like a cat could smell out a fish, Borda would always manage to find out money from the slightest whiff of it. Two days later when Kalu inspected his geography book, there was no money left in it. He turned the pages over and over frantically, but there was no mistake. The money saved over the weeks and months was gone.

Behind him Borda was grinning, 'Where did you get so much money from?'

Kalu lunged at him with impotent rage but Borda fled.

'I promise, I'll return you the money… with interest too!' he pleaded.

The promises pacified Kalu. But Borda never returned that money again.

The Little Tutor

'How will I earn money?'

The question dogged Kalu's mind from early childhood.

'Study… Study, you scoundrels, or else you will have to pull a rickshaw!' Samar often rebuked his children.

That thought kept haunting him all the time. Kalu was not even so daunted by the prospect of pulling a rickshaw as to the thought: 'Where would I find the money to buy a rickshaw?'

So he studied his lessons harder than his brothers. He was not the brightest boy in his class, but he wasn't a 'jackass' either, as Mr D'Cruz—the maths teacher—often liked calling him. As if to prove that point, by the time he was in the ninth standard, Kalu found a means to start earning.

His first source of income was two little children, the son and the daughter of one Mrs Mathur. He was appointed to tutor them in English and other subjects. Munna, the boy, studied in the second standard and Pinky was in the fourth. The family lived more than a kilometre away from Sulem Sarai, across the railway line in Subedargunj. Although sceptical at first—his students looked upon him as a boy not much older than they—Kalu turned out to be good at the job. The mother of the children, herself a teacher, was pleased with the result. The house had a lovely family photograph of a handsome man, posing with his wife and two children. It was an old photo and everyone looked much younger in it. Kalu, however, had never seen Mr Mathur and wondered where he could've been. Since Mathur Aunty did not wear a bindi, he presumed that Mr Mathur was dead. It made him feel very sad for the lady and her children. It was a sad house, he thought, particularly for the little girl with large, timid eyes. The man in the photo had looked extremely handsome and happy. That made Kalu sadder.

'How would he have died?' he wondered.

Then one day, he noticed a thin, dishevelled man around the house. He had dark rings around his eyes and an unkempt stubble.

Curious, Kalu asked the little girl, 'Who's that?'

'Father,' the girl whispered, as if afraid to mention him.

Kalu was incredulous. He looked from the photo to the man in real life and could not even find the faintest resemblance. The man was a ghostly shadow of his earlier bright self. It troubled Kalu to think that life could bring about such drastic change in a person. Mr Mathur had lost his job and went about the house in a daze, never talking to anyone.

Soon the children's final exams approached and Kalu had to teach his students for longer hours. When he returned home on Bappa's bicycle—which he had temporarily loaned from his brother—it would be dark. One day, the dogs from the Mehtar Patti—the sweepers' locality—chased him until he lost his balance on the cycle and fell into a roadside drain. Their mission accomplished, the dogs stopped barking and went back to their cosy snuggles. Returning from the tuitions after dark was a scary affair as he had to take a desolate road. Finally, the children passed their exams with extremely good marks and Kalu was given an extra ten-rupee bonus. The six-month teaching assignment fetched him one hundred and thirty rupees. But even this money he could not retain for long.

When summer became unbearable, with the hissing 'loo' winds sweeping over the dry, dusty landscape like a fiend, Samar and Basanti secretly decided on taking a vacation to the hills in Mussourie. It was not usual for parents to go travelling all by themselves. So when the news was out, the boys rebelled.

'We also want to come,' they demanded, feeling cheated of their share of the vacation.

But their parents explained that they did not have enough money to buy tickets for everyone. Kalu, especially, was inconsolable at this. He had always dreamed of going to the hills. He wanted to paint them.

Finally, Samar—moved by the boys' pleading—made a concession.

'Okay, if you can pay for your own tickets, you can come along,' he said.

Caught off-guard by the offer, Kalu had little option but to part with a large chunk of his tuition earning.

'I will pay for my tickets and come,' he decided with resignation.

But he was happy to be on the train to Haridwar, having recently finished with his Senior Cambridge exams, which had kept him awake and slogging for long nights. All through the journey he sat at the window, enjoying the changing landscape. He did not sleep even at night, staying awake and watching the moon and the trees that passed by. He took mental notes of the fleeting scenery that he wanted to paint later.

At Saharanpur, in the hours before sunrise, their compartment was detached from the rest of the train. Kalu sat awake in the darkness and the cold, watching the platform and the chai-wallahs on it calling out, 'Chai… chaai… garam chai… chaaai…'

He bought a cup of tea for his mother, who was always ready for tea. Samar went on snoring on the sleeper above. 'Strange man, he can sleep anywhere,' his wife complained.

Hours later, there was a loud bang and their coach began to roll. Everyone was jolted from their sleep, thinking there had been an accident.

'No, no… They're only coupling our bogie to the Haridwar train,' Samar assured.

Soon, around daybreak, their train began to move again. Shortly afterwards Kalu let out a shriek, 'The hills! Ma, we can see the hills!'

They all peered out of the train window to catch the faint blue outline of the hills against the dark blue sky. Kalu was fascinated and stayed glued to the window till Haridwar arrived. A tanga took them to the Bharat Seva Ashram dharamshala, where Samar made a ten-rupee donation and they were shown into a bare room with just a wooden bed near a window. The entire ashram was painted in a brick-red colour. For three days they lived in the hallowed precincts of the building, where early in the morning they were awakened to the holy chants at the adjoining temple. On two occasions they even ate bhog offered by the temple.

At other times, Basanti would light the stove they had brought along and cook rice. She would also put some potatoes and other vegetables into the pot, to be mashed and eaten with the rice when boiled. The ashram was strictly vegetarian. Even onions were not allowed inside the rooms. Soon, Basanti was tired of the tasteless fare.

'I cannot eat this food!' she declared.

Despite his feeling of guilt, Samar was quick to smuggle in some onions and eggs into their room. The green chillies from the ashram's kitchen garden added a little more variety to the food. The gushing Ganga nearby was a delight to bathe in in the afternoons, and sit by and watch in the evenings. Kalu also occasionally bought bhel-puri and other spicy snacks for his mother.

From Haridwar they went to Laxman Jhula, where they were fascinated by the sheer numbers of beggars lining the road. The monkeys too provided them with comic distraction. They made a stop at Rishikesh, and then travelled to Dehradun, where they stayed for a day. At night, as they sauntered through the streets of Dehradun, Samar suddenly pointed to a dense cluster of stars in the sky, like the facets of a massive diamond.

'Oh ma! What's that?' Basanti exclaimed.

'Mussourie,' Samar informed them.

Kalu was clearly fascinated.

'It's like some fairy tale...' he said, eager to see the town.

The next afternoon they took a bus for Mussourie, but not before the husband and the wife had had a fight. It was the result of Basanti expressing the desire to eat bhel-puri from a street vendor and Samar refusing to oblige with the money. Finally, Kalu stepped ahead and bought the bhel-puri and both mother and son relished the snack. Money had given Kalu the power to overrule even his father.

The winding mountain road that they travelled was a thrill to watch, particularly from their bus window as the bus climbed higher and higher. 'Those winding roads down there look like a jigsaw puzzle!' Kalu said, looking down from the bus window.

But the sharp twists and turns also made Basanti giddy. 'I want to vomit, I think,' she declared, and shifted to the window seat.

She did not eventually get sick, and soon the family was at Mussourie. As they descended from the bus, they could feel the mountain chill clinging to their bones. A bunch of Nepali coolies in dusty beggar-like clothes scrambled to pick up their luggage. After some haggling Samar settled for the one who agreed to the cheapest rates. Kalu was thrilled by the sight of coolies walking coolly up the steep hill road. He himself found it difficult to walk.

'Lean forward when you are going uphill,' his father advised him, resorting to a very simple principle of physics. 'And when you go downhill, you must lean backwards.'

Once he got the posture correct, it was fun to go up the hill road. Kalu even ran through some of his way. He ran down the Mall.

Following Samar's instructions, the coolie took them to a 'cheap hotel'. The entire hotel was built of wood and glass. When they climbed up the stairs, they made an unfamiliar wooden sound. Even the floor was wooden. When he went up to the balcony covered with glass windows, the view took Kalu's breath away.

'I want to paint this,' he told himself.

And through some strange coincidence, he saw a palette and a set of poster-colour bottles lying in a corner of the balcony.

'All I need is some paper,' he told the hotel owner.

Impressed by the boy's enthusiasm, the hotel owner told him, 'No worries. I'll bring you some art paper that was left behind by one of our previous lodgers.'

Soon after checking in and taking a quick wash, the family decided to go sightseeing.

As they wandered down the streets of Mussouri, what fascinated Kalu most were not the shops selling woollen clothes and other knickknacks, but the view of schoolchildren playing far down, at a level much lower than the streets. From the railings along the streets, they looked like Lilliputians from *Gulliver's Travels*.

By the end of the day they were tired, but their enthusiasm had not worn down at all.

The next day, Kalu refused to accompany his parents on their sightseeing tour. 'I want to stay at the hotel and paint,' he declared.

When his parents returned in the evening and took a look at his day's work, they were at a loss for words.

Finally his mother said, 'You made this!'

The green hills, dotted with red-roofed houses, had come alive on art paper. Even Samar was impressed, though he made no comment to show it.

'Your beta will be a famous artist one day,' the hotel owner told his parents.

Samar and Basanti looked at him and smiled in gratitude. They believed him.

Just that they were not sure how the vocation would feed their son. They had no idea at all of the enormous sums commanded by well-known artists.

His Father's Portrait

By 1976, painting had become a regular passion with Kalu. On the days when there was no school, he would sit in the barsati on the roof and paint all day. That was the best place to stay away from his father's eyes.

'Painting will not bring you food… Are you going to beg for a living?' Samar would rage indignantly, each time the subject was raised.

In the beginning Kalu painted from imagination, but slowly he graduated to reproducing the scenes that were visible from their rooftop in Sulem Sarai. Sunday mornings were his usual time for painting. When absorbed in his work, he would often become oblivious to everything else.

'Kalu … Kalu!' his mother would often scream from downstairs. 'Come and have your breakfast.'

Sometimes, Kalu could not even hear her. Unable to call him down, Basanti would finally have to come upstairs and give him his food. 'Just wait, I'm going to tell your father,' she would warn him before leaving.

But inwardly, she took great pride in her son's talent. She would often stay back at the barsati, quietly watching him at his work.

So immersed would he be in his work, that sometimes Kalu would dip his paintbrush into the glass of milk his mother had brought. At other times, he would break his reverie to discover that the tea Basanti had left him had gone cold and stale.

As the morning rolled on, Basanti would again yell from downstairs, 'Kalu, go and take your bath… It's time for lunch!'

A bath before lunch was compulsory in the Bengali household.

'Ma, I'm coming soon…' the boy would say.

But he immediately forgot about it, and after several futile calls the mother would plead, 'At least come and eat your lunch… This boy—what will I do with him?'

But Kalu was oblivious to the flow of time. Only around dusk, when the light was fading and everyone was waking up from their leisurely afternoon siesta, would he tiptoe downstairs and eat his cold food all alone.

Of course, such freedom could only be enjoyed on the days when Samar was not at home. When their father was at home, all Basanti had to do was to inform her husband, 'Are you listening… Kalu has still not—'

And the boy would abandon his painting and come downstairs to do as she said. At times when he didn't appear immediately, it was enough for his father to gently threaten once or twice, 'Do I have to come up?'

The penalty of having his father come upstairs to fetch him was usually heavy. Samar had little patience or appreciation for his son's 'idle' passion. If his father had the occasion to come upstairs, it would usually result in Kalu getting a sound thrashing at his hands. Kalu mostly suffered his father's indifference or tyranny in silence. But there was one occasion for which he could never forgive him.

It was another Sunday morning. His father lay sprawled on a mat, reading the *Northern India Patrika*. Kalu was sitting in the room with his sketchbook, when the sight of his father—wearing his spectacles and absorbed in the newspaper—caught his attention. Inspired, he asked his father to hold his position and made a quick sketch with a pencil. To his satisfaction, the sketch turned out to be a very good likeness. An idea quickly flashed through his mind—he wanted to give his father a pleasant surprise. He took the sketch upstairs to the barsati and began to apply colours.

As his father's portrait progressed, so did the frequency of calls from his mother downstairs, 'Kalu, finish your bath! Kalu…!'

But that day, Kalu was too absorbed with his idea to give in to other demands.

Then his father grunted, 'Kalu! Aren't you listening?'

'Five minutes, Baba,' he pleaded, 'I'm about to finish your portrait.'

Since he was making his father's portrait, Kalu presumed that his father would go easy with his permission. He was wrong. After several warnings Samar's patience wore thin, and he came by and grabbed Kalu by his hair.

'Baba, Baba…it's your portrait… I'm just about to complete it!'

Blinded with rage, his father snatched the sheet of paper and tore it to pieces. Kalu was shocked. Ignoring the physical assault, he began to frantically pick up the pieces of torn painting and tried to put them back together. His efforts were useless. He protested, refusing to eat lunch that afternoon.

Yet, none of these injustices could separate Kalu from his muse. In his heart, he had decided to become an artist. His latest inspiration was the father of Girish Shiksharthi. Girish also went to St Joseph's and was a friend of Bappa, although he was two classes senior to him. He would visit them very often at Afzal's Home, riding a rickety bicycle that was said to be thirty years old. Although Girish was much older than Kalu and Babu, he was friendly with everyone, even with their mother. He would hang around in their house for hours on end, but would disappear as soon as Samar came back home. Even then, he would stay back in the narrow lane downstairs leading to their door, standing and chatting with the boys.

Shiksharthi Uncle was well-known in Allahabad's literary circle, or at least, that was the impression Girish gave them. He was a painter, cartoonist and writer. Occasionally his cartoons appeared in *Northern India Patrika* and more often in some of the Hindi journals. Once Girish showed the boys a copy of *The Illustrated Weekly of India* in which his father's cartoon had appeared. Girish even said that his father might soon get the Sahitya Academy Award for literature. Ever since then, Kalu became curious to be acquainted with Mr Shiksharthi. But there was something forbidding and distant about the small, bald man who had a permanent scowl on his face. He appeared to hold the whole world in contempt.

Kalu often spotted Shiksharthi Uncle from the rooftop overlooking the G. T. Road, whizzing by on his red Lambretta scooter. The scooter made him more unapproachable. In the mid-seventies, not many people could afford a scooter. Sometimes there was a woman, riding pillion on his scooter. Kalu wondered who she was.

One day he was told by Bappa, 'She's Girish's chhoti amma—his stepmother. His father has two wives.'

After this revelation, Shiksharthi Uncle appeared even more mysterious to Kalu. And then, it suddenly dawned on him why he had never seen Uncle at Girish's home. The house was a sprawling white building with a portico, in the midst of a huge guava grove. Built on a grand scale it was somehow incomplete—as if it had been quit halfway through construction. In some rooms the windowpanes had not been put, in others the floor was not completely tiled. He learned that Mr Shiksharthi had originally planned the house for both his families, until his younger wife threw a rage and refused to live with her 'sauten' under the same roof. The younger wife was educated and held a senior government position. She had her way. An equally imposing house was built for her less than a few hundred yards away. When you climbed on to the roof of one of the houses you could see the other one. The two women never saw eye to eye.

Girish's Home

From the outside, Girish's house looked deserted. One of its few populated rooms was the kitchen, darkened by the perpetual smoke from the chullha. Here one found Girish's mother, a frail, timid middle-aged lady, who always had her head covered with the pallu of her sari. There was only another woman lurking about the house—Girish's grandmother. Dadi was bent with age and could not stand up, so she dragged herself around the house squatting. She looked like a ghost—her rough face spotted with deep pockmarks, her eyes like little slits, and her voice gruff, like that of a man.

'She could easily be in a horror flick without any need for make-up,' Bappa, who nursed filmy ambitions, observed.

Hard of hearing, Dadi spoke loudly and terrified first-time visitors.

Most of the time she would be shouting out, 'Dulahin... Dulahin!'

'Dulahin'—or bride—was what she called Girish's mother, who kept obeying her orders, which were usually to cook the dal or serve her rotis. Dadi often scolded her daughter-in-law, but Kalu later realized that a certain bonding existed between the two women. Dadi was possessive and protective about her Dulahin, whom her son had virtually abandoned for another woman.

On his first few visits, Kalu kept himself confined to Girish's room, which was full of encyclopaedias and other books bought by his father. Kalu would pore over the books all morning and afternoon. He loved the encyclopaedias, which also contained paintings by famous European artists, some of which Kalu reproduced with Indian variations. Many of the thick books had holes in them, cut through by termites, and the pages had gone brown with age. He fondled the pages with great care.

One day, when Kalu was intently reading *The Patriot* by Pearl S. Buck in Girish's room, Dadi crawled up behind him and shouted, 'Daktaar! Who is this boy?'

And she peered into his face.

Girish, who was called Doctor at home, screamed back so that Dadi could hear him, 'He is Bappa's brother.'

Satisfied, Dadi crawled back and ordered Dulahin to bring some rotis for Kalu. Soon, Dadi became friendly with Kalu. She would send him on little errands to fetch the tobacco leaves which she chewed most of the day. If Kalu did not turn up at Girish's house for a day or two, Dadi would reproach him. 'Where had you died?'

During winters Girish's house held another major attraction— guavas. The fruits would hang heavy from the guava trees and begin ripening around December. Kalu loved hanging around the garden, hunting for the ripe fruit. Allahabad was famous for its guavas, but the ones in Girish's orchard were the most delicious of all. Soft and milky inside, they contained no seed.

But Dadi kept a keen vigil on her 'amrud ka bagiya' and it was not often that Kalu could manage to steal. However, sometimes she would actually ask him to police the orchard, and he would go on a private rampage. The most hilarious part was during peak season, when Dadi would commission Kalu to pluck the fruit to save it from being eaten by the bats, birds and squirrels. She would crawl into the garden with a huge bag, Kalu following close behind with a hooked bamboo stick. While Dadi collected the fruit in her bag

Kalu would stand behind her and stuff his mouth, unnoticed by the old woman. Sometimes she would ask him a question, which he could not answer because his mouth was stuffed.

After an angry pause she would turn to him and say, 'Are you dumb!'

By then he would have gulped the fruit and got his voice back. Fortunately, he was never found out. After they had collected a huge pile of guavas, Dadi would repay the hard-working boy by giving him some of the best picks of the lot.

'Eat them!' she would order with affection.

Kalu, pretending that he never ate anything without sharing it with his mother and brothers, would say, 'Dadi, I'll take them home for Bappa, Babu and my mother.'

'Then take more some more.'

Kalu would fill a bag with all the fruit and take it home as quickly as his feet could carry him.

Charmed by the gift of the guavas, Basanti once asked Girish, 'Why don't you bring your Dadi to our house one day? Kalu keeps talking about her.'

The invitation was conveyed to Dadi and she agreed to come, crawling all the way from Dhumanganj to Afzal's Home in Sulem Sarai, accompanied by her Dulahin. It was a long distance for a woman who had to crawl all the way. Dadi had to pause several times on the way as Aunty stood beside her, plying her with water to soothe her parched throat. Bappa and Girish walked with their bicycles behind the ladies, prepared for any mishap. The G. T. Road was not easy to navigate, particularly for someone like Dadi.

When they finally turned into the narrow lane of Afzal's Home, Girish took over, carrying Dadi in his arms to the first floor. At the first sight, Basanti was aghast at the bundle of bones deposited at her door.

'This is Dadi,' Girish told her, and she welcomed them inside.

Soon the initial apprehension melted away, especially after Aunty handed Basanti a bag full of ripe guavas.

Though a city woman, Basanti quickly developed a rapport with the two rustic women, particularly with Dadi. She prepared halva and puri, which the guests devoured with delight, for the journey had been arduous and they were hungry. Served with samosas and tea before they left, Dadi and Aunty were pleased with the hospitality and invited Basanti to come to their house.

Not long after, Basanti paid them a return visit.

In the absence of Shiksharthi Uncle, Girish's house was great fun to be. But on the rare occasion when his father was in the house—marked by the scooter parked in the veranda—the atmosphere of fun would instantly evaporate. Everyone except the deaf Dadi spoke in whispers, lest they offend the man of the house. Seeing the scooter parked in the veranda would usually make Kalu turn on his heels and flee. He was terrified of coming face to face with Shiksharthi Uncle. But one day, he was trapped. He was reading one of the encyclopaedias in Girish's room when the splutter of a scooter was heard outside. Kalu was about to sneak out when Uncle walked into the house, and saw him.

'Why are you going away son, sit down,' he said.

Flustered, Kalu sat down, not knowing how to begin a conversation. Fortunately, Uncle asked him the usual questions about his name, where he stayed, what he studied, and so on. Once the ice was broken, Kalu told him how he admired his paintings and cartoons, and that he wanted to be an artist himself. He finally asked Uncle, 'Can I show you one of my paintings?'

'Yes indeed, I would love to see them,' Shiksharthi Uncle replied.

His heart leaping with joy, Kalu ran all the way back home and fetched the painting he had made over a week's time. Unlike his other paintings, this was a monochrome in brown and depicted a woman pining for her lover by the side of a river in the forest. It was a painting he had especially made for the Shankar's International Painting Competition, to be held in Delhi. He had planned to make it big—beginning with winning the Shankar's International prize.

When Shiksharthi Uncle saw the painting he claimed to be impressed, but his response was lukewarm compared to what Kalu had expected. He gave Kalu a tip or two on how to make the water look more vivid. On the way home, he comforted himself by saying, 'He must be jealous.'

But all the pains Kalu had taken over this painting were wasted. His father refused to give him the postage money for mailing the painting to Delhi. By the time he pulled together his other resources and organized the money, the deadline for the competition had expired. This time Kalu was so disappointed that he decided to give up painting altogether.

Besides, with his Senior Cambridge examinations approaching, the pressure of schoolwork had begun to weigh him down. He could not afford the additional fee for extra classes, which most of his classmates had joined. Bappa, who had barely scraped through his own Senior Cambridge exams with a second division, was of little help to his brother—especially with maths, the subject that made Kalu the most miserable.

So Kalu worked hard, sitting up late into the night, literally burning the midnight oil. Bappa would sometimes make him tea while he studied into the night. Then he too would fall off to sleep, and Kalu would be left all alone, cramming his lessons. Night was the best time, when his mother did not bother him with domestic chores and little Babu did not interrupt him with gossip from the school or the neighbourhood. Sometimes it was early morning by the time Kalu dozed off, book in hand.

The Peep Show

Late one night as he was poring over his biology book, the silence of the evening was broken by a soft creaking sound. Kalu pricked up his ears. The rhythmic creaking became faster and faster, reaching a crescendo, and then stopped. Kalu faintly recognized it as the creaking of a bed. Though he was not quite sure, the sound appeared to come from the adjacent room.

A new family had recently come to occupy the room next to theirs in Afzal's Home. Corporal Swamy was also from the air force, and he and his wife were recently married. The corporal was a dark-complexioned, pot-bellied man with a thick moustache. He had large, fierce-looking eyes, but the fierceness of his face was offset by the fact that he was soft-spoken and wore holy ash marks across his forehead. His wife was a fair and frail woman, small in built and pious-looking. She wore flowers in her hair like any traditional South Indian woman.

As the creaking ceased, Kalu started thinking, 'Could it have been Swamy Uncle and Aunty?'

But he drove the thought away. 'How could such pious people be copulating?' he told himself.

But then the sound of the creaking charpoy became frequent, occurring at odd times of the day. When it occurred while their father was at home, Samar would either quickly switch on the radio to high volume or order his sons, 'Read your lessons aloud!'

Kalu could barely concentrate on his studies.

'Could Swamy Uncle be bedding Aunty?' That was the question uppermost in his mind. He had to find out.

One afternoon, when his mother had gone to the rooftop to sit out in the sun and Kalu was alone in the house studying, the creaking next door started again. Kalu was aroused.

'I will find out today. This is the best opportunity,' he told himself.

He scanned the old wooden door that separated Swamy Uncle's room from theirs for cracks and holes. There were little holes here and there but too small to offer a substantial view. Finally he found a chink on the door large enough. He quietly peered through it and his suspicions were confirmed. His gaze caught two pairs of legs entangled with each other. Aroused, he wanted a better view. In his fervent search, Kalu lifted the hanger on the door that held his father's unused coat—and behold, it unearthed a gaping hole in the door between the two rooms! So the coat was used to camouflage the hole! But it was too high for Kalu to reach. So he got himself a stool and climbed over it. The view took his breath away.

In the other room, a naked Swamy Uncle was straddling his wife, who was wearing nothing but a petticoat. Bending over Aunty, he cupped her small white breasts in his hand, caressing them delicately as though they were breakable. Then he lowered himself further and began sucking her nipples. Tickled, Aunty kicked her legs in the air and suppressed a giggle. The petticoat was pushed up, revealing her fleshy thighs, white as ivory. Uncle began rubbing her thighs. Soon Aunty was completely aroused, and clasped Swamy Uncle in her arms. He entered her, making her sit up as he did so. They looked like a pair of Siamese twins, joined at birth. Even their mouths were sealed in a kiss. In this posture, they continued making love for a long time. Then finally Uncle laid Aunty flat on the bed and began thrusting himself into her. This is what produced the creaking sound—first in a slow rhythmic movement, then faster and faster until Swamy Uncle seemed to groan in pain. (Or was it delight? Kalu could not be sure.) After one long groan, he dropped in a heap upon his wife. They had passed out.

Masturbating as he watched, Kalu too passed out. Quickly cleaning up his semen with a piece of paper, he replaced his father's coat over the precious hole in the door. Then he unlocked the door he had bolted from inside. Showtime over, he picked up his history book and tried to continue revising his lessons. But it was difficult to concentrate. The only image haunting him was the newly discovered Siamese-twin posture. When his mother finally returned downstairs and found him with his book, she reproached him, 'You are still studying! At this rate this boy will fall ill. Shut your book and take a nap for now.'

Kalu obeyed his mother, covering himself up with a bed-sheet in preparation to take a nap. Under the bed-sheet, his mind replayed what he had just seen. Hot with passion, he masturbated again.

When Samar came home to find his son asleep, his reaction was sharp, 'He's sleeping and his board exams are not even a month away!'

Basanti hushed him, 'The poor boy has been studying all afternoon. I asked him to take a little rest. At this rate, he'll fall sick. Listen, why don't you get him some Bournvita? He will regain some of the energy he is losing with all this studying.'

It was true that Kalu was being sapped of his energy—but not so much by studies as much by his newly acquired habit. With every passing day, his concentration wandered further from his course books and gravitated more towards the 'keyhole view' of Swamy Uncle's room. Every time the creaking began he would get an erection, despite his best efforts to suppress it. His only outlet was a visit to the bathroom at odd hours.

'Do you have a loose motion?' his concerned mother would ask.

Soon, to the boy's utter disappointment, the peep show was over. Corporal Swamy was transferred out.

But after a short interval, the show came back to life again. Only, this time the participants were a new pair of tenants—a tall, robust man called Phool Singh and his short, buxom wife Neetu. They were followed by another newly wed couple, the Choubeys from Patna. While Choubey Uncle, in his thirties, was heavily built, the wife was just out of her teens. A sub-inspector in the police department, the man was clearly on overdrive. Returning from office he would undress and straightway head for the bed until the bewildered wife cried out for dear life. When not in a hurry, the couple, to the Peeping Tom's sheer delight, spent a lot of time in oral foreplay.

An Excursion with Classmates

Between the untimely visits to the loo, Kalu tried to work hard at his studies. Sometimes he read long enough to hear the factory siren go off. Then, in the wee hours of the morning, he would go out into the courtyard at the back of the house and watch the night-shift factory workers streaming homewards on their bicycles. It was still dark. After that, he would go upstairs and fall asleep.

It made Kalu feel wretched that despite working so hard, he was trailing behind the other boys in his class. At first the only subject he dreaded was maths, but he slowly started performing poorly in physics and chemistry, because of the mathematical calculations involved. Realizing that he was lagging behind in the valuable PCM group, Kalu tried to catch up with the boys who attended the extra classes. But the privileged lessons taught in the extra classes were closely guarded, and the boys only gave him vague answers. Those who attended the extra classes even seemed to know the questions that were likely to come in the prelims—the screening exams held by the school to filter out dull boys before they went on to take the actual board exams. The prelims ensured that the ISC results from St Joseph's were 'cent-percent', in keeping with the school's academic reputation. Despite not having attended the extra classes, Kalu did fairly well in the prelims.

Between the prelims and the actual ISC board exams—which the boys insisted on calling the Senior Cambridge exams and not the Indian School Certificate—there were a couple of weeks for preparation. Relieved at their good showing in the prelims, the English-speaking gang decided to go on an excursion before the last days of school were over. Since Allahabad offered very few options for entertainment, the boys finally settled on going to the Bamrauli Airport. There was to be an air display by the air force station and Mukul, whose family lived within the camp premises, offered to play host and show them around. The boys decided to make the trip on their bicycles. The party included Navroz, Babar, Ahmed, Rathore, Reginald, Keith—the entire English-speaking gang. While everyone was excited about the outing, Kalu was the lone dissenter.

'Why the airport? Why not the banks of the Ganga?' he suggested.

But the gang vetoed his idea. In fact, Kalu himself privately admitted that the air show was a great idea. His predicament was of a different kind—Sulem Sarai was on the way to the Bamrauli Airport from the main city. And he did not want his friends to pick him up from his house, as they would inevitably do if they were going to the airport. But the airport it was to be.

'Now tell us—how do we recognize your house?' Ahmed asked.

The image of Ahmed's mother, wearing sunglasses and driving a car, flashed past Kalu's eyes. In the flash of a second his mind was made up.

'It's a white house, three-storeyed. And it will be on your right after you cross the petrol pump,' he instructed Ahmed, who jotted down the details on a piece of paper.

In truth the house was two-storeyed, yellow, to the left of the road and well before the petrol pump.

Fortunately, Mukul was out of earshot when Kalu gave these instructions to Ahmed and the rest of the gang. The house he described was obviously not Afzal's Home but a figment of his imagination. The lie pricked at his conscience but he did not bat an eyelid telling it. There was too much at stake. He could not expose his 'station' in life to seven of his friends, some of them his closest friends. At one point he even thought of meeting his friends at a popular landmark which was way ahead of his house.

But once he had spoken, other possibilities began to whirl in his mind. What if someone felt thirsty and wanted to come over to his house for a glass of water? What if they wanted to come in and say hi to his mom? In any case, even if he managed to evade them on their way to the airport, they could still demand to stop over at his house during the return journey. There was only one way Kalu could prevent these situations—he would have to skip the outing altogether.

On the appointed day Rathore and Babar met up first at Navroz Dhondy's house. The three of them then left for Ahmed's house, where the rest of the gang members had congregated. The seven bicyclists then took a leisurely ride down the G. T. Road, heading towards Sulem Sarai. It took them fifteen minutes to reach. After crossing the petrol pump, the boys craned their necks in all directions but could not spot the 'three-storeyed white building' that Kalu had described to Ahmed.

Much ahead of the petrol pump, Kalu lay in ambush, hiding behind the wall of the rooftop, his eyes fixed on the road. Five minutes before the appointed time he saw the gang approaching, riding slowly, looking to all sides for the petrol pump that was to be their first point of reference. They were laughing away at the quaint rusticity of the place. Kalu ducked under the wall when they approached Afzal's Home, emerging from his hideout only when they had crossed his house. When they were gone, he watched them guiltily from behind. He would have loved nothing more than to entertain his friends at home, but he was too conscious of his poverty. He felt particularly bad for Rathore, whose homely hospitality he had enjoyed only a few days ago.

Rathore was a close friend of Kalu but he was also a 'guppi'— a spinner of yarns. And it was to find out the truth behind his gupps that Kalu and a friend had visited his house.

Rathore's tales about his ancestral riches were legion.

'Our fields are so big that when you stand at the centre, they extend right up to the horizon in whichever direction you look,' he would say.

Another of his tales was that, 'My dadi would never ride a car; she always went barefoot whenever she wanted to bathe in the Ganga. On one such visit, a babool thorn pricked one of her feet. Her sons—including my father—were so incensed that they ordered all the babool trees on the road to the Ganga to be chopped off.'

The last yarn was most ludicrous. Apparently, one time Rathore's grandfather wanted to light a fire to keep him warm through the cold night. But since there was no paper at hand, he had proceeded to light the fire with hundred-rupee notes!

Most of the boys refused to believe him and he was the butt of many jokes, but Rathore was unfazed. 'It's up to you to believe or not to believe,' he told everyone.

The last of Rathore's tales was about his father, who he claimed was one of the best-known lawyers of Allahabad. Apparently, he had even refused to become a judge because he earned much more as an advocate than a judge's salary would give him. According to Rathore, his father owned two Ambassador cars. It was to check the veracity of the two cars that Kalu and Mukul had decided to visit Rathore's house.

'Saala, he hasn't seen his black face in the mirror it seems,' Mukul said, and they laughed at their joke.

They were still giggling when they landed up at Rathore's address, as if they were detectives on their way to uncovering a truth they had already suspected. Rathore's house was in a posh colony adjacent to the Civil Lines, not too far away from where Kalu was dropped off by the city bus on the way to the school.

But the house—an old yellow-coloured bungalow—looked rather decrepit, the sagging tiles of the roof looking like they would cave in any moment. Kalu touched one of the walls and the flaky crisp whitewash peeled off at his touch. The two friends laughed, happy that their suspicion was coming true. They would tear Rathore apart, they thought. Then Kalu pressed a bell. A bunch of dogs began barking. And the two boys wanted to run for their lives. After a long wait a servant partially opened the door, to keep the dogs at bay. Through the chink he asked, 'Kisko chahiye?'

'Shivraj!' they said impatiently, for that was Rathore's first name.

'Oh Shibbu baba, ek minute,' the servant said, and disappeared.

After a long wait, another door opened and Rathore appeared, surrounded by five black Labradors encircling him as they wagged their tales.

'Take them away!' Kalu screamed.

And a servant led the dogs away.

'Hi, what a surprise!' Rathore welcomed them.

He led his friends into a dimly lit drawing room, furnished with glass tables and plush sofas. When Kalu sat on one of the sofas, he went in with a plonk—he had never known a couch so soft. Kalu and Mukul exchanged glances that seemed to say, 'This guy is not all gas…'

Later, on their way out, they saw two Ambassadors parked in the porch.

'Yaar, they really are rich,' Mukul whispered to Kalu after they had left Rathore's house. In the brief time they had spent at

Rathore's house, every few minutes a servant attended on them with snacks and cold drinks. Rathore's father was indeed one of Allahabad's best-known criminal lawyers.

Unlike his father, Rathore wanted to be a doctor.

'My sister and one of my brothers are also doctors,' he said, 'It's a noble profession.'

But he ended up as an unsuccessful lawyer.

Bappa Dreams of Films

By the time they reached the tenth standard most of the boys knew—or thought they knew—the career paths they would take. For most of them it was either engineering at the Indian Institute of Technology or medical college. Many of them planned to join the National Defence Academy or Armed Forces Medical College in Pune. Going with the conventional career choices, Kalu too wanted to be a doctor. But he could not give up the idea of becoming an artist either. He wanted to hang out in the streets of Paris, just like the characters in the novels of Somerset Maugham that he had read. But then, his ideas were only castles in the air. There were too many ground realities that held him back from his dreams.

'Who would fund my higher studies?' he considered.

There appeared to be no answer. In fact the answer was a loud and clear 'NO'.

His father was to retire in a year's time and had given an ultimatum to his sons, 'You have to fend for yourself. I cannot go on feeding you for the rest of your lives.'

The warnings were primarily directed at Bappa and Kalu. Bappa had finished his Intermediate exams by now, scraping through only after he had sent one of the papers for "scrutiny", a re-evaluation. Samar had tried to persuade his second son to become an airman like himself, but Bappa—after he was assigned the trade of medical assistant, in the third group, refused to join the air force.

'Airman…and that too in the third group…I would prefer to beg in the streets of Allahabad', he said with disdain.

Bappa had other ambitions. One of them was to become a film actor. His interest in this direction began with a photo of his that was taken at a studio. He had the photo enlarged and sent it to a few ad agencies. One of them had asked him to attend a screening test. That was enough for him to start planning a career in films.

'I'll do modelling just for a few years, and then I'll join films,' he told his audience, consisting usually of Kalu and Babu. He would spend a great deal of time in front of the mirror, touching up the pimples on his face with Clearasil, the most popular brand of anti-pimple creams of that time. It was Borda who secretly supplied him the money to buy Clearasil and other facial aids. While the rest of the family oiled their hair with ordinary coconut oil, Bappa bought Brylcreem for his exclusive use. He applied the cream with great patience, after his hair had completely dried up. Then he would style his hair like his idol, Rajesh Khanna. He had also tried to acquire some of Khanna's mannerisms. To be updated on his idol and other film stars he read the *Stardust* from cover to cover.

Before he left the house in the evenings Bappa, would always ask his brothers or mother, 'How am I looking?'

He looked handsome, in a slightly effeminate sort of way, particularly after he got rid of his moustache. After a few visits to the modelling agencies Bappa soon realized the futility of it all. But he kept hoping to make it big in the film world. Once, on a visit to Calcutta, he attended a shoot at a film studio in Tollygunge and came back excited.

'All the technicians and even the leading lady were looking at me,' he told Kalu when he was back in Allahabad.

The brothers were greatly impressed. But the promised call

from the director never materialized. What did was a job on probation with a well-known paint company. Bappa was to be a sales representative. Somehow, like everything else about him, he even made out the job of a sales rep sound like it was something fancy. The effect was not lost on his younger brothers, particularly on Kalu. 'Some day I too would like to become a sales rep,' Kalu confided to his older brother.

With his first pay packet Bappa brought himself a nice pink-coloured shirt-piece. He had it stitched from Shankar Tailors with large 'dog collars' that were in fashion those days. With his next pay, he bought a pair of black bell-bottomed trousers. During the next Durga Puja Bappa strutted about proudly, telling everyone how challenging his new job was. Kalu wondered if he could ever make it to a career as a sales rep.

'How trendy it sounds,' he thought.

Bappa discouraged him, saying, 'You have to be fair and handsome to be a sales rep.'

But by the third month, he was thoroughly bored with the job. After he got his pay for the third month, he stopped going to the office.

Samar began nagging him, 'How long will you carry on in your father's hotel? I have less than a year to retire.'

Tired of nothing to do and his father's constant nagging, Bappa finally managed to get admission at the ITI for a diploma in civil engineering. Girish had joined the printing technology course at the same institute and the two of them enjoyed their time there. Both made it sound as if their respective courses would take them places. Kalu wondered what he would do. He wanted to be an artist or a textile designer. He hoped to join either the J. J. School of Art in Bombay or the National Institute of Design in Ahmedabad. He knew for sure that the cost of studying at either of these institutes was way beyond his father's humble means. The cost of a five-year medical degree was even more prohibitive. He wondered if some rich man could appear out of nowhere and agree to support his ambition to study at the J. J. School of Art.

Senior Cambridge—Kalu Gets
a Second Division

It was among these turmoils that the Senior Cambridge exams approached. On the first morning of the exams, his mother fed Kalu a spoonful of curd before he left the house.

'Swallow it… It's auspicious,' she said.

Basanti always reminded him to touch the feet of the idol of Goddess Saraswati before he left to write an exam.

'She is the goddess of education and wisdom. She will help you in your exam,' his mother would say.

At school, there was tension in the morning air. Just before the exam started, the boys would huddle together and discuss their last-minute problems. Kalu always avoided these problem-solving sessions, because they confused and terrified him more. He always ended up feeling he had not revised properly.

The exams went more or less along expected lines. Kalu didn't do too well in physics and maths, but the paper in English literature made him happy. He came out of the examination hall early, grinning from ear to ear. He was still gloating happily when the other boys started streaming out, but the smile was wiped off his face when he realized some of the boys were discussing a question he had no clue about. He looked through his question paper, but could not find the question they were discussing. Finally he asked Rathore, 'Which question are you talking about?'

Rathore snatched the question paper from his hand and turned it over.

'This one!' he said.

Kalu was shattered. He had missed out a twenty-mark question printed on the reverse side of the paper! That meant he had written for only for eighty marks of the exam. English had been his trump card and now it was lost. Kalu had a sinking feeling, as if the entire world was closing in around him.

The staggering impact of that oversight was felt two months later, when the Senior Cambridge results were declared. Fearing the worst, Kalu did not go to the school in the morning with the rest of his classmates.

'I do not have the courage to face them,' he told himself.

He went alone in the blinding afternoon sun, after everyone else had left. The results were hung up on a sheet outside Father Rego's office. He searched for his name in the list of those who had made it to the first division. It was not there. When he found himself finally, it was in the list of second-divisioners! Out of fifty-seven students in their batch, only eleven had got a second division. Kalu looked around to see if anyone was watching him. He wanted to hide from the rest of the world.

Luckily, there was no one else around. For one last time he looked for what marks his friends had got. They had all scored in the first division. Rathore had sixty-three percent, Ahmed sixty-six, Navroz sixty-eight, Reginald seventy-two and—what hurt his pride the most—Mukul had done the best among them with seventy-five percent! Kalu had always fancied himself a better student that Mukul. But now his marks seemed to mock at him. The world was mocking at him.

Kalu went back home and never returned to his school. He made no attempt to meet any of his friends. Once, Rathore sent word through Babu inviting him for a meet-up at his place. But Kalu was too ashamed to meet any of his school friends. He spent the summer vacation all alone, brooding most of the time. He occasionally yearned to see some of his school friends, particularly Rathore, but the slur of being a second-divisioner held him back.

Meanwhile, most of his classmates started to migrate from Allahabad, either for the NDA or the AFMC in Pune or some other medical college. A few got admitted to the St Stephen's College in Delhi. There were a few others who went to study at Oxford and Cambridge. Kalu cocooned himself at home, wondering how he could become an artist. He began to apply colour to many of the sketches he had made at Mussoorie. But he could concentrate on nothing.

'I want to go to the J. J. School of Art in Bombay,' he finally told his father.

'Go wherever you want,' his father replied, 'but don't expect any financial help from me. I have to build a house. My retirement is close.'

After a few more futile arguments with his father, Kalu wrote a long, moving letter to the principal of the J. J. School of Art. In his letter he pleaded with the principal that he was a poor student, but art was his passion and he had always dreamed of being a student, at his prestigious school. He concluded the letter by writing, 'Sir, I will be indebted to you for the rest of my life if you could please arrange for my schooling. As for my fees, I will try my best to repay you through the paintings that I will make and sell during my course.'

It was such a moving letter that anybody would have melted. After he sent it off, Kalu waited for a few days with bated breath. Finally, the postman brought in a sealed envelope from the J. J. School of Art. Kalu tore it open impatiently. It turned out to be just a brochure from the art school, not a letter from the principal, no acknowledgement that his own letter had been read or considered. There was no way he could get a free admission. Aimlessly, he whiled away his time playing cricket in the day and watching Lucky's parents copulate by night.

With the spectre of his father's retirement looming, Kalu worried about what would happen of their family. 'If only Bappa was working, I could have studied further,' he told himself.

Bappa showed no sign of getting a job until he completed his diploma, and that was a good two years away. Kalu felt burdened with the responsibility of helping his father. He had a few friends in Sulem Sarai, and those were mostly Bappa's friends. There were Raja and Prashant—both good fun but good for nothing. They didn't inspire him, and he felt actively repulsed by the stories of their sexual conquests, which both the boys aired publicly. In their turn, the boys treated Kalu in a patronizing manner, which he didn't quite like. Girish was the only one of Bappa's friends with whom he shared a certain mental wavelength. Girish sympathized with his situation, but advised him against joining the air force as an airman.

'You have done your Senior Cambridge from St Joseph's, don't forget that!' he would tell Kalu, who wanted to hear precisely that.

Girish was privy to the most of their domestic problems and knew that Kalu was being pressurized to join the air force. One evening when Girish, Bappa and Kalu were having a chat about their respective futures the question came up.

'Kalu, what will you like to become?'

Since becoming an artist for a living was ruled out, he said without hesitation, 'A journalist!'

Bappa and Girish guffawed. 'Journalist… Ha! Ha!'

His pride was injured once again.

Basanti too was against the idea of her son becoming an airman.

'If this is what you had in mind, why did you send them to a convent? You want them to lead a life like you,' she chided her husband.

Samar tried to explain, 'Once he joins, he can try and get the commission and become an officer.'

'Just the way you became one,' his wife mocked.

The sons laughed. Samar was one against four.

Unable to make them see his reason, he would lose his temper and warn Kalu, 'I do not know anything... After my retirement I will not let you stay in my "hotel" even for a day!'

Despite himself, Kalu sympathized with his father. He did not want to bring on one more heart attack on him. Finally, Samar had his way. The father and the son boarded a train for Kanpur. Kalu was to take his tests for entering the air force.

Recruitment Office

The duo of father and son reached the Air Force Recruitment Centre in Kanpur early in the morning. A large crowd of young village boys, accompanied by their guardians, was gathered outside the barbed wire fencing of the recruiting office. Samar, dressed in his khaki sergeant's uniform, went right inside the office while Kalu waited outside. He stood out like a city boy among the rustics. Some of the boys came up to him and asked if the man accompanying him was his father. He nodded condescendingly. They looked at him with awe and he felt privileged to be the son of an airman.

'This is all about relativity—in school I used to feel inferior to my rich friends,' he thought to himself.

Eventually, an airman appeared at the gate and announced in Hindi, 'All those who wish to appear for the written tests should give me their names.'

There was a scramble for registering. Kalu hated to join the crowd, so didn't register his name. After a while his father appeared and took him directly into the recruiting office. The two waited in a room and an officer—a squadron leader—walked in.

Samar stood up and saluted.

'This is my son, sir,' he introduced Kalu.

The officer looked at the boy and said, 'How do you do, young man?'

Kalu looked at the officer and smiled. They were led to another room where a sergeant asked Kalu to step on to a weighing machine.

'Forty-four, he is short by one kilo,' he said.

Then he took his height and measured his chest—165 and 35 centimetres.

'Go and eat a lot of bananas,' the sergeant told him, adding to his father, 'Bring him back after an hour.'

They went outside the gate where a hawker with a bicycle cart was selling bananas.

'Eat as many as you can!' Samar urged Kalu.

At home, they never got to eat more that half a banana at a time. So swallowing six full bananas one after the other was quite a task. Kalu refused the seventh, which his father had already peeled. Glancing at Kalu's face—which looked as if he would puke—his father did not insist. He ate the seventh banana himself.

'Drink a lot of water after this,' the banana seller advised.

He knew the weight-increasing trick. Many of the skinny young boys were thrusting bananas down their throats. After an hour, Kalu weighed 45.5 kilograms on the weighing machine. The bananas had saved his day.

The boys who had met the physical requirements were then herded into an open veranda and made to sit on the floor. Each boy was given a sheet of answer paper.

Then the sergeant who had taken his weight announced, 'Anybody found copying or asking questions to his neighbours will be debarred!'

After that, the question papers were distributed. The questions were so basic that they made Kalu smile with sarcasm. He found it insulting to his academic background to have to answer such simple, stupid questions. He was the first to submit his answer sheet.

By the afternoon, the written examination was over. The boys were then herded out of the compounds of the recruiting office and asked to wait for the results. A hawker selling roti-sabzi made good business. Kalu and his father had their lunch inside the recruiting office canteen with dosas and idli-vada.

Outside, the sun became unbearably hot. The waiting crowds outside the fence huddled into little groups under the shade of trees. Finally the sergeant appeared at the gate with a sheet of paper. The groups scrambled to their feet and swarmed towards the sergeant. He read out the names of some twenty boys who had passed the written exams. The ones whose names were on the list were ecstatic. Those who had not made it became crestfallen. Kalu's name was on top of the list, but he did not feel the least bit excited about it.

'Among the blind, the one-eyed is the king,' he told himself.

The sergeant announced, 'Those whose names have been announced today should report to the recruiting office tomorrow by seven. You will undergo the oral interview, and those who pass will have a final medical examination.'

He was mobbed with a barrage of questions from the aspirants.

Those who had failed the written examination melted away into the hot afternoon. It was dusk by the time Kalu and his father left for his Mama's home in Kanpur, where they were lodging.

Early the next morning, Samar and Kalu returned to the recruiting office. The crowd outside the office was a much shrunken one this time. The interview was nothing more than a tête-à-tête with the recruiting officer, one Squadron Leader Baxi.

Among the questions he asked was, 'Why do you want to join the air force?'

Kalu had the impulse to say that he was not at all interested. Instead, he lied, 'I want to serve my country.'

The recruiting officer was impressed. As he walked out of the room, another boy walked in. After the round of interviews was over, there were only twelve boys left in the fray. They were then lined up on the veranda and asked to strip down to their underwear. Kalu was embarrassed by the 'striptease'. One by one the boys went inside a room, where a medical assistant examined them. When the medical assistant asked Kalu to remove his underwear, he blushed with shame and refused to oblige.

Impatiently, the medical assistant grabbed his underwear and yanked it down. He ordered, 'Okay, cough now!'

He coughed. Then he was asked to bend over and the medical assistant focused the torchlight on his anus. Eventually, he declared, 'All normal.'

Kalu was relieved that he could get back into his trousers. By the end of the day, nine of the boys had been selected. Since it was a non-technical batch, Kalu had to be satisfied with a third-group trade. He and four others were recruited as Radio Telephone Operators—RTO, in short. Three were MTDs or Mechanical Transport Drivers—fourth group. Another one was a musician—fifth group. Finally the group of nine was met by the recruiting officer himself, who congratulated the boys. Each of the boys was given a provisional selection letter.

'You will be receiving your final call letters soon through post,' the recruiting officer informed them. On a final note, he added, 'I welcome you all to the air force family and wish you good luck.'

It was Kalu who said, 'Thank you, sir,' on behalf of the boys.

Since he was the only one of them who spoke English fluently, he became the group leader of sorts, even though he was the youngest of the nine. The musician was the oldest, being at least six years older than Kalu. That afternoon, the group of new recruits felt like adults. The recruiting office handed over some money to each of the boys—two-way train fares between their respective railway stations and Kanpur and also some contingency money.

The small amount of money gave them a sense of freedom. They went to watch a popular movie. The next day, Samar and Kalu took the train back to Allahabad.

His First (and Last) Solo Exhibition

Out of the remaining allowance he got from the recruiting office, Kalu bought a set of watercolours and paintbrushes. In the following days and weeks, with nothing to do, he painted passionately. Some of these works were replicas of paintings that he had seen in the encyclopaedias at Girish's house, but there were others that were products of a fertile imagination. Most of them had a man and woman in them with the moon or the river in the background. An undercurrent of love ran through each of them. Did Kalu yearn for love? He did not know.

Then one day, a dark-complexioned mendicant in orange robes came to their lane begging for alms. '*Beta kuchh de do, bhagwan tera bhala karega!*'

With his white beard and yellow, shining eyes, the sadhu looked picturesque. The wrinkles on his face added to its strong character. Kalu decided that he wanted to paint a portrait of the mendicant.

'Baba, I'll give you food and water...but you will have to sit with me for a while. I'll paint a picture of you,' he said.

The sadhu happily agreed and Kalu took him up to his barsati on the rooftop, fed him a proper meal and asked him to pose. Basanti was livid at the antics of her son.

'What is this nonsense...I do not have any extra food cooked,' she shouted.

With some cajoling, she quickly gave way. After the meal, the beggar sat quiet in a pose. Kalu was quick, first with his pencil and then with his paint and brush. As he silently worked, the portrait came to life, but not until it was dusk. When he got up from his sprawled position on the floor, his legs and arms ached. As he stretched his back, Kalu took a look at his work and was amazed. It had turned out to be a vivid portrait.

'Baba, this is you!' he showed the portrait to the beggar.

'Wah!' the beggar said, 'You are a real artist.'

His mother and brothers too were impressed. In the evening when Samar returned from his work, it was Basanti who enthusiastically showed him the portrait. As before, Samar was quietly impressed with his son's talent. He said, as if musing to himself, 'If only I had the money, son, I would have sent you to an art school.' For once, he felt guilty that he would be wasting his son's talent by sending him to the Indian Air Force.

It was just about that time that Guha Kaki—wife of the junior warrant officer Guha, who lived in the same building and became close family friends with the Biswases—came up with a surprise offer.

An ardent fan of Kalu's talent with paint and brush, Kaki asked him, 'Kalu, would you like to exhibit your paintings?'

'What—an exhibition of my paintings?' Kalu was sceptical.

He remembered the time when the Lion's Club had organized a painting competition at his school. He had participated in it. As he worked away absorbed, all those who passed by would stop at his table and spend some time admiring his work.

'He will take the first prize, mark my words,' an onlooker had said.

And indeed, when the prize was announced, Kalu had come first.

At another competition organized by the Nehru Museum at Allahabad, he had again come first. But a solo exhibition was not the same thing as participating in a competition.

After the initial hesitation, he agreed to go along with Kaki's offer. She was ecstatic. 'Great! In about a week from now, there will be an Air Force Day fête. There I'll have one room dedicated entirely for your exhibition.'

Guha Kaki taught the kindergarten class at the air force school in Bamrauli where the fête was to be held. She was one of the key organizers of the event.

Kalu was finally caught up in the excitement. This was, after all, going to be his first solo exhibition!

'But you will have to frame up the paintings,' Kaki had declared to him.

This unforeseen condition left Kalu crestfallen. The leftover money from the recruiting office was exhausted and he just could not afford the cost of framing his paintings. When he conveyed this problem to Kaki, she said, 'Don't worry, I'll loan you the money. You can return it to me after you have sold some of your paintings.'

Kalu was so happy he hugged Kaki, exclaiming, 'You're so good!'

He then rode to the Chowk Bazar on his cycle to check out prices of the frames. He would need were eleven of them, in all. Initially, the shopkeeper demanded, 'Eighty rupees. Not one paisa less.'

But when he saw that Kalu was only a young boy trying to frame his paintings for the first time, he gave him a discount of twenty rupees. Two days later, Kalu carted home the framed pictures on a rickshaw.

On the evening before the fête, Kalu felt excited when he and Guha Kaki took the paintings to Bamrauli on a rickshaw. Even Bappa and Babu chipped in, carrying a few of the paintings as they followed the rickshaw on a bicycle. Everyone helped with the nails, the hammer and the other paraphernalia needed to put the paintings up on the walls of the exhibition room. By the time they were done, it was night and they were ravenous. All day they had not eaten anything except for a cup of tea and samosas, which Bappa had organized from the air force *wet* canteen. By the time they found a rickshaw and returned home to Sulem Sarai, it was past eight. Samar began to shout at the boys, 'What time do you think it is?'

But he sobered down the moment he saw that Mrs Guha had been accompanying the boys.

Kalu could not sleep that night because of the excitement. He was busy calculating the money he would make from his paintings. His calculations came to over five hundred rupees! He was already dreaming of buying a shirt and a pair of trousers trouser for himself and a sari for his mother. With the remaining money, he would buy a gift for Guha Kaki and some paint and brushes. For a long time he had realized that he needed good-quality brushes and art paper, if he wanted to improve the quality of his paintings.

The next morning, there were huge crowds at the Air Force Day fête. The Air Officer Commanding Air Vice-Marshal Latif and his wife Bilkees inaugurated the fête and Kalu's exhibition with it. The couple were pleasantly surprised when Guha Kaki introduced him to the artist.

'I'm very proud of you, young man,' AVM Latif told Kalu, whose chest swelled with pride.

A host of senior officers and their wives followed in after AVM Latif. They all shook Kalu's hand vigourously and patted him on the back. 'Well done, young boy!'

When some of them inquired about the prices of the paintings, Kalu felt almost feverish with excitement and joy.

'I'll make a killing selling these paintings!' he told himself.

He was soon to realize that the enquiries did not necessarily materialize into sales. In the beginning he was enjoying the praise and the adulation—everyone wanted to know who the artist was and was surprised to find it was someone as young as him; everyone came to him and shook his hand and made him feel like a celebrity—but slowly his father's words begin to sink their teeth into his skin.

'Where are the buyers?' Kalu kept asking himself.

He would have no face to show his father who would say, 'Didn't I tell you, paintings will not fill your stomach!'

So the next time an admirer extended his hand towards Kalu, he took the initiative and asked, 'Thank you, but will you buy one of the paintings?'

People fumbled at the question. Some said they hadn't brought the money with them, but if Kalu told them they could take the painting and he would pick up the money later, they would hesitantly head for the door without seeing the entire exhibition. After a while, he decided not to press any more people to buy.

But as the day wore on, the morning surge of visitors dried up to a trickle. Kalu hadn't managed to sell a single painting. He was so disappointed that the next time someone asked who the artist was he did not even bother to introduce himself. His chief worry now was that he wouldn't be able to return the money borrowed from Guha Kaki.

Kalu was just preparing himself mentally to face the humiliation of everyone he knew, when an elderly couple pointed at a painting and asked, 'How much does this one cost?'

The gentleman introduced himself as one Squadron Leader Puri.

'Why are you wasting my time?' Kalu wanted to tell him. But he held back his irritation. Instead, he informed the man disinterestedly, 'Seventy-five rupees.'

To his surprise, the gentleman simply counted out the notes and gave them to him. Kalu could not believe his eyes. He quickly pulled down the painting from the wall and handed it over to the couple, afraid that they may change their minds. They did not. A smile spread across the faces of Kalu and Guha Kaki.

'Didn't I tell you to be patient,' Kaki said.

At last they were happy—at least one painting had sold. But on hindsight Kalu realized that he suddenly felt sorry, for the painting that had sold had been his favourite. The brown monochrome had been made for the Shankar's international competition.

When the last of the visitors had left the makeshift gallery, the remaining paintings were dismounted and carefully stacked against a wall. Later, when Kalu and Guha Kaki carted back the paintings home in a rickshaw, it was in silence. They had sold just one painting. Overall, they were disappointed. It had been good to receive the gushing reviews and praise, but the sales were a huge let-down for the boy.

Guha Kaki refused to take back the money she had loaned him. When Kalu insisted, she found a respectable exit route. 'Okay, give me two of your paintings. That would cover my cost.'

It was an agreeable solution, Kalu thought. The exhibition had left him disillusioned and tired.

'Maybe my father was right,' he said to himself. 'Painting as a hobby is fine, but not as the source of one's livelihood. Perhaps joining the air force was the right thing to do, after all.'

A few days after the exhibition, Kalu was sitting in the house and pondering about his future. He hated the idea of becoming an airman. But he also knew that pursuing art was an option that would be full of uncertainties. The poor sales at his recent exhibition had only helped to reinforce doubts that assailed his little mind. He wished there was someone he could turn to for guidance. That's when the silence of the afternoon was meekly interrupted by the *crin-crin* of the postman's bicycle.

'*Kalu Biswas, chhithi hai!*' he heard the postman shout.

Kalu ran down the dark stairs.

'There is a registered letter for you,' the postman said, and gave him a paper to sign on.

The letter was from the Air Force Recruiting Office in Kanpur. Kalu tore it open. It was his final call letter, asking him to report to Kanpur latest by 15 February 1977.

'You are also advised to collect your warrant for the journey from Kanpur to Bangalore,' the letter said. 'In addition to your salary of Rs 339 per month, you will be given free food and lodging.'

Kalu recalled the long discussions he used to have with friends in school. 'If it's at least a four-figure salary, that would be okay,' one of his friends had once mentioned. 'Nothing less is even imaginable.'

For a moment he had the impulse to tear up the letter, so that nobody would get to know about it. But then he thought of his father who had invested in him, sending him to an expensive school he could hardly afford. 'Would you like to cheat your father?' a small voice inside him asked.

The answer was an emphatic 'No.'

He accepted the letter and went upstairs into the house. When his father came home later that afternoon, Kalu resignedly handed over the letter to him. A smile spread across Samar's face. He had been waiting for the letter expectantly.

Like a man who knew his fate has been sealed, Kalu silently started preparing for his departure. His father bought him a tin box to pack his belongings in. Basanti flung it away.

'That box is fit for a barber's son!' Basanti yelled at her husband.

With the money she had saved up for years, she bought Kalu a more respectable leather suitcase, swearing at her husband for his poor taste. Samar also bought him a shaving kit, a pair of shorts and canvas shoes.

'You will need these at the training centre,' he said, with the air of one who knew from experience.

Kalu also packed some paintbrushes and poster colours into his suitcase. At the last minute, Guha Kaki bought him a sketchbook made of art paper.

'Don't give up painting, whatever your calling in life,' she said, a trifle sad.

Kalu was grateful. The sketchbook would provide a valuable diversion to overcome the long days at the training centre. Etching and painting would make life a little more bearable.

'You are the only one, Kaki, who has understood my passion,' he said, with tears welling in his eyes.

His mother prepared him a box of salt-and-sweet cookies for the journey. Two days later, with the leather suitcase and a bed-roll, Kalu boarded the train for Kanpur. The entire family came to see him off at the Allahabad station. But it was his mother's tears that wrenched his heart and made him want to return.

At Bangalore's Air Force No. 3 Ground Training School, in Jallahalli, a new and strange life awaited Kalu. All the boy had asked for in life was a pen or a paintbrush. Instead, thrust upon him was a rifle and a bayonet. In his heavy leather boots he plodded along.

Author's Note

If it was not for Peter Godwin, my English boss in UNDP, who allowed me to carry home the office laptop in 1994, the book would perhaps never have happened. Peter Godwin was also the first person to see my unfinished manuscript. He was thrilled, insisting that he too be featured in the book. I was, honestly, flattered. I also wish to thank Shashi Tharoor, who despite his senior position and busy schedule with the UN in 1997 not only agreed to go through my manuscript, but also reverted with some encouraging comments, 'I found it extremely interesting, full of evocative detail and deeply felt.'

I'm also grateful to Khushwant Singh for going through my manuscript and suggesting that I cut down on the descriptions. He was one of the directors at Penguin then and suggested that I submit the manuscript to Penguin—they never got back. I gave up. Dejected, I went to Rupa who said they liked it, but never got back with a contract. By 1999 I had left UNHCR and was desperately looking for work that only came in bits and pieces. The book was virtually shelved.

Between 2004 and 2008 I did my stints with the UN missions in Liberia and Sudan, the book a distant dream by now. After Sudan I was back in India waiting to go back to Darfur. The wait that was supposed to be a few weeks, turned into months and years. With over two years of waiting, and diminishing coffers, I began to get desperate. It was in one of those idle moments that I sent

Rajat Banerji, a friend from my journalism days, the manuscript. He responded quickly on email, 'You bum... With your kind of talent, I would take this to a publisher.' He also asked me to get in touch with Nandita Bhardwaj, his friend's wife, who was in the publishing business. She was working with Roli then. By the time Nandita got back to me saying, 'We have liked what we read... Can you please send us the full manuscript,' she was at Rupa.

In June 2011, Rupa sent a contract that I signed without an advance. The rest, as they say, is history.

Along the way I have many people to thank apart from those already mentioned. Thanks is due to Abid Shah's wife whom I have never met. She, if Abid is to be believed, said after reading the book, 'This is like Premchand in English.'

Others who have helped me keep my faith in the book include Sohail Hashmi, Max Martin, Debashish Sen and Vinod Dhavan, all friends and colleagues in the profession. Although, in a different context, I also wish to thank Vinod Dua, who after reading an article of mine said—hold your breath—'I was reminded of Bernard Shaw.' I was sure he was pulling my leg and scrutinized his expression. It wasn't funny.

Special thanks is also due to that lovely and precious institution called family. My wife who, even though she did not act as my first reviewer, had confidence in me and, more importantly, has stood by me even through very trying (financial) times. I must also thank my children Indraneil, Shubham and Shreya, who are the fulcrum of my life; who still dote on me. More importantly, I wish to thank all my readers. If you enjoy reading the book, I urge you to recommend it to friends and foes alike. After all, dear reader, it's your duty to ensure that no author dies in penury.

Ashim Choudhury